# Revenge and Re

# Revenge, Relatives and Retribution

## A Trio of Novellas

G. Alan Brooks

**To order additional copies of this book, contact:**
Xlibris
1-888-795-4274
www.Xlibris.com
Orders@Xlibris.com
815536

I dedicate this book to my wife Nancy, with deep love and appreciation for sharing a wonderful life.

# CONTENTS

# THE FIVE-HUNDRED-ACRE RANCH

*Revenge requires a plan.*

# The Interview

S TEVE WALLACE WAS seated in a beautifully decorated private room in the offices of Platinum Singles, a high-end dating service. He had previously completed an application and paid his $10,000 fee.

This brief meeting was a required face-to-face interview before they would begin their search process for the perfect woman. He needed to answer a few more questions.

An attractive, well-dressed thirty-something female interviewer entered the room, took a seat, said hello, and began her questioning without hesitation, "What do you want in a woman?"

"I want a woman who understands me and shares my dreams," Steve said.

"What do you mean? What is it you need her to understand?" asked the dating counselor while taking notes on her laptop.

"My desire for simpler things. For a rural life, not a hectic urban existence," Steve said.

Steve continued, "My former wife only cared about urban activities, and what she thought her friends would like. She focused on what would impress others, and make her more important in the city social circle," Steve said with a sigh.

"What are your dreams to share with a new woman in your life?" she continued.

"To find a home where we can be alone most of the time, and enjoy the relaxation of solitude. A place filled with the natural beauty of grass, water, livestock, fish, birds, and a ton of tranquility in a warm climate," he said.

"Where would you find a place like that?" She prodded.

"A ranch in Central Florida. It will be a beautiful property not too far from Orlando but far enough to avoid the crowds. I want a woman who is in her forties, fit, and energetic who loves to ride horses, shoot guns, go hunting and still be sophisticated enough to enjoy fine wine and food. Being near Orlando will give us easy access to an international airport for global travel activities," he smiled and continued.

"I am sick and tired of city-sophisticated women who want to be pampered and praised for looking good but are so self-centered they cannot understand and appreciate their man," he said.

"Thank you for your input today. I will enter your profile into our exclusive database of single women. I feel sure we will find a few good candidates who would love to share your dream," the dating counselor said confidently. She got up, indicated the short meeting was over and escorted Steve to the elevator.

Steve left the interview, feeling embarrassed that he had shared so many feelings with a total stranger. He had been divorced for six months and was tired of the bar scene and the dates set up by his Miami friends. He had heard stories about the success of people using the dating services of Platinum Singles to find a good match for long-term companionship. He was surprised at how a few simple questions had enabled him to clearly express the kind of person he wanted in his life.

As he walked to the valet to retrieve his Range Rover, Steve reminded himself that he had one more deal to complete before he could retire in happiness. Maybe the right woman would give him everything he needed.

# CHAPTER 1

# Steve's Childhood History

STEVE WAS RAISED in the Redlands, a rural community thirty miles south of Miami and just a few miles north of the Florida Keys. His father had been a hardworking farmer who struggled to make ends meet while raising a variety of vegetables on their two-hundred-acre farm.

Steve had helped with farm chores most of his childhood. From the time he could walk, his father taught him how to plant and harvest beans, tomatoes, potatoes, squash, watermelon, and cucumbers. He learned to plow the fertile soil, use the proper fertilizers, apply the necessary insecticides, and where to buy the supplies needed to run a small farm. Both Steve and his father loved to ride horses, and they kept two well-trained quarter horses, which they rode all over the rural areas of the Redlands.

Steve thought that one day, he would study agriculture and animal husbandry at the University of Florida and join his farming family. He and his father had talked about buying more land and getting more advanced farming tools like irrigation and harvesting equipment. They would call the new, larger farm Wallace and Son.

When Steve was in the eleventh grade, his father fell ill one afternoon after spraying the tomato plants with a powerful new insecticide; and he died the next week. The doctors think he must have inhaled chemicals that quickly destroyed his lungs, and he died of a rapid-onset of pneumonia. Steve was devastated by the death of his father, and he decided he did not want to farm without his dad. A lawyer told them they could sue the chemical manufacturer, but Steve and his mom did not believe his father would approve of that action.

Steve attended a small high school in Homestead, where he was an academic athlete who played every sport: basketball, football, track, golf, and tennis. The idea of farming was forgotten and abandoned, so Steve changed his plans and worked hard to win a golf scholarship to an elite college.

Steve had outstanding grades, maxed out the SAT exams, and won a golf scholarship to Stanford, which had the best golf program in the country. At one time, he had visions of being a golf pro; but he ultimately majored in finance and systems design. He was a natural at design and coding complex projects and would later use those skills to achieve financial success.

Steve's mother, an uneducated but pretty housewife, was lost and emotionally devastated when her husband died. She adored Steve; and while he was in school, she kept the farm. They continued to struggle financially; and when Steve left for California, she decided to sell the farm. She moved in with her divorced sister in Tampa and sold the farm to one of the largest landowners in the Redlands.

His mother received more money than she had ever had in her life, and it was more than enough to live well. She could also help Steve with college expenses and travel with her sister to exotic places. His mother and father had always loved to travel, but most of their travel was within the USA on a frugal budget. Now, his mother and sister were flying all over the world, visiting fabulous sights and meeting beautiful hip and exciting people.

# CHAPTER 2

# A Childhood History of Marie

MARIE ROBINSON WAS born into a family with three generations of roots and financial success in New York City. Her great-grandfather, a Harvard-educated anesthesiologist, discovered and patented several drugs that became widely used in the operating room. After the initial success of the drugs, he started a pharmaceutical business; and his Wharton-educated son joined the company. Her grandfather proved to be an exceptional manager and took the company public. The company was listed on the New York Stock Exchange and was one of the premier drug companies in the USA. Marie's father was the current CEO, and the business continued to be enormously successful.

Marie attended Trinity, a K-12 private coeducational school on the Upper West Side of NYC. It is one of the most elite schools in a city filled with high-quality preparatory schools.

Marie's parents had both gone to Yale as undergraduates and then to the Wharton School of Business for MBA's in finance. As expected of affluent people, they immediately became active in civic affairs and gave large sums of money to their alma maters, several hospitals, and many other charitable institutions. Her father was on the board of numerous institutions, and her mother was well-known in local politics. Her mother's political activities primarily focused on developing programs to address domestic violence. In short, her parents were movers and shakers in New York City.

Marie was a good student throughout her school years. She planned to attend an elite university and then marry a high-powered, successful man who would likely come from a family similar to hers. She did not expect to work more than a few years; then she would stop work altogether to raise a family with two children. After the kids were in school, she would become active in civic affairs like her parents.

She was always physically active and played tennis all four of her high school years. She was remarkably attractive, with a movie-star face and a fabulous body. Needless to say, she was one of the popular girls at Trinity, and the boys chased her constantly. During her high school years, she had many boyfriends and attended countless galas and parties at spectacular venues. She always planned to meet her husband in college, and so the high school relationships were never that important to her.

Marie applied to several Ivy League schools and Stanford. Stanford accepted her; and, for the first time in her life, she was out from under the close supervision of her family and friends. California was far from New York, and it would prove to have a significant impact on her marriage and life plans.

At Trinity, she also had a wide range of girlfriends; and in the summer between her junior and senior years, she had traveled to Europe with several of them. She remained a good friend and felt wonderfully comfortable with her New York relationships. She expected to return to NYC to live after college.

She had one brother, Mark, who was three years older than Marie. They were not exactly close but loved each other and had a good rapport. Mark was a practicing oncologist after attending Harvard undergraduate and medical school. She and Mark had traveled extensively with their parents both in the United States and abroad, and they were indeed a couple of cosmopolitan New Yorkers.

# CHAPTER 3

# Marie and Steve Together

S TEVE MET MARIE through a fraternity brother in his junior year. He discovered she was from NYC, and her family had been living in Manhattan for four generations. She grew up in the city, attended elite schools, and was beautiful. She was smart, ambitious, upper class, and as urbane as they come. She never bragged about her wealthy parents, and Steve was surprised to see how they lived when she took him home the first time.

Marie found Steve to be utterly fantastic! He was clean-cut and good-looking, smart, and tanned from playing golf. He dressed like a golfer with his khaki slacks, polo shirts, and loafers without socks. Steve was a gentleman in every way, excellent manners, soft-spoken, and popular with everyone he met. He was the president of the computer science fraternity and admired for his grasp of the latest technology trends. He was ambitious, and she was sure he would be successful. She changed her mind about marrying a man with money and chose one with obvious potential.

They fell in love almost immediately, surprised everyone by getting married during their senior year, but they stayed the course, and both graduated college with honors. They promptly left for jobs in New York. Steve started in an executive training program with Microsoft, and she began with a small boutique art gallery specializing in Egyptian antiquities. Marie knew they needed two incomes for a while.

Her parents had been disappointed that she married a man without family money, but they accepted Steve as a man with potential. They were thrilled to have the young couple in the city; and when the twins were born, her parents provided a reliable support system.

She had long dreamed of being a New York socialite, but now she knew that she would need to wait for a while. Steve needed to become successful for her dreams to come true. She knew she would inherit some substantial money when her parents died, so she took a chance on a poor boy. Early in their marriage, Marie quietly took plenty of money from her parents to make sure they had many of the beautiful things she enjoyed as a child. To her credit, she kept working for a few years after the birth of Dan and Ann.

As she had hoped, Steve was soon doing well, moving up rapidly in the Microsoft management hierarchy; and everyone decided it was time for her to become a full-time stay-at-home mom. Her father made her an advisor to his drug company, and she earned substantial money while staying home.

Steve was promoted to an international marketing position and traveled extensively. Meanwhile, Marie was beyond bored staying at home, so she hired a nanny to help with the kids. With the support provided by her parents and the nanny, Marie was rarely home. The kids attended Trinity just like their mom, went to college, and both were now finishing law school. Marie was alone far too much of the time to be happy.

On one of his many trips to California, Steve spent two weeks at a wine seminar in Napa Valley, which focused on the best wines from all regions of the world. He learned many things that enabled him to enjoy a wide range of fine wines. He was taught how to appreciate the different attributes of grape varieties and blends. The seminar gave the students samples of the finest wines from the USA, France, Italy, Spain, Argentina, Australia, and New Zealand. Steve became a wine lover, joined several wine societies, and built an extensive collection of world-renowned wines.

Marie became a docent at the Metropolitan Museum. She had studied Egyptian art at Stanford and was a talented, beloved volunteer at the museum. She specialized in mummies and artifacts of the Middle and New Kingdoms, which spanned the timeline from 2055 to 1070 BC.

It was at the Metropolitan Museum where she met a new love who became her intellectual and physical soulmate. He was the curator of

Egyptian antiquities and the son of a prominent NY financial dynasty. After she took the docent position and met her new secret love, Marie was now ecstatic with her life. She had the lover she had always envisioned and a successful husband.

While Marie was happier than ever, dark clouds were gathering in Steve's head. Although he had a high-paying job and was well positioned for a more significant role at Microsoft, Steve had lost the spark in his marriage and his career. He had been with the same company for over twenty years, and he felt it was time for something new. Unknown to Marie, he had been thinking of starting his own company when he accidentally met Clint.

# CHAPTER 4

# The End of Steve and Marie

WHILE ON A business trip to Mexico City, Steve met an IBM engineer, Clint, who was working on a new Internet-based tool for supply chain management. They spoke nonstop for two days on the need for a system that would connect the raw material suppliers to the finished-product producers and greatly enhance the effectiveness of global manufacturing.

Steve returned home and continued to work for Microsoft while also talking on the phone almost daily with Clint. After four months of dialog and detailed systems design, they both decided to leave their current employers.

Steve quickly formulated a plan to launch the new company in Florida. He told Marie his plans and resigned from Microsoft; and within two months, they were in Miami. Steve did not ask Marie for her opinion about the change because he was utterly absorbed with the idea of his new company. This period was a happy time for Steve and a shocking and upsetting time for Marie.

Steve and Clint decided to start their software development company in Miami so they could easily hire programmers in both Miami and Mexico. The flights from Miami to Mexico were quick, and the cost of highly skilled programmers in Mexico was one-fourth the price of a coder in the USA. Another reason for choosing Miami was that it had a very robust Internet data center connection.

They named the company Supply Chain Max (SCX). With two brilliant minds, a powerful Internet connection, and an affordable development team, it did not take them long to get their business up and running profitably. Steve was also a good salesman, while Clint was a master at systems design and a genius for getting productive work from his programming staff. Steve had never been happier; and he was seldom home while traveling the globe, looking for prospective clients to purchase their software.

Marie was furious that Steve had made these decisions with little regard for her desire to stay in NYC. He did not care that her parents provided a significant support network, that she loved her position at the Met, and that she had many close friends in New York. Of course, he was not aware of her love affair with the Egyptian curator. Even if he had known, he probably would not have given it much thought or concern. He had found his new love in his company.

Although they turned a profit after a couple of years and had a few small customers, it took them two more years to develop a product that was exceptional enough to be purchased by a single major global manufacturer. They knew they must make this early user a success story or the reputation of the new company would be tarnished. This trusting customer was the key to more just like them, and they must do everything to make the CEO happy. During this time, Steve and Clint worked eighty-hour weeks.

The day they incorporated SCX, Steve and Clint had worked with an attorney to create a comprehensive buy-and-sell agreement. They had been advised it was the correct thing to do upfront to avoid conflict. If either wanted to leave the company, they would receive a one-time payment of two times the net profit of the last certified financial statement. If either of them died, the stock of the deceased would go to the living partner; and the family would get the same dollar payout. Neither had wanted any new partners or family members to own stock.

They often talked about selling the business as their sales volume increased, but they kept pouring their revenue back into development, and their profits stayed low. They did not think they were ready to maximize profits until they had a top-notch product that beat the competition hands down.

It was this environment of increasing sales but low profits when a shark attack killed Clint. Nobody in SCX or Clint's social circle could believe that such an exceptional young person had been so brutally killed while on a fun-filled fishing trip.

Steve had recently returned from a fabulously successful fly-fishing trip to the Abaco Islands in the Bahamas. The Abacos have some world-class bonefishing destinations both in the marls and on the oceanside where the fish can be huge. He and Clint had been working long stressful hours, and he had found the fishing camp environment and their superb guides to be the most relaxing experience he could remember. He insisted that Clint take a week off and go to the same place and enjoy the same relaxing pause in their work schedule.

Clint found the Abaco trip to be just as relaxing and fun as Steve described; and on his third day, he and his guide decided to fish the Atlantic Ocean side of the island. There were bigger bonefish there, and he had caught so many small- and medium-sized fish that he wanted a shot at a larger fish. He and the guide were both wading for bonefish up to their waists, each had a rod, and they separated to search in different areas of the long beach. They were out of sight of each other; and apparently, Clint was attacked by a large shark, pulled into the water, partially eaten, and then it discarded his mangled body. Maybe the shark had first bitten his legs, which created a blood frenzy for other sharks in the area also to attack, but it was impossible to know for sure.

When the guide returned to retrieve Clint for the trip back to the fish camp, he discovered Clint's lifeless body. It was unusual for sharks to attack so close to shore, but it did occur occasionally. It is well known that big sharks can come in as shallow as two feet of water.

His partner's death saddened Steve; and for a few months, he was also lost trying to replace Clint's role in the business. Luckily, one of Clint's strong points was his team-building skills, and his system design and programming teams were filled with competent workers and managers. Soon, the company regained its momentum.

Steve paid Clint's wife $5 million, and he now owned 100 percent of the company. The wife was happy with the settlement and left Miami to be with her parents in Michigan.

SCX announced the latest version of the software six months after the death of Clint, and it was soon a real hit in the supply-chain software world. Two years later, they had implemented systems at a dozen large international companies. The news rapidly spread about their intelligent

G. ALAN BROOKS

and effective new way to manage supply chains, and the SCX business exploded.

Three years later, Steve sold SCX for $50 million to a large German software company that was providing business systems to multinational companies. Steve had a two-year earn-out contract, which provided even more income. Two years after he sold the business, Steve had a net worth of over $60 million. He invested his money with two wealth managers from different financial institutions, and his fortune continued to grow nicely.

Steve was fifty-five when he was finished working with SRX and the buyout company. The twins were both attorneys with law degrees from Ivy League schools, and they were working for different prestigious law firms in Miami. Neither was married, but both had significant partners and seemed happy enough. The twins were close to both parents but appeared to be more attracted to their father than their mother.

Marie filed for divorce as soon as Steve sold the business. She saw an opportunity to get some meaningful money and live in New York. She had never liked Miami, and she had grown tired of the simple life in this cow town compared to her exciting and culture-rich New York. New York was her city and her planned destination for the rest of her life.

On her many trips to visit her parents, she had also maintained a wonderful relationship with her lover at the Met. She saw how she could have just what she wanted: money, New York, and her true love.

The divorce was completed in two years; and when she moved back to New York, it was with an $18 million settlement. This was entirely her own money: separate from the money she was to receive from her inheritance. She was set for a happy life.

# CHAPTER 5

# Steve's Complaints

S TEVE WAS HAPPY to give Marie the divorce. He spoke to the twins about it, and they had their own lives to live, and it did not seem to upset them very much. When they were young, Steve was always away on business, and their mother was rarely home, so they felt closer to their long-term nanny than to either of their parents. Ann was a little concerned since her mother was moving away, and they had recently spent Saturdays together at the upscale Bal Harbour Malls, but she felt she would get over it quickly.

For most of their married life, Steve and Marie lived in NYC and spent their time attending cultural events, eating at Michelin-starred restaurants, socializing with New Yorkers, and visiting every museum in the city. Steve had tried often during their thirty years of marriage to interest Marie in travel to rural locations for some of their holidays. Still, she only wanted Paris, Rome, London, Geneva, Saint Petersburg, and other such cosmopolitan destinations.

She was not interested in traveling to the national parks, the Grand Canyon, Yellowstone, dude ranches, Montana, Jackson Hole, the Everglades, or other outdoor destinations. She would not go fly fishing. She had no interest in golf, which was a sport Steve loved. She was happy to let Steve and the twins spend as much time as they wanted "in the outdoors." While Steve and the kids were enjoying fun in rural areas, she would go to the famous cities with her girlfriends and of course, on her own to her beloved New York.

When her mother left for New York, Ann hired the family nanny because she was thinking of marriage. Ann wanted her kids to have the same love she had gotten during her childhood. Steve was glad to be rid of Marie, and Marie was delighted to have her own money and the freedom to live well in Manhattan.

Things were different in one regard: Marie had a relationship and someone to love her, but Steve had only loved the business. Steve yearned for someone he could enjoy spending time with; but he hated the dating scene in Miami bars, discos, and the fixups by friends.

He had found Platinum Singles and was ready to try something new.

# CHAPTER 6

# False Starts

TWO WEEKS AFTER his interview, Steve got his first call for a lunch date. The dating counselor told him they located a forty-eight-year-old woman from Jacksonville who looked like a good match. If he agreed, she would travel to Miami for a lunch date and possibly dinner if the lunch meeting was a positive experience.

He agreed, and Platinum Singles set up a luncheon appointment at an upscale Italian restaurant on Miami Beach. The dating counselor made sure neither of them had ever eaten there previously.

They arrived at the same time and were escorted to a table specially selected and prepared for them. The restaurant was in an old mansion with beautiful period furniture, and majestic palm trees filled the courtyard. They had a private table between the palms and next to a fountain with gently falling water seeping from the mouth of a stone nymph.

Her name was Naomi, and she looked fit and confident. Steve ordered a bottle of champagne, and they toasted each other with a clink of their glasses. Naomi had been raised in Alabama, attended Auburn, and married five years after graduation. She had two children who were both students at the University of Florida.

Naomi was a CPA and a partner in a midsized accounting firm in Jacksonville. She lived in the small nearby community of Orange Park. She had been divorced for two years.

Steve asked where she had recently traveled. She told him of her recent trip to Rome, Florence, and Milan, where she had seen some of the incredible art and world-class museums. She said her journey the year before had been on a cruise to the Baltic leaving from London, and she had loved the sophistication of Saint Petersburg.

He asked her to tell him the last time she had been fishing, and she thought he was making a joke. She said she had fished from her grandfather's dock when she was eight. He asked when she had last been horseback riding, and she looked at him with concern that this lunch was not going in the right direction.

They stopped talking long enough for each to order a Caesar salad with shrimp. While waiting for the salad, she asked him a few questions. She wondered when he last went to Europe or Asia on vacation. He said that he had traveled all over the world; but when going on a vacation, he wanted an outdoor experience. The salads came, the conversation cooled, and they decided that dinner was not a good idea. He walked with her to the valet and said good-bye as she left for Orange Park.

He called the dating counselor and told her that Naomi was lovely but that she was not interested in the rural life he envisioned.

"Please find someone that shares my idea of a rustic and outdoor retirement," he complained and insisted.

The next lunch date was so depressing that Steve started to give up on Platinum Singles. The woman was a divorcee from Mississippi who owned a chain of casinos she had inherited from her father. She was interested in the outdoors, and she was not unattractive, but she wanted him to move to Mississippi to help her manage her casinos. She had been attracted to him because his profile said he was a successful business executive. They parted ways with a smile and a laugh that being single was no fun.

# CHAPTER 7

# Hello, Karen

AFTER THE LAST two meetings, Steve had gone over the head of the dating counselor and called the owner of Platinum Singles. Steve was polite but very forceful with his opinion they were sending him anyone with any interest in any aspect of his profile. He was not happy with their service, and he told them he would not give them a good recommendation unless things improved.

"I was very clear in my interview and in my written application about what kind of woman I wanted to meet. Either look for what I requested, or I will stop using your service," he said forcefully.

A few weeks later, Steve received a call directly from the owner. She had an exciting prospect who lived in Idaho and was visiting Miami. The candidate had expressed an interest in meeting Steve, and the owner was confident this would be a better match than the prior lunch dates.

This time they sent Steve a photo, a summary of her interests, and her education before the date. She was forty-six, had been divorced for three years, loved the outdoors, and was in public relations with a small firm in Idaho.

The owner took the time to review her profile carefully with Steve so he would feel comfortable meeting with her. She suggested that he meet her for lunch at Joe's Stone Crab restaurant. Joe's is a well-known establishment on Miami Beach where the rich and famous go for lunch and dinner. Steve agreed to meet her for lunch after continued assurances that she was interested in sharing the ideas he had expressed in his original interview.

Steve was not sure how long it would take to get seated at Joe's, which is famous for the long wait. However, Platinum Singles had prearranged for a quiet table near the back of the restaurant, out of sight from most diners.

Steve arrived first and rose to greet Karen when she approached the table. She was wearing a pair of jeans, a simple sleeveless black top, little makeup, and her hair was in a ponytail. She looked twenty-five, not forty-six. She was a knockout!

"Karen, I am pleased to meet you, and I am delighted we could meet for lunch," Steve said as he smiled brightly.

Karen replied, "I have been looking forward to meeting you since the dating counselor gave me your profile. I very much love horses, farms, ranches, and animals."

"Wow! I may have met the perfect lady." Steve laughed as he marveled at her early declaration of interest in the things he liked. He felt sure the owner of Platinum Singles had coached her, but he would listen carefully.

"Steve, I grew up on a three-hundred-acre sheep farm in Idaho near the Wood River valley. We had some of the best hunting and fishing spots in the USA. My father was an avid sportsman who enjoyed the great outdoors," she said.

"I grew up on a farm in South Florida, and my father and I hunted and fished throughout the state. We rode horses to hunt deer and wild hogs in Central Florida. I fell in love with that part of the state." Steve smiled.

"So you want to buy a ranch in Central Florida?" she asked.

"Yes, I found a nice piece of land with around five hundred acres, good pastureland that has 250 acres completely cleared, and several hundred acres of wild woodland," he said.

"I want to raise a few cows and buy a few well-trained quarter horses to ride and use for hunting," he said.

"What kind of living quarters are on the property?" She smiled as she asked.

"There is a rustic three-bedroom main house with two bathrooms, a modern kitchen, and a large great room for entertaining," he said.

"That sounds super. Have you bought the property already?" she asked.

"No, I wanted to meet my potential female partner and take her to see the land and buildings before I close on the deal," Steve continued.

"I gave a sizable deposit, and the owner agreed to hold the property for six months. It is owned by a widow who has been trying to sell it for two years," he said.

"How will you make enough money on such a small farm to support your lifestyle?" she asked.

"I have plenty of money from the sale of my former business. I do not need income from the ranch to support me," he said.

"Well, that is a good thing because I saw how hard it was for my parents to make a living on a three-hundred-acre sheep farm. The big sheep farmers had so much more efficiency and buying power than we could manage. We tried to specialize in extra high-quality lamb and wool, but it was a struggle to make any real money," she said.

"Are your parents alive?" he asked.

"No. One of the reasons I wanted to meet you is because of your desire to live in a place where it is warm. My father broke a leg during a bad snowstorm, and he froze to death because he could not get back to his truck. He was only sixty-five. My mother had always been fraught with aliments, and she had a frail body. She took an overdose of some pain medicine six months after he died," she said.

"I saw on your profile that you like golf, and I also enjoy golf but not as much as other outdoor sports," she said.

"You seem too good to be true," he said with a smile and wink.

# CHAPTER 8

# Playing Games

"HOW WOULD YOU like to play a round of golf with me this afternoon? I am a member of a beautiful club in Coral Gables, right on the bay. We have many interesting holes and a unique array of wildlife, saltwater crocodiles, iguanas, peacocks, ibis, heron, cormorants, and Egyptian geese. It is an Audubon sanctuary and one of the toughest courses in South Florida," he asked.

"I will take you up on your offer, but I need to make a couple of business calls to cancel some other phone meetings," she said.

They finished lunch; and he gave her the address of the country club so she could make her calls, change into some golf clothes, and meet him at the club. They would have time for nine holes, maybe eighteen, if she did not spend too much time looking for lost balls.

Steve was incredibly pleased with their first meeting, and he thought he saw potential in this woman. She was cute and seemed to like everything he liked. Almost too good to be true, but Karen was surely a possibility for his eventual plans.

Karen was impressed with Steve. He was nice-looking, seemed to have money, enjoyed the outdoors, and was an interesting conversationalist.

Just as planned, she met Steve at his club at three o'clock. She was a good, not great, golfer with a fifteen handicap. He was a superb golfer with a two handicap. Remember, he had been the captain of his golf team at Stanford in his senior year. To his surprise, her golf was far better than he expected; and he was delighted. They played fifteen holes before darkness forced them to stop.

"That was a lot of fun. Karen, you are an excellent golfer. You and I could team up and beat almost any couple I know," he bragged.

"I had so much fun. The course was beautiful and challenging. Plus, the wildlife was astonishing. I can't believe those crocodiles are real. I have never played with anyone as good as you played today. You are amazing." She smiled.

Steve offered to take Karen back to her hotel, but she chose to go back by Uber so she could catch up on some work for one of her best clients. Before leaving, she told Steve she would be busy the next day with phone calls; and she also had a dinner appointment that evening with a prospective customer. She told him to call her the following day, and maybe they could do something together.

Steve was intrigued by his initial meeting and decided to spend more time with Karen. She seemed nice and at least pretended to like the things he did. He called and asked if she would like to try a day of fishing in the Gulfstream for sailfish and dolphin. She said it would be fun, and she would meet him at the boat docks he described.

Steve chartered a popular sailfish captain who owned a sixty-five-foot Viking sport fisher. It was a real fishing machine, equipped with every marine device available and supported by a captain and two mates who helped with the rods and bait.

It was a perfect day for sail fishing. The wind was out of the north at fifteen knots, and the Gulfstream current was moving fast in a northerly direction. The two opposing forces of nature caused the baitfish to be pushed into massive schools, which made a gourmet buffet for the sailfish and other gamefish like dolphinfish (mahi-mahi), wahoo, and tuna.

They caught six sailfish, twelve dolphinfish, and one large wahoo. Karen landed eight fish herself and was exhausted when they stopped fishing for the day.

"I never knew offshore fishing could be so much fun. The size of those fish was amazing. All my prior fishing has been in the lakes and rivers of Idaho," said Karen.

"I am glad you enjoyed today. I love to fish everywhere: oceans, backcountry, rivers, streams, and lakes," said Steve.

"I could learn a lot about fishing from you, but it will be hard to have more fun than we had today," she said.

"There are many lakes and some rivers in Central Florida near the ranch. Plus, we are only a couple of hours from either coast. I plan on taking my twenty-five-foot center-console Contender on a trailer to the ranch. We can fish almost anywhere, except super-shallow water, in that boat," he said.

"Your plans sound so wonderful. It seems you have thought of everything," she said.

They had a quick dinner at a small pizza joint that made a delicious pizza and veggie lasagna. On the way back to her hotel, Steve asked if she was free the next day; and she said the morning would be taken up with business calls, but her afternoon would be open.

"What do you have in mind?" she asked.

"I want to show you my horses. I keep two quarter horses in the Redlands at a small ranch owned by a friend. Plus, I have a horse trailer that accommodates two horses. I want to take you horseback riding in the Everglades," he said.

"I have never seen the Everglades. Aren't the bugs bad out there?" she asked.

"Not this time of the year. You will love the beauty and natural environment where I plan to take you," he said.

"I am game," she said.

Steve was beginning to be infatuated with this amazing young woman who seemed to be his vision of an ideal mate.

When she arrived at the hotel, Karen tried hard to reach Brad; but his phone was busy every time she called. She left a short voice mail: "Brad, things are progressing better and faster than I expected. I will keep you posted."

# CHAPTER 9

# More Fun in South Florida

THEY LOADED THE horses onto the trailer and took the remote road toward Flamingo. They soon entered Everglades National Park and stopped at the welcome station. Steve explained the exhibits to Karen, and they shared their amazement at some of the park wonders.

After leaving the welcome station, they turned off the main road and took a small unpaved road south into one of the remote unvisited areas of the everglades. Steve had obtained a special permit from the chief ranger to ride horses in the park.

"Steve, I feel we are all alone in a wonderland of cypress trees, water, and pines!" she exclaimed.

"I wanted you to see this marvel of nature on horseback the way the Seminole Indians and early settlers saw this river of grass," he said as he led the horses off the dirt road into the cypress-and-pine swamp.

The horses were well trained, and Karen showed she was a superb rider. The wet cypress swamps were ankle-deep to the horses, and they needed to work their way around the cypress knees that dominated the wetland, but it was a comfortable ride. Steve was once again amazed at this woman who was a golfer, horse lover, fisherwoman, and a beauty to boot.

Interspersed among the swamps were islands of pine trees that grew on solid ground, and they spotted frequent deer and even saw a glimpse of a rare Florida panther. They saw alligators in the swampy areas, but the gators did not seem aggressive. There were also abundant water birds, and Steve knew the names of most.

They were returning to the horse trailer when Karen's horse jumped sideways so suddenly that she was thrown from the saddle. She was riding a western saddle with a saddle horn, and she grabbed the horn in time to avoid falling entirely off her horse. The horse jumped twice more; but she regained her position in the saddle, demonstrating once again her riding skills.

She and Steve instantly searched the area to see if they could find what the horse had smelled or seen. After a few moments of searching, they saw a diamondback rattlesnake coiled and ready to strike. The Everglades is filled with rattlesnakes, and horseback riders and hikers need to be careful to avoid getting close to them. The snakes rarely strike unless they are threatened; but if bitten, a human can get extremely ill or die without prompt medical attention.

Karen was not hurt, but she had torn one of her nails in the struggle to regain her position in the saddle. She did not complain about the broken nail, but Steve could see some blood on her left hand. He did not comment but mentally noted her toughness.

Steve decided it was time to see if she would join him at the ranch for a visit and to continue his exploration of how well she matched his wants and needs.

"Karen, I would love to show you the ranch. I know you would enjoy the entire experience. Will you please come with me for a few days?" he asked.

"Yes, I will go with you to the ranch, but I must go back to Idaho for three weeks. I am working on a special project for our biggest client, and I must finish it," she said without much hesitation.

"However, I have two weeks of vacation coming before the end of the year. I can use that time to come back and go to the ranch with you. I have enjoyed these last few days, and I want to see the ranch and you again," Karen said.

"I am sorry you must go back, but I will plan some great things for us to do together when you return," he said.

They loaded the horses, dropped the trailer and horses in the Redlands, and returned to Miami for a farewell dinner. He dropped her at her hotel and sent an Uber to bring her to one of his favorite restaurants after she showered and dressed. He bathed and put on nice slacks, a long-sleeve dress shirt without a tie, and a navy blazer.

Florida does not have a Michelin representative, so Miami does not have starred restaurants. However, they had dinner at a beautiful restaurant that would have had two stars, if they gave them out in Miami. The food was superb, and Steve selected a vintage Bordeaux cabernet sauvignon to complement their grilled lamb chops and assorted vegetables. The buttery madeleines with rich coffee were excellent as a finishing touch.

"Steve, I cannot remember a more wonderful evening. You have given me so much to remember, and my anticipation of spending two weeks with you will keep my mind in a spin," she said.

"I have never had more fun and genuine enjoyment with any woman. I so much look forward to your return," he said.

# CHAPTER 10

# Karen and Brad Make Their Plans

KAREN RETURNED HOME to the open arms of Brad, her longtime lover.

"How was the trip? Did you set the hook in our new fish?" he asked.

"Oh, Brad, you will not believe how much fun I had. This guy is so nice. He is a true sportsman, and I enjoyed every minute with him. He fell head over heels for me," she said.

"So what is our plan?" asked Brad.

"I am going back for a two-week visit. Steve is taking me to a ranch he wants to buy for some horseback riding, hunting, and fishing. I suspect he will also expect some romantic experiences as we spend more time together," she said.

"I don't care how much romance you give him if he can deliver a big payday," said Brad.

"The last guy was not nearly as rich as Steve, and we got $500,000 from him. Steve is brilliant, but he is so focused on finding the right woman that his brain is not in gear. I will prove to be the right woman," she said.

"Do you think you will need to marry him to get his money?" Brad asked.

"Oh, Brad! I don't have a feel yet for how this will play out, but I am sure we can get a big part of his net worth in the next two years. He is our ticket to financial security," she said.

"I want to spend our retirement years in luxury. If you think Steve is our best shot of all the single guys you have met for lunch, then let's make this a home run. How much money do you think he has?" Brad asked.

"He is the best candidate of all. He will be fun to be with while we are setting up our end game. I did many Google searches to find out his net worth and found that he sold his company for $50 million, but his wife got some. Maybe he has $40 million left. Whatever it is, he has a lot." She laughed, thinking of how much would be hers one day.

"Don't have too much fun. Remember, we are in this for the money, not the honey," said Brad.

Brad and Karen had been lovers for a dozen years. They had planned for her divorce, and the settlement was much bigger than usual because Brad had photographed her husband with two women in a moment of wild abandonment. Brad had paid the women $1,000 each to entice her straight husband to have a little fun after a night of drinking at his favorite waterhole with an old friend. Her husband's law firm would not want their partners to behave like that.

Her husband was happy to get rid of Karen anyhow and was eager to make the photos go away. Karen came away from the divorce with $1.5 million and alimony of $30,000 per year for ten years. The alimony payments were about to stop.

Since the divorce, Brad and Karen were living together in a condo in Boise. They were saving their money, while both were signing up at dating agencies to search for vulnerable targets. They also watched cruises that appealed to singles of all ages. They had enough money to invest some of it to find wealthy, lonely suckers.

They were both attractive, well educated, well-traveled, and the perfect date. Karen and Brad were also athletic and skilled at many sporting activities, which made them even more exciting. They had their deceitful life stories down perfectly; and for five years, they had been learning how to effectively fleece their dating partners. Each had made several scores. They would probably have succeeded at legitimate businesses, but they had chosen a life of deceit.

Brad had succeeded at scamming $1.5 million from an older widow who had fallen in love with him. He met her on a cruise to the Caribbean two years ago and convinced her to invest in a nonexistent company. He told her the company went bust and that he was too embarrassed to stay around. She was still in love with him, so he stayed in touch with her to see if there might be more he could steal.

They had no problem with each other being intimate with their target. It was all part of the game. There were no rules except to make money! Their goal was a retirement nest egg of $20 million, and they jointly decided Steve could make it come true.

# CHAPTER 11

# The Introduction to the Ranch

THEY MET AT the Orlando Airport baggage claim. Steve was dressed in his worn jeans, a long-sleeve plaid shirt worn outside of his pants, boots, and a tan cowboy hat. He looked like a real modern-day cowboy or rancher, and a few women near the carousel gave him smiles and flirtatious looks before Karen arrived. Karen showed up in her tight jeans and a sleeveless top that highlighted her fit and curvaceous body. The women laughed at their foolish thoughts and looked away.

After they retrieved her luggage, a valet helped them to an outdoor parking lot. Karen was elated when she saw the horse trailer behind the Range Rover.

"You brought your horses!" she exclaimed.

"I wanted them with us for the next couple of weeks. I plan to show you some terrific riding trails in the forests close to the ranch. Besides, I want to show you the ranch by horseback," he said as he gave her a hug and a kiss.

"The ranch is only an hour north of Orlando, but the difference in vibe could be a thousand miles away," he said.

"I can't wait to see everything. The land and foliage in Florida are so different compared to Idaho," she said.

"We need to stop by the widow's home in a small community called Hernando to get the key and say hello. She knows I am interested in buying the ranch because I gave her a substantial deposit. I also told her I might close the deal in two weeks if we enjoy it as much as I hope," he said as he reached over to hold Karen's hand.

"She was kind enough to stock the house with enough food for a few days until we have time to shop for ourselves, and I need to pay her for the groceries," he said.

"It seems like you have planned every detail, and it impresses me that you are so thoughtful," she said.

There was a small family-owned restaurant near Hernando, and they stopped for a home-cooked meal of meatloaf and mashed potatoes. After lunch, they met the ranch owner at her modest home, where she served them a glass of iced tea while Steve reviewed their plans to use the ranch house and facilities for two weeks. The widow was thrilled to see Steve and excited that he might buy the ranch she had been trying to sell for the past two years since her husband died. Steve paid her for the groceries, and she gave him the key and a set of papers that explained how to work the ranch house appliances and the lights for the outbuildings.

When the GPS said they were at the turnoff to the ranch, they saw a wooden archway and a sign that said Mossy Oak Ranch. Majestic oak trees filled with Spanish moss waving in the gentle wind, bordered the two-track dirt road that led to the house. Along the way, there were cleared pastures with green grass and a few black Angus cattle grazing lazily. Just in front of the house was a blue-tinted spring-fed pond that looked like an inviting spot for an evening swim.

The house was a typical 1950s-style Florida ranch house with one level, wooden sidings, a large front porch, and a tin roof. It was unpretentious but looked exactly as Steve had described to Karen.

"It looks just like I expected, and I can't wait to see what is inside," she said.

They unloaded the horses into the corral and put the trailer away. They took their luggage into the house.

"There are three bedrooms. The master has a bath, and the two others share a bath. Would you like your own room?" Steve asked.

"I think I would like to share the master bedroom with you," she said, smiling.

Her simple response was the beginning of their commitment to an intimate relationship. During the next two weeks, they would spend a lot of time in the master bedroom.

After unpacking, they walked around the property near the house. The oak trees seemed even more massive when they were up so close, and they guessed the trees must be over three hundred years old. The grass near the house had been recently mowed, and the air was fresh with the smell of cut grass. The pond sparkled in the afternoon sun, and it was the perfect vision of a country ranch house.

"Let's saddle the horses and make a scouting expedition around the entire ranch. We still have five hours before nightfall, and we can cover a lot of ground in that amount of time. I will put a blanket, some bread, cheese, and a bottle of wine in the saddlebags, and if we find a nice spot, we could have a picnic," said Steve.

As they roamed around the perimeter of the ranch, they saw more cattle, which the owner had agreed to include as part of the sale. There was a surprising amount of wildlife: deer, turkey, rabbits, and even a few coyotes. The southeast corner of the ranch abutted the Withlacoochee State Forest, which was a favorite hunting preserve for many Floridians. Inside the forest was a vast network of connected navigable lakes. The ranch had a dirt boat ramp that would enable Steve to launch his boat into a small creek that led to the big lakes for some incredible bass fishing.

Just before sundown, Steve stopped at a spot near one of the lakes adjacent to a green grass meadow, surrounded by the big oaks with their swaying Spanish moss. He tossed the blanket on the ground, opened his saddlebags, and retrieved the picnic supplies. After a few glasses of wine and many kisses, they consummated their relationship.

On the way back to the ranch house, they sang "You've Got a Friend" from the top of their lungs in total ecstasy!

G. ALAN BROOKS

# CHAPTER 12

# Preparing for Year One at the Ranch

T HE INITIAL TWO weeks at the ranch went by rapidly for the two lovers as they explored the entire property and the neighboring wilderness areas. They went riding almost every day; the season for mourning doves was active, and they did some afternoon dove hunting. Steve loved to eat the doves; and he often created a tasty meal by covering the birds with a unique mix of flour and seasoning, which he dropped into hot oil for three minutes and served the perfectly browned doves with cheese and grits. They fished the lakes and often had fresh grilled bass and bream for dinner with an assortment of locally grown vegetables and of course, a white French burgundy.

One day they took the hour-long drive to Orlando and spent most of the day at Disney World. They had enough of the park around five o'clock, and they ate an early meal upstairs at the Grand Floridian Hotel restaurant named Victoria & Albert's. The restaurant prides itself on providing an elegant setting, service, and food. After their leisurely dinner, they drove back to the ranch and were in bed by ten o'clock. The contrast between the bustle at Disney and the tranquility of the ranch was extreme, and it was fun to experience both in a single day.

Several days before she was scheduled to return to Idaho, Steve asked Karen if she would live with him permanently. No promise of marriage but a commitment to have fun and enjoy life. He said they would spend time at the ranch, fish around the world, enjoy the beaches, ride popular horse trails, travel anywhere she wanted, and eat wonderful meals. Karen said yes, and Steve drove to Hernando and bought the ranch from the owner.

"Steve, when I go back to Idaho, I will let my company know that I am moving to Florida. I would like to work part-time from the ranch if they agree. I can do my PR work from anywhere, and I like having some of my own money," she said.

"I don't want you to work. Please spend all your time with me. I will make sure you have all the money you need for whatever you want. For example, when you return, we must buy you a vehicle. I want you to think about what you will choose while you are gone," Steve replied.

"Oh, Steve, are you sure? I do not want to be a burden while we are together," she said earnestly.

"I am sure. Let's have as much fun and enjoyment as we can without the worry of client commitments or phone-call deadlines," he said.

"Okay, let's do it your way." She smiled.

When she returned to Idaho, Brad was waiting anxiously for her at the airport. She gave Brad an update on her progress, and they decided she would go back to Florida in one month. This would give them time to plan their strategy.

She told Steve she needed a month to wrap up her business affairs, arrange for her things to be shipped, terminate her lease, and say good-bye to her friends. He was happy with that idea and was excited that they would be spending a long time together. He had found his dream woman!

"Do you think he has any idea that you are not really in love with him?" asked Brad.

"No way! He is totally enchanted with me. He can't do enough to make me happy, and he is considerate of my every need. I have played this perfectly so far, and I think we will get a big payoff," Karen said gleefully.

"I ask you again. How long will it take to find a way into his pockets?" asked Brad.

"Well, he has offered to buy me a new car when I return. He said I could have any car I want. What do you think I should buy?" she asked

"I think an SUV is best since you are going to be in the country, but a Mercedes GL is going overboard and may seem too greedy. Maybe a Ford Explorer or Jeep with all the electronics would be comfortable and make you seem more reasonable," Brad suggested.

"I think you are right. I will call Steve and suggest he buy an Explorer or a Jeep for when I arrive," she agreed.

"I don't care about the car, but how are we going to get his money?" asked Brad.

"I have a plan that is slowly emerging. It will take a while, perhaps a year or two, but I think it is a solid strategy. It might involve marriage or not, but it will require me to find some legal mechanism to enforce his payment whether he wants to pay or not," she said.

"What could that be if not a marriage?" Brad asked.

"It is too early yet, but I read in the Miami papers about the accidental death of his business partner a few years before he sold his business, and it gave me a couple of ideas that need to be worked out. Think how fortunate it was for him to have 100 percent of the company stock when he sold the business," said she with an evil smile.

"I don't know what you are thinking, but I am happy you are exploring ideas so that you can get this deal done without taking so long that I forget you," he said.

Karen and Brad spent the month enjoying each other and lamenting the time they would be apart. Their relationship was strong, and both believed that they could keep their love intact while Karen was making the score they needed to retire together in comfort. It would not be easy, but they wanted big money more than anything else, and this was the only way they knew to get it.

Karen shipped a few personal items that would not fit in her luggage to the ranch. She left Idaho with three large suitcases, said a tearful good-bye to Brad, boarded the plane to Orlando, and started her new life as Steve's girlfriend.

On one of their favorite websites, Brad had found a likely candidate, whom he had met for lunch two weeks ago; and he was preparing to go to Atlanta for the con. His target was a divorcee who had been single for less than a year and was looking for a playmate. Her ex-husband was a successful developer of commercial property who had given her a significant divorce settlement. She had no kids, so it looked like a solid prospect with little downside. His new sting would keep him busy enough to avoid thinking of Karen every minute and might bring home some more bacon.

# CHAPTER 13

# Together at the Ranch

THE YEAR WAS just as Steve had promised. He had a long list of things to do and places to go. He showed the list to Karen, which included an unbelievable array of local, out-of-state, and international destinations. He asked Karen to pick what she liked, tell him when she wanted to go, and he would make the arrangements.

If she wanted to stay at home, that was fine with him. She could be alone in the house if she wished; and he would go riding, hunting, fishing, or just puttering around the ranch. They settled into an unrushed but active life of adventure and relaxation.

Besides their joint excursions, she loved to read on the front porch with a glass of tea or wine and gently rock in one of the old-fashioned rockers they had purchased together. She used her new white Ford Explorer to go into town to get whatever food or supplies she needed and to get her hair done once a month.

The drive into town also gave her a chance to call Brad on her burner phone. It was an idyllic life with no stress unless, of course you were plotting a sting on your new lover.

After nine months, she was no closer to a plan to get Steve's money, but she was beginning to fall for this wonderful guy. She started to ask herself why she should go back to Brad when she could have this beautiful existence for the rest of her life. She became conflicted but told neither man her thoughts.

Meanwhile, Brad lost control of the situation in Atlanta because his sting went back to her husband. He was left without a score of any money, plus he was getting angry with Karen's lack of progress or formulation of a plan to fleece Steve. Brad was in a foul mood.

After trying unsuccessfully for two days to reach Karen on the phone, Brad finally got her to answer his call.

"Are you crazy? Why are you calling me on my mobile? You know I will call you from a burner phone when I am in town. This is nuts!" she yelled.

"I am coming to Florida to see you, and you must find a reason to get away from the ranch. I have missed you too much, I must hold you, and I want to help you formulate a plan," demanded Brad.

"You cannot just come here and disrupt things. You can spoil it all with your nonsense," she said.

"I will be there tomorrow whether you like it or not. Where can we meet? I will not take no for an answer," he said.

She gave him the name of a small feed store in Citrus Springs, where she had picked up some sweet feed for the horses a month ago. She asked what he was driving, told him to wait in his car, and she would honk when she drove past the store in her white Explorer. He would follow her, and she would stop somewhere she felt was safe to meet. She was furious at Brad and did not know what she would do when she saw him tomorrow. He was a damn fool to risk everything.

She honked as she passed Brad's red rental car. She had told Steve she was going to get a few more bags of sweet feed for the two horses, who loved the special mix they made at this feed store. Brad followed her as she turned off on a dirt road several miles from the feed store. She drove down the two-track dirt road until it ended at the edge of a large lake. Karen and Steve had picnicked at this spot one afternoon a few months ago. There were no cars in sight, and she and Brad got out of their vehicles.

"I am so mad at you. I cannot speak. I simply do not know what to say to you, except you are a fool!" Karen shouted.

"Calm down. I will not mess things up. I just needed to see you. Come to me," he said as he pulled her close for a kiss. "I have been thinking about a plan that could help us both," Brad said.

"What is it? There must be some good reason for this visit other than to see me," she said as she pulled away.

"Do you think you could convince Steve that you guys need someone to help with the multitude of tasks you have with the mowing of the fields, the feeding of the horses and cows, and other ranch-related things?" he asked.

"You are totally crazy. First, Steve likes doing those things. Second, if you were there, you would not keep your hands off me. Third, he would surely see through our antics," she said.

"Who helps with the farm chores when you guys are out and about traveling?" he asked.

"We have an old Mexican gentleman who is available when we travel," she said.

"Maybe I could be hired to help when you are gone rather than him. You can tell him I am a cousin who found out you are living in Central Florida and wanted to be near you. Tell him I lost my job in Atlanta selling real estate, and I want to chill for a while. Tell him we grew up together, and I am a fine person who never made it in the business world but knows a lot about animals and farm life," he said.

"If he says okay, I will rent a cheap place in one of the local towns, get a job doing low-level work at a restaurant or store, and work part-time until you guys need me at the ranch," Brad said.

"Think about it, if I am there to observe, we will have two eyes and brains thinking about how to get some of his money," Brad commented.

"I will think about it. In the meantime, go away! Go to Orlando and rent a cheap room and wait for me to call. Do not call me on my mobile. He is very tech-savvy and frequently picks up my phone to make a call rather than his," she said.

"I will float the idea of a helper other than the one we have now. It will not be easy, but I will see his reaction and let you know in a couple of weeks. Next week, we are planning a trip to South Carolina for camping and riding in one of the national forests, which has a few hundred miles of remote trails," she said.

Brad was interested in some romance, but she was so upset she got in her Explorer and burned rubber as she was leaving. She had a sinking feeling that this would not turn out well, but she knew she could not stop Brad once he made up his mind. She returned to the ranch with some sweet feed and a worried brow.

# CHAPTER 14

# Brad Arrives

ONE NIGHT IN a South Carolina forest, Karen mentioned she was worried about the guy taking care of the ranch while they were gone. She said she was concerned they knew little about him or his background, and they had many valuable things in the house and outbuildings. She also suggested that if they had a reliable full-time man to tend the ranch, they might have more time to spend together. She only mentioned it once and let it drop.

"I've been thinking about what you said regarding a full-time ranch worker, and I think you might be right. We should start looking for someone with a good background who is willing to work hard," Steve said when they were on the way back to the ranch.

"Good. Let's put out the word and see what we can find. The right person could free us up while taking good care of the horses and cows while we are gone," Karen replied.

When they returned to the ranch, Steve posted some help-wanted flyers on the poster boards at the local restaurants, general stores, and feed stores. He spoke to the owners and staff of each business and explained what kind of help he was looking to hire. He left both his and Karen's mobile numbers for anyone interested.

They received a few inquiries, but they only found two men they felt might be a good fit. They interviewed both potential candidates and hired a young twenty-two-year-old who lived in a nearby town named Brooksville. He appeared to know animals and said he was handy with most farm tools. He had grown up on a small farm that raised hogs and goats. He graduated from high school and spent four years in the army. He had just arrived home from a tour of duty in Iraq and decided not to reenlist. His name was Terry Jackson.

Karen told Brad she was working on a plan to get him hired at the ranch, but it would take a little effort and time. She suggested he find a job in Orlando until she could work things out on her end. Brad was not happy, and he let her know it with a string of expletives.

Terry, the new hire, had been working at the ranch for three weeks when things started to go downhill for him. He arrived late, his work was spotty, and he seemed to lose interest in his job. After four weeks, he said thanks for the work but told Steve he did not like the commute from Brooksville, and he had found other work. Karen had made it easy for Terry to leave and find another job when she presented him with an envelope containing ten $100 bills.

Karen called Brad to let him know that the job was now open, and her next step was taking place. She was going to tell Steve that her cousin wanted to visit them at the ranch for a few days and get his reaction. She hoped Steve would say okay to a visit and that once Brad was visiting, he would impress Steve enough to get the job.

"Steve, I got a call from a cousin of mine who grew up on the farm next to ours in Idaho. He is my age, educated, and well mannered. He loves the outdoors, just like me, and he would love to visit me here at the ranch. Do you think that would be okay?" she asked sweetly.

"We have three bedrooms, and only one is being used. Of course, he can visit. It might be fun to have another man around to help a little now that Terry has gone. When does he want to come?" Steve asked.

"He can leave Idaho in a couple of days and be here next week. Can he stay for a couple of weeks?" she asked.

"Sure. If he is as nice as you say, a few weeks should be no problem," answered Steve.

Karen called Brad the next day and let him know to pretend to arrive the following Monday, and she would meet him at the Orlando Airport. Get rid of his rental car, and their hour drive to the ranch would give them time to develop their strategy for getting Brad hired as the ranch hand.

Karen acted so excited about seeing her cousin while pretending they had gone to their small school together for twelve years. She constantly talked about how nice it was that Brad wanted to visit and that Steve had agreed to let him. She was in a great mood and skipped around the house and property like a young schoolgirl. She could not believe that she would have both lovers in one place at the same time. She just needed to be careful not to spoil the con. Damn Brad, she thought, but it might be fun to have him around.

# CHAPTER 15

# Brad Is Surprisingly Helpful

KAREN MET BRAD at the Orlando Airport rental car lot. They quickly embraced, put his luggage in her Explorer, and headed for the ranch. Karen was still aggravated at Brad for rushing her plans but glad to see him.

"Karen, I have missed you so much. I can't wait to hold you in my arms!" Brad exclaimed.

"I am glad to see you too, Brad, but you have pushed me to move too fast. We need to be extra careful around Steve because he is super smart and will pick up on any affectionate moves you might make toward me. I know you, and you are going to have a hard time seeing me with him while keeping your distance. This is the biggest possible score we have ever had, and we can't mess it up for some short-term romance," she cautioned.

"I understand, but I still need to be intimate with you from time to time. We will find a way when he is away, I am sure," Brad said.

"That is the stupid damn thing I'm talking about! If you spoil this deal, I think I will kill you with an ax!" she shouted.

"Calm down. I will not spoil this deal. I am only visiting my cousin for a couple of weeks, and then I'm going back to Idaho, where I'm starting a new job as a hardware store manager. I will be the perfect guest, and you can count on that," he said.

When they arrived at the ranch, Steve was waiting for them at the front door. The winding dirt road up to the ranch house is almost a mile from the paved turnoff, and it was normal to hear any approaching vehicles. He bounded down the stairs and went to the car to help unload Brad's luggage.

"Welcome to Mossy Oak Ranch. We are happy to have you here as a guest for a few weeks. Karen has told me a lot about you, and I am anxious to learn more. We look forward to your visit," said Steve with an enthusiastic handshake.

"I am excited to be here. The ranch property looks so beautiful, and to see my close childhood cousin is a treat. I thank you for your hospitality," Brad said, looking Steve straight in the eye and with a firm handshake.

"I had another well-trained quarter horse dropped off at the ranch this morning so we can all ride together. Get settled in your room, and let's take a ride around the property and have a picnic like Karen and I did on her first day here. Karen, do you remember the spot of our first picnic?" Steve asked.

"Of course, I remember it well! That is a great idea. Brad, put your stuff in your room, hurry up, and let's all go for a ride. What a great idea," Karen said with bubbling excitement.

Brad knew his way around horses, and he helped saddle the three powerfully built quarter horses, which were the breed most local people owned and admired. Most quarter horses were trained to herd cattle, and they learned to move based on the knee pressure of the rider. They are among the fastest horses in the world for a quarter of a mile. Some have been timed at fifty-five miles per hour. Many young people like the fantastic sport of barrel racing using the quick-cutting ability of the horses to move around barrels at an amazing speed. In the South, they are a beloved breed.

Not far from the ranch is the city of Ocala, which is known all over the world for its thoroughbred horse farms. These horses are bred specifically for racing over the distance of one mile. They have a different purpose when compared to the quarter horse that is bred to be quick and agile for short distances. Ocala and Kentucky are the two major breeding areas for USA thoroughbreds. Both are beautiful breeds but have different capabilities, and they are ridden differently.

"Brad, if you want a quarter horse to move right, press with your left knee and turn slightly to the right. If you want the horse to move left, press with your right knee and turn slightly to the left. Of course, you can also neck rein the horse by doing basically the same. It is a simple process once you do it a few times," advised Steve.

"That is different from my farm learning, but I think it makes sense. I can tell these are special horses from their behavior and powerful stature. I will do my best to ride them properly." Brad smiled.

They rode through the ranch side by side and chatted about the beauty of the trees, cows, and grass. It was a pleasant ride without any rider having trouble even when they galloped or ran the horses hard for the sheer excitement of it. Brad rode with skills, and Steve tipped his hat to Brad after a five-minute fast run.

The cattle on the ranch were mostly two breeds: Angus and Hereford. The Angus is almost always solid black; but occasionally, a few red-colored cows will appear. It is the most common breed of beef cattle in the United States; they are very hardy and can take the Florida heat without complaint. They are regarded as medium sized. They have large muscle content and excellent marbling qualities. The Hereford usually has a deep red body with a white face; they are easy to raise and adaptable to many ranch temperatures. They are also middle sized, very productive breeders; and many believe their marbling qualities are superior to the Angus meat. Many ranchers raise both breeds successfully in the Florida heat.

When they got to the picnic spot, they dismounted, tossed the blanket on the ground, and toasted one another as they had a glass of wine. Brad could not believe how beautiful everything was, including Steve. He liked the ranch environment and Steve's natural way of living and behaving. Brad quickly understood how Karen could have fallen under his influence. He would need all his charm to keep Karen for himself, not lose her to this remarkable man, and not lose the money.

# CHAPTER 16

# Steve and Brad Create a Bond

B RAD SETTLED IN comfortably to their daily routine, and everyone seemed to get along great. Brad asked Steve for permission to ride alone when he was not needed or included in one of their trips away from the ranch. Brad quickly learned the layout of the ranch, the best trails, and the time it took to go from one place to another. After a few days, he was comfortable with his assigned horse and had no fear or concern about riding alone for hours. He also used his horse to help take care of the cattle.

Brad knew how to feed and water the horses and how to groom them after a ride. He was also handy with all the tasks necessary to keep the cows properly fed and watered. There were watering troughs in the fields with windmill-driven pumps to keep the troughs filled with water. Sometimes there was not enough wind to fill the troughs, and he would manually pump the necessary water into the troughs to fill them completely. On several days, he drove the old pickup truck Steve had purchased to take feed and hay to the cattle in the remote pastures.

He and Steve worked together to repair damaged parts of the roof on the old barn that housed the feed, hay, and a variety of ranch equipment. It required them to spend close time together and to assist each in various tasks. They had also successfully fished for bass several early mornings in the adjoining streams and lakes. They enjoyed spending time together, and neither found it necessary to speak continuously. Each enjoyed fishing, riding, and working with just the noise of nature in the background.

After ten days, the time for his departure was rapidly approaching; and Brad was worried he had not impressed Steve enough for him to be hired as the ranch hand. Nervously, he decided to broach the subject one evening after they had changed a large flat tractor tire that was a tough and cumbersome job. They were both sweating and laughing at the difficulty in lifting and managing that big massive tire.

"Steve, I am enjoying this vacation experience. I hate to leave in a couple of days, and I was wondering if you would have any interest in letting me do the job you hired Terry to do. I would give up my job in Idaho to stay here because I love this life," Brad said.

"I'm glad you brought it up. I was wondering if you would be interested in the job. I think it would be a great idea if you would stay a while longer. How about a six-month trial? If you still like it, we can think of making it permanent. Let's tell the good news to Karen. I am sure she will be happy," he said.

"Oh, how wonderful! I will have two of my favorite guys right here on the ranch with me." She smiled as she hugged Steve.

During the next two months, Brad, Karen, and Steve spent a lot of time together and alone. Brad did the ranch work without any complaints and did not interfere with Karen and Steve when they wanted to do something that did not include him. Late one afternoon, Steve approached Brad with an idea.

"Brad, let's build you a small cabin. It will give us more room in the house, and it will provide a lot more privacy for you. I know it is not easy for us to be on top of each other all the time. What do you think?" asked Steve.

"That would be terrific! I think you and I can do a lot of it ourselves if we hire someone to put in the foundation, framing, and roof. We can do the finishing work on both the interior and exterior!" exclaimed Brad excitedly.

"Okay, let's pick a spot. I think I would like it to be a log cabin, and we will get a contractor to do as much as needed, and we will do the rest," said Steve.

It took only two months from start to finish to build a nice five-room log cabin, which consisted of a great room with a kitchen, a bedroom, a bathroom, a laundry room, and a small office. The great room would serve as the living room, dining room, and kitchen. The floors were synthetic wood, and they decorated the inside with rustic furniture and fixtures.

When finished, it was a simple but attractive cabin that kept the ambiance of the ranch intact. Brad was happy to have his own place, and he also felt that the effort Steve took to build the cabin was a positive indication of their solid relationship. Now, Brad and Karen could take their time to figure the best way to get their score. Maybe they could also use the new cabin for some fun when Steve was not around. Things were working out great.

"My daughter Ann is coming to visit for a week. I invited her to come up from Miami and take a few days off from her crazy, busy job as a criminal defense attorney," announced Steve to Brad, who was cleaning one of the horse's hooves.

"Great! I hope she likes to ride because the weather is perfect, and pastures are beautifully green and lush." Brad smiled while wondering what this development would bring to the happy threesome.

Ann's relationship with her fiancé had turned sour, and she was having a difficult time getting over it. Steve had visited her three weeks ago shortly after the breakup, and Ann was distraught but still working and going about her daily life. Steve thought she would benefit from a few days of riding, fishing, shooting, and just hanging out.

Ann was twenty-nine, and she kept herself in excellent physical condition. She had her mother's good looks and a perky personality. Maybe she would enjoy meeting Brad. He was older than she, but he was fun to be around. They could certainly do some riding together, and Steve knew it would help take her mind off the breakup.

When Ann arrived, she took one of the spare bedrooms, quickly unpacked, and immediately asked for a glass of wine.

"I need a glass of wine and a snack of anything. The drive from Miami was tough today because of so much construction and traffic. I am starved and ready to party." She laughed.

"We are prepared for you. Look at this display of cheeses, crackers, loaves of bread, olives, shrimp, and a lobster tail just waiting for your arrival," said Karen as she took the platter from the refrigerator.

"Thanks. Dad, what kind of wine do you have open?" she asked.

"I am opening one of your favorites right now," said Steve as he opened a vintage California chardonnay from Napa Valley.

Karen had met Ann several times before on the trips to Miami, and she had found Ann to be high strung. Ann seemed stressed out all the time because of her work defending criminals. She always seemed to be behind in her assignments. Karen thought Ann was in over her head with the complicated cases, but she knew Ann had attended elite schools, and she must be smart. Karen did not really like Ann but never let it show, and she knew she could put up with anything for a week.

# CHAPTER 17

# Seeing Too Much

"ANN, GET YOUR pistol and let's do some target practice. I am rusty and need to fire a few hundred rounds. I set up two lanes of targets behind the barn at varying distances, and we will see who can shoot the best kill patterns," said Steve.

Ann and Steve had both received their Florida concealed-weapon carry permits three years ago. With the permit, a concealed weapon can be carried in most places except federal buildings, airports, bars, voting stations, and schools.

They both bought Sig Sauer P365 pistols that were specifically designed for concealed carry because they are small and easily hidden. They shoot 9-millimeter rounds with a magazine capacity of ten, with one in the barrel, giving the shooter eleven rounds in the small pistol configuration.

"Okay. Let's go. I have it in my purse, and I am ready," Ann replied.

Ann usually carried her pistol in her purse, and Steve regularly carried his in his right pocket using a specially designed pocket holster. They were both typically armed each day wherever they went.

Steve and Ann were both excellent, but not great, shooters. It took hours and hours of constant practice to be outstanding with any firearm. However, you did not need to be an expert to protect yourself in close quarters. You did need to know a few of the essential skills: maintaining a solid proper grip, extending the arms the right distance, focusing on the front sight, keeping a steady pull of the trigger, and learning not to be alarmed by the noise and recoil of each round.

"I have provided one hundred rounds of ammo for each of us, three fully loaded magazines each, and some manual easy-to-use magazine loaders when we need to reload the mags. Let's start with some slow-fire of fifty rounds, then move up to rapid-fire for the last fifty," said Steve.

"I bet you a bottle of wine that my total score will be better than yours, and I will finish the one hundred rounds before you." She laughed and laid her pistol and ammo on the little shooting table he had set up for each shooter.

They had fun competing on the range Steve had recently built. He hired a local farmer with a Caterpillar and blade who made a large hill by pushing dirt twenty feet high, thirty feet wide, and ten feet deep. Because Steve also loved to practice with his rifles, he made the range four hundred yards long. Of course, long-range rifles can shoot much longer distances, but most hunters do not shoot game over 150 yards.

"I think I beat you by eleven points because I was better on the rapid-fire at fifty yards," bragged Ann.

"Yep, you win. That was a lot of fun, and I am impressed that you are still quite capable with that small pistol," Steve said.

"Dad, I am amazed that such a short barrel can be so accurate and that we can group the shots so tightly. I'm glad this was our pistol choice. I love it," she said.

The next day, Ann and Brad were up early to take a morning ride. The horses were anxious and spirited since they had not been ridden for a while and were eager to gallop and take a good run or two. They let the horses have their way, and they flew past fence posts and the majestic oaks as if the world were a spinning top. After the long run, they let the horses blow for a few minutes; and then they walked and talked.

Ann told Brad that she had just ended a four-year relationship she thought would end in marriage. She was sure she would ultimately be better off, but she had trouble getting her mind clear of breakup thoughts. He was sympathetic and mentioned that it had happened to him a few times, but the pain diminished quickly. They rode for a couple of more hours before returning to the ranch house. They unsaddled the horses and went to the house for lunch.

Karen had made a large fresh salad with grilled salmon, and she served it with a chilled Sauvignon Blanc white wine. Steve had gone to the feed store, and Ann decided she wanted to take another ride by herself. Ann saddled her horse, got her pistol, put some water in the saddlebags, and said she would be back in several hours.

As soon as Ann left, Brad started caressing and kissing Karen. They went to the cabin and began making love. At that moment, Ann returned because she had forgotten her cowboy hat to keep away the sun. Ann was walking from the barn to the house when she heard the lovemaking noise and stopped to peer in the windows of the cabin. She saw them together in an intimate embrace, and she wondered how her father had come to trust Karen. Ann would need to think about how to deal with this. She got her hat and resumed her ride.

"Brad, this is crazy. If anyone were to see us, it would ruin everything. I told you many times. You must leave me alone. This is madness, and I am mad at myself for letting you entice me," Karen barked as she put on her clothes.

Things would never be the same for Brad and Karen.

# CHAPTER 18

# A New Plan

WHEN ANN FINISHED her ride, Brad joined her at the barn and helped unsaddle her horse. He was happy to be helpful and chatted with her about her trip while mentioning he wished he had gone with her. He said it was boring when he had no chores, and Steve was away. Ann said she understood as she marveled at his deceit and easy way of lying to her. Ann decided to tell her father what she had seen. She did not think he would be very understanding since he had invested so much time and effort courting Karen.

"Dad, I had such an interesting ride today. I found a new path to one of the lakes, and I think it could be a good place to fish for bass from the shore. Will you ride with me?" she asked when Steve returned and unloaded the sweet feed into the barn.

"Sure. Let me grab a snack from the fridge, and I will be ready in ten minutes. Ask Brad to saddle our horses, and I will bring a rod and reel with us in case you are correct about shore fishing. That would be an easy way to catch our dinner." He laughed.

They rode for a while, and Ann took him to a familiar spot near one of the small streams. Steve looked surprised when she asked him to dismount and sit with her on a fallen log near the edge of the water.

"What's the matter, Ann? Are you upset about your breakup?" asked Steve.

"Dad, this is not easy for me to do, but I am going to give you some awful news. This afternoon I saw Brad and Karen making love when they thought you were at the feed store, and I was on a long ride. I do not think this was their first time either," she said.

Ann told Steve the whole story about returning for her hat and what she saw. To Ann's surprise, he did not seem so alarmed or devastated.

He smiled a little and scratched his chin, which was a habit she had often see him do when he was amused and thinking of how to respond to a situation.

"Well, I guess you and I need to think about a little reward for those guys. Let's put our heads together and see if we can have some fun without letting them know that we are aware of their intimate relationship. I guess I now know why Karen wanted Brad to visit and stay here," he said without emotion.

"What do you think they were trying to do here? Do you think they knew each other from the beginning? Do you think Brad is her cousin? What kind of people are we living with?" asked Ann.

"It is time to do a little more investigation into their backgrounds and try to answer those questions you just asked. Our advantage is they do not know we know. Let's catch some fish." He laughed as he unpacked his rod and reel.

"I knew something was up two weeks ago when I saw Terry, our former ranch hand, at the feed store, and he told me Karen gave him $1,000 to quit the job." He sighed as he made a long cast into the calm water.

"After Terry told me that she paid him to leave, I have still been having fun with Karen, and I decided to see how this little game played out. I was worried about the possibility of what you saw today, but I have been hoping I was wrong," Steve said.

They returned to the ranch house with one medium-sized bass, which was not enough for dinner; but it was a fun appetizer when Steve put it on the grill after covering it with butter and lemon juice. Steve had decided they would grill steaks and an assortment of fresh vegetables. They had a pleasant dinner, and everyone was relaxed after a few glasses of wine.

There was no tension in the air, and Ann was stunned at the casual way all three of them seem to ignore the terrible relationship behavior and deceit. She thought about her recent breakup and the tremendous emotion it had created for her and her fiancé. Something extraordinary was happening at this dinner table, and she hoped her dad would not get hurt by these scumbags.

Steve contacted a friend in Miami who knew some good investigative agencies. He asked for a complete detailed investigation of both Karen and Brad. He said he did not care what it cost, but he wanted to get to the truth of who they were and what they had been doing before meeting him.

Ann returned to her job in Miami, but she kept in daily contact with her dad. They had begun the development of a plan to have some fun at the expense of Karen and Brad. They waited for three weeks before hearing from the investigator.

The investigator's report was very damaging to the character of Brad and Karen, who had told Steve almost nothing but lies. They were not cousins but longtime lovers. Neither had a job in Idaho, they spent their life trying to con lonely single people of all ages, and they had stolen money from several unsuspecting people in the last three years. They had gone to college but decided to live a life of scamming rather than trying to make a good living through hard work as most graduates spend their life trying to achieve. Karen had decided after cheating her husband that scamming was easier than work and more fun.

Steve decided they were a lousy couple who needed a harsh lesson.

"Ann, I want you to take a leave of absence for six months. I want you here, and if you lose your job, I will double the lost earnings. Please tell your firm that I need you, and if they need to speak to me, I will be happy to explain that I desperately need your help," Steve pleaded.

"Okay, Dad, I think I can get leave without losing my job. I will be at the ranch in ten days. Is our plan ready?" she asked.

"Yes, and I think you will enjoy it and love being a part of the lesson we are going to teach them," Steve said.

# CHAPTER 19

# The Plan Starts to Develop

STEVE ASKED ANN to contact his ex-wife and speak to her about a portion of the plan. He was not sure Marie would help them, but Ann did as Steve asked; and in a few days, a package arrived from New York City addressed to Ann. It came from Bloomingdale's and was gift-wrapped like a present for a special occasion.

"Who is that from?" Karen asked when she saw the beautifully wrapped box.

"One of my recent clients who narrowly escaped jail time wants to thank me for saving his butt," Ann answered untruthfully.

Ann took the package in her bedroom to open. Inside the box was a lovely blouse and the item Ann had asked her mother to send. When Ann showed the article to Steve, he smiled and put it in the barn, well hidden. They could now implement step one of the plan.

Ann had asked her mother, who was a part-time dealer in Egyptian antiquities, to send several ancient parchments to the ranch. Ann wanted a parchment that Marie believed was authentic enough to be authorized for sale by the Cairo Museum of Egyptian Antiquities. She also wanted a string of bogus letters that explained what had been happening with the parchments.

A few days later, Steve encouraged the group to take a late-afternoon horseback ride and then fish from the shoreline for bass. He took the usual picnic supplies and an extra bottle of wine. The group was in a jovial mood and decided to ride along the southeast perimeter of the ranch, where they rarely rode because it was often wet and swampy. Steve chose this section to ride because he wanted them to see the huge quantity of birds that made this their home. The wetland area was filled with water birds of all descriptions: heron, ibis, anhinga, osprey, and countless songbirds. It was unusually wet this day, and the horses were often knee-deep in the dark water.

As they were leaving one of the extra deep spots and just getting back on solid ground, Steve's horse stumbled over an old black object. He dismounted to check the horse's leg and to pick up the small box. It had looked old because it was covered in dark mud, but Steve cleaned it using some Spanish moss that had been hanging from one of the nearby oak trees. When it was cleaned, they could see it was a leather handbag or purse with a Fendi design on the lid. Everyone was eager to see what was in the handbag, and all dismounted to look closely. It looked like a purse that would be carried by an affluent lady.

Steve opened the purse and was surprised to see an elongated clear glass tube with a cap on one end that made it waterproof, and there were also some paper documents or manuscripts. There were several letters with postmarks dated two years ago that had been partially damaged by the wet area.

"How did that thing get here and survive in this water and mud?" asked Ann.

"Someone must have dropped it while riding because it could not float here from the streams or lakes, and it is too wet for anyone to walk along this spot," suggested Steve.

"Who could it be? Who else would be riding out here?" asked Karen.

"I think the widow rented the ranch to a few wealthy New Yorkers before we bought it. Maybe one of them lost their purse, and I bet they looked everywhere for it, but it could have been underwater when they dropped the bag," offered Steve.

"Let's wait until we get back to the house to open the tube and see if the letters can give us any information that would enable us to return it to the owner," said Steve.

They rode to the shoreline, tossed out the picnic supplies, and fished for a few minutes. Everyone was so anxious to examine the purse that the fishing was cut short, and they returned home earlier than planned.

Steve put the purse on the dining room table with everyone standing around. He opened it, removed the five letters, spread them across the table, unscrewed the glass tube, and put a strange-looking set of old parchments next to the letters. The parchments looked ancient and were filled with hieroglyphics, which everyone quickly assumed were Egyptian.

They looked at the addressee's name and address and the sender's names and addresses. All five letters were directed to the same person: Ms. Penelope Matthews at 201 Madison Avenue, New York. They had been sent from a museum in Egypt and an Egyptian antique dealer in New York.

Steve opened the letters and began reading them aloud. It seemed each letter was discussing the rare documents that had been in the glass tube. Ms. Matthews had purchased the documents from an antiquities dealer in Cairo for $500,000, and she was trying to sell them to the dealer in New York for a significant profit. She had returned to the USA without obtaining the necessary certification of authenticity and the authorization from the museum to leave Egypt and be offered for sale.

The dealer in New York was suspicious and required certification from the museum in Cairo before he would buy the documents. The last letter was from the director of the Cairo Museum, who said he would not certify and authorize the documents unless he could physically see them. He had suggested that Ms. Matthews bring them to Cairo herself, and he would look at them immediately upon her arrival.

The director promised it would be a short trip because he was a specialist in ancient Egyptian New Kingdom artifacts and documents. He would be able to certify very quickly, and then she could easily sell them if they were authentic. He said that based on the photos Ms. Matthews had sent to him, they looked real and could be extremely valuable.

"What should we do with the documents? They might be unbelievably valuable, and I guess we should contact Ms. Matthews and attempt to return the documents," said Steve.

"Dad, I think a little differently. These documents are on our property, and being the lawyer that I am, I think possession is nine-tenth of the law. They have been here a while, and I am suspicious that if she really paid $500,000, she would never have stopped looking for that purse. I would not be surprised if she stole the documents and did not know how to get them certified. I think we should make the trip to Cairo, get them certified ourselves, and determine their value. Then we can decide what to do with them," said Ann.

"Well, that is a point of view that surprises me. Maybe she would give us a reward if we give them back to her," said Steve.

"I agree with Ann. We don't know what they are worth, and neither does Ms. Matthews, so she would be reluctant to give a meaningful reward. Let's go to Cairo and see if they are worth anything. They sure look old and impressive," said Karen.

"It seems like a no-brainer to me. I agree with Ann and Karen," said Brad.

"Okay, since you guys all agree and you are ready for an adventure to sort this out, I do hereby grant all financial interest in these documents and their subsequent value to the three of you," said Steve while smiling at the three of them.

"But I have a slightly different idea than going to Cairo right away. I think we need to do a little more examination before we go to Egypt on a boondoggle," he continued.

"I think Karen and Ann should visit a specialist in Egyptian New Kingdom antiquities at the world-renowned Metropolitan Museum in NY. I am sure the museum would be happy to have one of their experts look at these documents. They might not certify them, but they could probably give a scholarly observation. That way, we can get an opinion before anyone takes the trip to Egypt," said Steve.

"I think that is an excellent idea. I will make some calls to the museum and get the name of an expert. Then I will contact them to set an appointment as soon as possible," said Ann.

"This sounds like a lot of fun. I look forward to working with Ann to solve this mystery and make some money." Karen laughed.

# CHAPTER 20

# The Metropolitan Museum

ANN AND KAREN had to wait ten days to get an answer from one of the Egyptian experts at the Met. It was a woman named Mar, and she had agreed to meet them one week later in New York at 2:00 p.m. They were excited to have the appointment because they had spent hours on Google and other search engines to learn more about the documents in their possession. One of the letters mentioned the papers were likely from the New Kingdom period.

The New Kingdom of Egypt began around 1570 BC and lasted until 1069 BC. It was one of the most prosperous times in Egypt, the peak of its power; and it was the period of the famous warrior Pharaohs. The documents looked like they described some decisive battle or battles, and it could have been written by one of the Pharaoh's scribes to preserve his victories. They saw some characters on the bottom of each page that looked like a date notation, and they hoped it would further identify the period in which the documents were created.

Ann and Karen left the ranch and drove to Orlando for their flight to La Guardia Airport that was followed by a twenty-minute drive to New York City. Karen had been to NYC on only one prior occasion, and she was eager to see the famous city and to visit with the expert. Ann had grown up in New York and been back many times to visit her mother. She falsely told Karen she had been to the city a few times but was not a real New Yorker, and Karen would need to help navigate their way around town.

They stayed at the Mark Hotel, which was on Madison Avenue and Seventy-Seventh Street, just a few blocks south of the museum, which was on Fifth Avenue and Eighty-Second Street. The Mark was an upscale hotel with an excellent restaurant by Jean-Georges and a happening bar with a real New York vibe. The two women went to the bar, and soon several young traveling executives flirted with them and offered drinks.

They smiled back at the handsome men, had two drinks each, and went to the fancy restaurant for dinner without any male companionship. They had each taken a separate room; and after dinner, they went to their respective rooms and agreed to meet for breakfast and do some touring before their afternoon meeting the next day.

"Brad, this is the coolest hotel ever! You should see this place, the fancy restaurant, and an active bar scene. Ann is picking up the tab for everything. How are things going with you and Steve?" Karen asked.

"We went pistol shooting today on the range. It was fun, and I was amazed at how good Steve is at hitting the kill zone in the targets. I did okay but not nearly as good as him. Tonight, we had dinner together, and I am headed to bed," answered Brad.

"I hope we get some solid authentication from the museum expert tomorrow. The value of these documents could be some serious money. Steve said we could divide it among the three of us, and that is a generous offer that might add some real sweetness to our main objective," said Karen.

"When are we going to get big money from Steve? I am tired of waiting, and I don't see that you are making any progress," said Brad.

"You are wrong. Just a few days before we left, Steve said he was thinking about making our relationship permanent with marriage. He asked if I thought it was time to stop living together and tie the knot. Of course, I said I would think about it, but it sounded like a nice offer," she answered.

"Well, what happens after the marriage?" asked Brad.

"It will not take but six months or a year for him to have an accident on one of our international adventures. I will make sure he has made me his beneficiary shortly after the marriage," she said.

After completing the call with Brad, Karen called Steve to say good night. She told him about her day and evening with Ann and their plans for tomorrow. He wished her good luck, said he loved her, and they hung up.

The next morning, they met for breakfast at the Mark. Then they did a real touristy thing and purchased two hop-on-hop-off bus tickets. The buses, with an upper deck for viewing, take tourists all over the city. Using a loudspeaker, the driver explains the sights and tells stories as he drives along the streets of the city. When the passengers see something that they want to investigate in more detail, they get off the bus and visit the new scene. When finished with that attraction, they wait at a designated spot until another bus comes, and they hop on and stay until they find another exciting venue to visit and hop off. It sounds silly, but it is an effective way to learn a lot about a new city, and Karen loved it.

They hopped off the bus in Chinatown and found a family-owned restaurant that made a delicious variety of dim sum dishes. After lunch, they walked the streets headed north until they saw it was almost time to meet the expert. They took an Uber to the Mark to get the manuscripts and then to the museum.

They waited until an attractive lady with black hair met them by the staircase in the Great Hall and took them to her small office near the Egyptian exhibits. The met has over twenty-five thousand historical Egyptian artifacts, and many came from the exhaustive thirty-five years the museum's own archaeologists spent in Egypt. Without any doubt, the Metropolitan Museum houses a team of the most knowledgeable Egyptian experts in the world.

"Hi, everyone calls me Mar, and I am happy to meet with the two of you. I understand you have some ancient documents that need certification by the Cairo Museum. I am friends with the director at the Cairo Museum, and if you go there, please give him my regards," said Mar.

"May I see the documents? I am familiar with most of the periods in ancient Egypt, but I am most skilled in the New Kingdom period, which was the apex of the Pharaoh's power," she explained.

Ann took the documents from her briefcase and handed them to Mar. Mar put on her glasses, took a magnifying glass, and slowly examined each page. She made no comments as she studied the old papers, and Karen was worried she would say she did not recognize the work. After a full fifteen minutes, Mar said she was surprised at the beautiful hieroglyphs and the impressive preservation of the documents.

"I am not the one who needs to make the certification of these documents to guarantee their authenticity and authorization for sale, but I think they are the real deal. Before I could be sure, I would need to share them with some of my associates, but I think they are real enough for you to visit my friend at the Cairo Museum and get the certification you need. They could be worth a fortune unless the Egyptian government confiscates them as a national treasure. Be careful not to leave them with anyone, or they might disappear." Mar explained.

Ann and Karen left the museum and high-fived each other as they descended the front steps of the impressive Met. They had thanked Mar and immediately left for Kennedy Airport. Steve had booked them on a direct flight to Cairo, assuming they would get a positive reaction from the Met expert.

They were on their way to a fortune and lots of excitement.

Secretly, Ann called her mother and thanked her for being "Mar" for the morning!

# CHAPTER 21

# Time in Cairo

THE FLIGHT FROM Kennedy to Cairo is just under sixteen hours and exhausting even if you are tucked away in first-class. When the plane landed, Karen and Ann got their luggage and headed directly to the Four Seasons Hotel. The hotel was in the heart of Cairo, with views of the Nile, the city skyline, and the Great Pyramids. It had an array of restaurants, a fancy mall attached, and beautiful boutiques around the corner. It was a great place to stay while they waited to meet with the director of the museum.

After checking in, they went to their bedrooms; and both slept soundly for eight hours before showering and meeting for lunch downstairs. Their appointment was the next day, so they looked around at the amazing sights and sounds of Cairo. They visited Giza and rode camels with a knowledgeable guide around the Great Pyramid and the Sphinx, that mythical creature with a lion's body and the head of a Pharaoh. Neither of them could believe such massive construction could have been conceived and accomplished so many thousands of years ago, with only manual methods.

"I don't think I have ever seen anything as impressive as these structures, and to think they were built over 4,500 years ago blows my mind," said Karen.

"I agree. There were some very skilled architects in those days, and I guess they used a lot of slave labor to build them," said Ann.

They wanted to go to Luxor to see the ruins and tombs that were so famous, but Luxor was four hundred miles away, and they did not have time to go on the first day. If things went well tomorrow with the authentication, maybe they would go on day three.

The next day, they met the director at the Cairo Museum of Egyptian Antiquities, which houses the world's most extensive collection of antiquities from the time of the ancient Pharaohs. Their collection exceeds 120,000 items. A few hours before meeting with the director, they had an unforgettable visit to the mummy rooms. The rooms contained countless mummies, and they learned about the rituals of mummification that had lasted for several thousand years. It was a mind-blowing experience to see so many ancient dead mummified people over four thousand years old still wrapped in cloth.

The director was a small man with rimless glasses and a polite manner. He greeted them, offered a glass of tea, and suggested they go into his private quarters to analyze the documents.

"I am anxious to see what you have. We are always looking for new and interesting artifacts from the ancient periods. We are also careful to make sure the artifacts we certify are real. You have no idea how clever crooks create many fraudulent Egyptian objects," he said.

They had been warned by Mar not to leave the documents with anyone, and they were careful not to let them out of their sight. If he asked to keep them overnight, they were prepared to say no. They planned to tell him they would keep them overnight and bring them back again, if necessary. They were also concerned he might confiscate them and keep them as Egyptian state property.

He studied the documents for at least an hour. He carefully compared their papers to images in several large textbooks; and when he looked up, he had a curious expression. Neither Ann nor Karen could determine what the strange look was meant to convey, but it made them nervous.

"These documents are real. They are some of the remnants of parchments we have on display downstairs. I am not surprised at Mar for thinking they might be real. She is such a fine expert, and from my experience, she is rarely in error," he said.

"How can you be so sure?" asked Karen.

"Is there a chance you can be mistaken?" asked Ann.

"No, there is no chance I am mistaken. Let me show you something I think you will find interesting. I will bring your papers, and we will compare them to some parchments we have on display," he said as he stood up and led them out of his office.

He took them to a display of New Kingdom parchments and pointed to several sheets that looked almost identical to the ones they had given him to authenticate. After he pointed out the similarities, it was clear, even to them, these documents were part of the parchments on display. Ann and Karen were elated to know they were real. Now they needed his stamp of authorization for them to be taken out of the country and offered for sale.

"Because we have so many of these same parchments already in our collection, I am happy to authorize your papers as authentic and approved for sale. You may take them home with you, and I wish you good luck in your endeavors," he said as he stamped the back of each parchment with his approval symbol. He also gave them a letter authorizing the exit of the documents from Egypt and their approval for sale anywhere in the world.

"Sir, do you have any idea of the retail value of these parchments in the world market?" asked Ann.

"No, I am not involved in commercial activities. My job is simply to protect the antiquities that are found in our country," he said.

Karen put the documents back in her attaché case, and they thanked the director and returned to their hotel. They went directly to the bar and had a few drinks to celebrate and then called Steve and Brad to give them the good news. They were so excited they did not know what to do, but they wanted to have some fun.

"Ann, how much money do you think we get for the parchments?" asked Karen.

"I don't know, but if we get $500,000 or more, that will be a lot of money for the three of us to split," said Ann.

"I can use the money. Maybe I will buy a fur coat." Karen laughed.

"Me too," said Ann.

They rested in their rooms for a few hours and then decided to go for a night on the town to celebrate the good news. They met downstairs at the casual restaurant around 9:00 p.m. and had a simple dinner of burgers, fries, and a bottle of average wine. They were dressed in attractive evening outfits, and they asked the hotel concierge where they might find a couple of safe nightclubs to enjoy a night out. He gave them a few nightclub names, suggested they take a driver from the hotel who would wait for them, and warned them not to leave the clubs with strangers. They promised to listen to his recommendations and warning.

When they arrived at the first nightclub on the list, they were amazed at the clean, attractive, and modern interior. The DJ was good, and the bar was filled with energetic young couples and clean-cut single men and women. They were given a table with four chairs, and soon the men were flocking to the table for chances to dance with these pretty American women. They had three martinis each; and after two hours of dancing, they went back to the hotel and got ready for their flight home tomorrow. They were too excited to spend any more time in nightclubs; they just wanted to get home and try to sell the parchments.

The next morning, after a brief ride to the airport, they flew back to New York and then to Orlando and then drove to the ranch.

# CHAPTER 22

# Back at the Ranch

W HEN ANN AND Karen returned to the ranch, there was high-fiving and joyful screaming. They celebrated with champagne toasts to a successful trip and to the profitable sale of the documents.

"I will call Mar and tell her that we received a certification of authenticity and approval to sell the parchments. I will ask if she can introduce us to potential buyers," said Ann.

"Did you find out the value of the documents from the director?" asked Steve.

"No, he said he did not know the dollar value of the parchments," Karen said.

Ann called Mar with Karen also on the phone. Mar gave them the names and phone numbers of three potential dealers, and all of whom were in Manhattan. They called each dealer and described the parchments and told them they were approved for sale by Egyptian authorities. The dealers asked to see images, and they sent photos taken on their phones to each dealer.

Two of the dealers would give no suggestions of price without physically looking at the documents. One dealer suggested that the parchments could be worth $600,000, but he would like to inspect them in person. He said he was confident he had a buyer if they were what they appeared to be.

They arranged to fly back to Manhattan; and two days later, they met the interested dealer. He offered them $600,000, and they asked for one day to think over the offer. They took the parchments to the other two dealers, but they did not get a better offer.

Unbeknownst to anyone, Steve immediately wired a check for the full amount to the dealer; and the documents were given to Marie for safekeeping. Now Brad and Karen would have some money that would enable the plan to continue.

Ann and Karen returned home with a cashier's check for $600,000, and again there was a champagne celebration and fancy dinner.

"What will you guys do with this money?' asked Steve while enjoying one of his red wines.

"I have not had time to think about that," answered Karen.

"Neither have I. I am so tired from our recent travels that I can't think straight," said Ann.

"I might buy a car with some of it," said Brad.

"Well, $200,000 each is a nice little nest egg but not enough to change your life, is it?" asked Steve.

"Maybe not, but it will give me something to build on. I think I will add this to some money I have in a savings account," said Karen.

"I will probably do the same," said Ann.

"I think I will just keep mine in a checking account for now because I may want to buy some things in the near term," said Brad.

"Karen, how much interest are you earning on the money in your savings account?" asked Steve.

"I'm not sure because I never think about it much," she answered.

"Well, I always think about getting the best return I can on my money. I think it is silly to let the money sit idle when it can be working," said Steve.

"What do you mean?" asked Brad.

"I mean, I put my money to work. I look upon money like a tree or a flower. It needs to multiply to have a purpose," said Steve.

"How do you make it multiply?" asked Ann.

"I make solid investments with people I trust who understand the intricacies of the financial markets," Steve said.

"Well, you have experience in the financial world, but neither Brad nor I have had the opportunity to learn about growing money," said Karen.

"Someday, if you ever want to learn a little, I can let you invest some of your new money along with my investments, and you can start to understand the idea and the beneficial results of smart investing," offered Steve.

"That would be great," said Karen.

"I would be interested in that," said Ann.

"Me too," said Brad.

"Well, the next time I have a good opportunity, I will tell you about it, and you can decide if you want to invest a little with me," said Steve.

They all agreed to think about investing with Steve if he found something that he thought was special and safe.

Steve had set the hook, and he just needed to create the right situation to continue to execute his plan.

Ann returned to Miami and resumed her work at the criminal defense law firm.

# CHAPTER 23

# Taking Time to Make
# the First Investment

F ROM THE MOMENT he saw the ranch, Steve was enamored by the beauty of the blue-tinted spring-fed pond that could be seen from the dirt road leading to the house. When he first saw the pond, Steve was not familiar with the sinkhole problems of Central Florida, including Hernando, which was known as sinkhole alley.

He later learned that Central Florida is filled with sinkholes that can be only a few feet wide or sometimes several hundred acres. They can be one foot deep or several hundred feet deep. Some have vertical walls, and some like Blue Sink near Williston can have caves that run parallel to the ground for long distances. Many scuba divers have been killed diving these deep sinkholes while exploring the caves, losing their direction, and running out of air.

A friendly neighbor confirmed to Steve that his blue-tinted pond was really a sinkhole. Steve had enjoyed swimming in the blue hole on a few occasions and the water was always refreshing. It was fed by underground aquifers that had been penetrated when the soil collapsed and sunk deep into the earth's surface.

One day, Steve was curious, and he free dived as far as he could and then used scuba gear to explore the sides and bottom of the sinkhole. He found there was only one horizontal tunnel at a depth of eighty feet and that the bottom of the sinkhole was probably two hundred feet deep.

"Brad and Karen, I feel like swimming today. How would you like to join me at the blue pond?" Steve asked.

"Sure, I would love to take a swim. You have never taken me to the blue pond, but I always wondered if it was a place to swim because it looks so pretty from a distance," said Brad.

"I went diving one time on a trip to Acapulco, but I was so scared that I did not enjoy it. Is there anything that bites in that pond?" asked Karen as she pretended to be frightened.

"Only me!" Steve laughed as he pushed Karen into the water.

They spent the afternoon swimming and diving. Steve had brought three sets of scuba gear, and he taught Brad how to use the equipment. Steve took each one of them separately on the dive so he could teach them buddy diving. They only went down twenty feet with the scuba gear, but Brad and Karen were excited at how much fun it was to have breathing equipment underwater. Steve explained the need for a buddy when you are diving in case there is a problem with your equipment, or you get sick. Steve was the buddy as they dived around the sinkhole, and he advised them to never dive alone.

At such a shallow depth, a tank of air will last for more than an hour; and together they explored the sides of the sinkhole, looked in all the crevices, and saw fish of all sizes. Someone must have stocked the sinkhole with bass and bream because they could be seen everywhere. The pond quickly became a new activity for the group to spend relaxing hours together.

Karen spent some of her time preparing meals, riding her horse, and hanging out with the guys. She liked to read on the front porch and did not mind being alone some of the time.

"I think maybe we should find a project to occupy our minds and bodies, and I have an idea that will take a lot of muscle and sweat," Steve said to Brad one morning.

"What do you have in mind?" asked Brad.

"You know that overgrown area near the back pasture with the black Angus cattle?" asked Steve.

"Yes, of course, I do," answered Brad.

"I think we can use chainsaws, machetes, and saws to cut down the brush and small trees. Rather than try to burn the downed trees and bushes, I would prefer to feed them to a woodchipper," said Steve.

"That makes sense to me," answered Brad.

"There is a rental shop in Hernando with a Carlton 1712 portable woodchipper, and I can tow it out here with my Range Rover. It has a forty-eight-inch-wide feed chute, and that should take even the biggest of our treetops and grind them up small enough for us to use in the horse stalls as bedding," explained Steve.

"That would be a good project for us, I bet we can get that done in a couple of weeks, and it will improve access to that pasture," said Brad.

A few days later, Steve and Brad sharpened the blades on the equipment, rented the woodchipper, and began their project. It was October, and the weather was perfect for hard work. They worked long hours for more than ten days, often cooling off at the end of the day by a swim in the blue pond. It was a big job but satisfying when a tree fell and within an hour became wood chips for the horse stalls.

Meanwhile, Brad and Karen were preparing for their next move, but it was moving too slowly for Brad. Brad was pushing her to ask Steve about marriage, and he was getting terribly angry and impatient with all the delays.

"You must get this marriage deal moving. What is the problem? You said he asked you if you wanted to get married, and it is time you said yes. You are not going to get on his beneficiary list right away, and then he cannot have a fatal accident too soon after, or it will be suspicious. Hurry up. I don't want to spend the rest of my life on this damn ranch," Brad insisted.

"Okay, I will say yes tomorrow on a horseback ride to our picnic spot," she said.

That afternoon, they all went for a swim in the blue hole. Because it was chilly in the air and in the water, they did not stay long; but they came out super refreshed and ready for a hearty meal. Karen was an excellent cook; Steve loved to grill; and he selected the wines for the three courses of octopus ceviche, bison steaks, and homemade carrot cake. There was laughter all around, and Steve was sure they did not suspect he and Ann had any knowledge of their deceit and dangerous plans.

The next day, Karen suggested a picnic at their favorite spot; and after a brief snack, she kissed Steve gently and agreed to marry him. He returned the kiss, gave her a big hug, and acted ecstatic. He told her he would need some time to finish one of his business deals so he would have nothing else on his mind.

"What kind of business deal would take up your time?" she asked, a little disappointed in his answer.

"I am working with a quant in NY on a special project," he said.

"What is a *quant* for heaven sakes?" Karen asked.

"*Quant* is short for *quantitative analyst*. These specialists have been trained in mathematics and technology, and they know a lot of fancy math like calculus, differential equations, and statistics. They also know how to program in mathematical languages. I don't expect you to understand the details, but they are the new geniuses in the financial markets," said Steve.

"How long do you think it will take to finish this quant thing?" she asked impatiently.

"No more than two months the quant told me last night. It should be done by then, and if it works like I think, we will have a great deal of new money for our honeymoon," he said.

"If you think it is a good deal, can I invest with you?" Karen asked.

"Let me check it out more carefully, but this might be a good chance for the three of you to risk some of the parchment money," he suggested.

# CHAPTER 24

# The Big Investment

S TEVE WENT TO town for some horse feed; and while he was there, he decided to buy the woodchipper and keep it permanently for more land clearing. He paid the rental office the full retail price and was happy he could now clear the land at his leisure and dispose of the wood without burning it. He did not want to be bothered with continually coming to town to rent the woodchipper.

This gave Brad and Karen time to be alone again in the cabin. After their lovemaking, Brad acted depressed.

"I am frustrated at the time this is taking with no end in sight. I keep telling you, but you do not seem to understand that I miss you, and I hate that you spend more time with him than with me. I am jealous! I didn't think I would be, but I am," he explained.

"You need to get a grip. We agreed that we would handle this with marriage and an accident. Now, don't you start backing out at the moment we are about to enter our final stage," she snarled.

"I am going to say it one more time to you, Brad. If you don't stop this complaining, I will just stay married to this wonderful man, and you can go to hell!" she shouted, put her clothes on, and left the cabin.

Brad was confused with his feelings and his conflict between jealousy and greed and simply did not know how to handle Karen anymore. She was becoming too independent to suit him.

Steve returned with the feed and put it in the barn with Brad's help. Together, they fed the horses some sweet feed and fresh hay. They spread some of the new wood chips for bedding and then went to the ranch house for dinner.

"I got a phone call from my quant today, and he told me he was finished with his latest program. He thinks he can execute the new program on Friday, which is the last day of trading for the week," said Steve.

"What does his program do that will help you?" Brad asked.

"His program has taken years to develop, and it is designed to capitalize on unique stock market trading opportunities. It can execute high-frequency trading, which detects slight variations between liquid and illiquid securities. It can make millions of trades in just a few minutes," Steve said.

"I have no idea what all of that means," said Karen.

"Listen, I do not understand the details myself, but he has been a superstar at the hedge fund where he works. He has made a fortune for the fund investors by running this program. He has just added some new features that make it even more profitable. I have been investing with this hedge fund for years, but I have never seen returns like this guy is producing," Steve said.

"How do you know it will work properly? Is it risky?" asked Karen.

"Everything in the market is risky, but I think this is low risk because of the performance I have seen over the last two years with them. Anyway, I am investing a million dollars with them for the run he plans to make on Friday," said Steve.

"By the way, Ann is also investing $150,000 of her new money in this run," said Steve.

"I will also put in $150,000 of my money if you think it is safe, and we can get a good return," said Karen.

"Me too," said Brad.

Steve collected the money and wired it to the hedge fund on Wednesday. They waited together for the end-of-the-day trading results on Friday. Steve got a phone call at eight o'clock Friday night that they had doubled their money and that they would receive a wire transfer with the proceeds on Monday.

"I can't believe that I made $150,000 in two days!" exclaimed both Karen and Brad.

"What about Steve? He made a million dollars in two days," said Brad.

They wanted to celebrate, so the next day was Saturday, and they went to Orlando for a dining extravaganza at a French restaurant near Disney. It was a fun evening, and they had called Ann while they waited in the bar to have a tele-drink toast.

Karen and Brad drank more alcohol than usual because they knew Steve was driving, so they fell asleep on the way home. It was a special evening with lots of laughter about how easy it was to make a lot of money.

They repeated the investment two more times until all three had $500,000 each. Each time the three of them got a wire with the profit, Steve had wired the amount of the make-believe profits to the hedge fund in advance. Steve was funding the unbelievable winnings, and there was no quant involved. Steve knew how greedy they were, and he hoped their chance to make an even bigger score would be irresistible.

"I want to ask you guys a question. Do you have any more money in your bank or investment accounts back home in Idaho? The reason I am asking is that I am about to make a large investment with the hedge fund because the quant is quitting the firm and retiring. He tweaked the program to make an even bigger return just before he leaves," said Steve.

"How much are you investing?" Karen asked.

"I am going to give them $5 million. I want to make a big hit before he leaves. If you have any extra money at home and want to invest with me again, this is the last chance we will have," he said.

"I have around $1.5 million in two different accounts," said Karen.

"I have just about $1 million, and I sure would be sad to lose it," said Brad.

"If we combine our investment, we can get some extra attention, and maybe he will start the program a minute or two earlier, and the return will be even bigger. I will talk to him and see what he says," Steve said.

They got the money together, and Steve sent the money and made the investment. The quant ran the program, but it was a disaster. They lost all but 10 percent of their investment. Karen got $150,000 returned and Brad got $100,000. Brad and Karen were angry and stunned beyond what they could really comprehend. How did they let this happen? They had worked so hard to scam others, and to lose their hard-earned money was unbelievable.

Of course, Steve lost $4.5 million, and he was furious at the quant and the hedge fund owner. He took Karen with him to New York and met with the hedge fund management and the owner, who was distraught himself at having lost an enormous sum of money. The hedge fund owner promised to find a way to help them recover some of the money, but it was gone for now. They left furious but convinced there was little hope in getting their money back.

When Steve and Karen returned to the ranch, there was some intense tension in the air. Karen and Brad were depressed and angry at Steve for suggesting they make the last investment. Steve apologized and reminded them he had lost much more than either of them. His apology did not mean anything to them, nor did it reduce their anger.

As he had planned for months, Steve now had the money Brad and Karen had invested with the quant in his personal bank account. Steve sent a case of wine to his friends in New York, including the imaginary quant.

# CHAPTER 25

# A Change of Plans

KAREN AND BRAD were furious with Steve, although they did not suspect him of treachery. They thought he was just a rich guy who could afford to lose big money and not be affected like them. They were wiped out unless they could make this scam work. Brad pushed Karen every time they were alone to force the marriage.

Karen was about to lose her mind! She had Brad pushing her, and Steve seemed in no hurry to marry her, although she had said yes. What in the hell was she supposed to do? she asked herself. She decided to push things and take a risk her aggressive move would work.

"Steve, I am disappointed that we are not already married. I love you and have spent a long time with you in our relationship. We love one another. I agreed to marry you, and yet you seem hesitant to go forward with the marriage. Is there some problem?" she asked.

"I have enjoyed our time together, and of course, I have given serious thoughts to marriage. I have never had so much pleasure being with a woman as I have with you. I asked you if you would marry me, yet I am reluctant to go forward," Steve agreed.

"What do you mean by that?" she asked.

"We are so happy together, and maybe that is the way to keep it. My last marriage was not so successful, and maybe ours would turn sour also," he said.

"No, Steve, no! I have given my last few years to you in love and happiness. You were the one who asked about marriage, and now that I have agreed, you are changing your mind. Is that fair to me?" she asked with tears rolling down her cheeks.

"I don't know about fair, but I want you to ask yourself what difference being married would make. You are here with me, we do everything together, you can have anything you want, and have I ever told you no on any purchase?" he asked.

"You know it is not the same! I want to be your wife, not your mistress!" she shouted.

"It was my goal when I signed up with Platinum Singles to find a man to marry, not just to date until I grow old and get discarded like garbage," she cried.

"I will not discard you. I think you should consider what you are saying and how you are behaving. I have treated you and even your cousin with all the love I have. You are making me nervous with your insistence on marriage," he finally said.

"I am making you nervous! You are moving the world from under my feet, you idiot," she said.

"Karen, you have never spoken to me like that. I did not know you had that kind of hostility in your body," he said unhappily.

"I am sorry, but you have hurt me," she said.

"I think you and Brad should take a horseback ride. Go relax and talk to your cousin. Everything can stay the same. We are all happy here, without marriage or any change. Brad seems happy, and you can have anything you want," he said.

Karen left with a spinning head. *What am I going to do now? Brad will kill me if I don't marry Steve after all of this effort. We will lose everything and start over. We have no money after the loss in the market, and if we get nothing from Steve, we will be broke.* Karen was feeling totally desperate and dizzy with the fear of being broke. She was also afraid of Brad when he got super angry.

She went on the ride with Brad as angry as a person can be.

"Brad, I do not know what to do. He does not want to marry me. He wants to keep things the way they are. I do not believe that I can change his mind," she said.

"You are a damn failure and a tramp. You gave yourself to him for more than a year, and what did we get from your efforts? You enjoyed the time with him, and you lost sight of our goal!" he screamed.

"I did not forget. He changed his mind after saying he would marry me. I don't know what the hell happened, but he was hell-bent for marriage, and then he changed his mind!" she screamed back at Brad.

"Well, we are broke. If we leave now, we will go back to Idaho without any money in the bank and no prospects in sight. I do not mean to be critical, but you are not looking as hot as when you met Steve. You are getting too old to hit it big with guys who are looking for forty-year-olds," Brad said.

"Thanks for the insult, and I must say you are no longer any great catch either," she replied.

"It serves no purpose to go against each other right now. We need to put our heads together to figure out how to score. There must still be a way," Brad said.

Brad suddenly made a wild suggestion. "What if we kidnapped Ann and held her for ransom? It would be easy to do, and Steve would pay big time to get her back."

"That sounds dangerous as hell and stupid on top of that. How would it end without us going to jail?" asked Karen.

"I have a simple idea. Before we would release Ann, we get Steve to agree in writing that the money he is giving us is to replace the money we lost and the money we should have made. If he gave us back double our invested money, we would be okay," said Brad.

"Will anyone believe that story if Ann says she was kidnapped?" asked Karen.

"She will not say she was kidnapped, if we can get her to sign a paper that says she was not taken against her will but that we just took a ride together," Brad said.

"I think it is too risky. Let's forget about that idea and try another," said Karen.

Two frustrated, angry, desperate, and deceitful people rode back to the ranch without a plan.

# CHAPTER 26

# Ann Is in Trouble

IT WAS HUNTING season, and Steve bagged a buck in the forest near the ranch. After skinning the deer and expertly cutting the quarters and the backstrap steaks, he put the meat in the freezers.

Afterward, he prepared a venison meal for the three of them and complemented it with a bottle of robust burgundy wine. They talked about the weather and the chores that needed to be done in the next few days. They could each discern that their relationship had somehow changed and that the old friendship and love affair had diminished.

Brad saw they had to leave or take some serious action. There was no con left and nothing else he could envision to get money from Steve. He contemplated hurting Steve in a pretended accident so that he would be needed to do more at the ranch. Then maybe Steve would increase his salary or maybe make him a partner.

Brad had dropped that idea because, deep down, he was afraid of Steve. He suspected that Steve was tougher and a more hard-hearted man than he appeared. Without any other ideas, Brad decided he would leave for Idaho next month if Karen would not go along with his kidnapping idea.

There were alligators on many parts of his land, and Steve saw them frequently on his horseback rides and while doing the ranch chores. Alligators are widespread though out the Southern states, and Florida alone had over one million gators. They live in lakes, swamps, rivers, canals, and slow-moving streams. They eat a wide range of food, including snails, turtles, birds, deer, and other small mammals. They are aggressive, opportunistic feeders; and they will take advantage of any new food source. They kill over ten people each year in Florida; and last year an alligator killed a woman while swimming in Hernando Lake, which was just a few miles away. A Florida state record was recently set when a trapper killed a fourteen-foot male alligator weighing over one thousand pounds. The strength in their jaws creates the most powerful bite in the animal kingdom. In short, they are large powerful creatures with a hearty appetite for meat.

Steve was incredibly angry at Karen and Brad. Their deceit was despicable, and he had wondered countless times how to best get his revenge. He did not know for sure if they had planned to kill him, but he suspected it was part of their plan.

Apparently, Karen cared nothing about his feelings and their relationship. He had loved her, and he had liked Brad. He had been hurt emotionally by their devious actions.

When he initially discovered their plans, he thought of throwing Brad and Karen to the alligators in one of the swamps but quickly decided against it. He even considered tossing them into the woodchipper and scattering their remains to the gators. He had also once dreamed of tossing them into the blue pond to be drowned. But basically, he was a good guy and did not want to harm anyone physically. He had decided to hurt them financially like they had planned to damage him.

He had mostly completed his goal, and now he just wanted to get rid of them.

There were clearly two angry sides at the ranch. Steve wanted them to go, and Karen and Brad were waiting around and plotting to get their hands on some money before they left. It was a boiling cauldron of disgust for one another and danger on both sides.

"I want to go to Miami for a holiday as soon as possible," Karen told Steve.

"Okay, let's go in the next few days," Steve answered.

"I think I want to go alone or maybe with Brad," she said.

"You hurt my feelings by not wanting me along," said Steve.

"We have not been so loving in the last few days, and I need to clear my head. I am sorry, but I feel like I need some time alone. I want to stay on Fisher Island and be left alone," she said.

"Okay, but be careful and don't stay long," Steve said.

Steve sent Ann an e-mail message and a pair of new sandals. He asked her to keep them in her purse along with her pistol. He told her he thought things were getting dangerous and that Brad and Karen were on their way to Miami. He told her to be prepared for anything and that he would be in Miami and nearby if needed.

Steve got in his Range Rover and headed for Miami. On the way, he called the detectives he had used before to investigate the scandalous background of Brad and Karen. He asked them to follow Brad and Karen when they arrived at the ferry to Fisher Island. There is only one way on and off the exclusive enclave called Fisher Island, and that is by ferry. The detectives waited by the ferry until they saw Brad and Ann, and they began their surveillance.

Brad and Karen settled into one of the villas at Fisher Island and had heated arguments over what to do next. They discussed either leaving right away for Idaho or trying the kidnapping scheme, as crazy as it might be. After consuming a bottle of wine, Brad decided to go forward with the kidnapping.

"I think we should ask Ann if she would like to have dinner at one of the Miami restaurants she likes," said Brad.

"Are you still convinced that kidnapping her is our best option? I definitely do not want to hurt her, and I don't feel good about our chances that this will work," Karen said, still worried about this choice.

"I do not think we will need to hurt her. We just want her to tell Steve to wire $5 million to our accounts in Idaho. She will promise not to press any charges, and Steve will write a letter stating that he is giving us the money because he feels badly about recommending the quant to us. Remember, he does not know we planned to con him," said Brad.

"I think I agree if we can get those documents from them. Steve will not miss the money, we will go away and leave him alone, and we will be able to live a nice life as we had planned. Everything will be okay for all involved," said Karen finally.

They called Ann and arranged for dinner at a terrific upscale Italian restaurant in Coral Gables with a beautiful ambiance, an unrivaled staff, and a remarkable wine selection. They all arrived at about the same time and were seated at a lovely table with elegant table settings, fine china, a soft linen tablecloth, and beautiful silver.

Ann was dressed more casually than they expected for dining at such a fancy place. She had on a pair of jeans, a rather worn-looking T-shirt, and a pair of sandals. She apologized for her clothes and said she was at a fellow lawyer's house working on a case when they called for dinner.

"I am glad to see you, guys. How have you been? I've been so busy I forgot about the ranch for a while and that terrible financial loss we all experienced. I guess I will have to work harder to make up for that disappointment," Ann said.

"We have not been good because we were completely wiped out by that debacle your father put us into. We are still reeling from that," said Karen.

"Oh well, there doesn't seem to be much we can do about it," said Ann.

They had a tension-filled meal; and when they were leaving, Brad asked if Ann wanted to have coffee at a local Starbucks, and she said sure. They asked her to follow them, and they met a few blocks away for coffee. When they had finished their coffee and were walking back to their cars, Brad put a gun in Ann's back and told her to get in his car. He said they were taking a drive to the Keys.

"Brad, are you crazy? Are you going to kidnap me? We have been friends, and we have shared so many wonderful times. Why would you do such a thing? Karen, aren't you still living with my dad and planning to stay at the ranch with him?" Ann asked.

"Things have changed. Your dad is throwing me out. He does not want to marry me anymore, and there is no future for me. We are broke and have nothing left. Your father is rich, and we want $5 million, and you guys can go back to your normal life," said Karen.

"How will this end unless you do me harm?" Ann asked.

"Just get in the car and shut up for a while," said Brad.

After tying her hands, Brad also removed her gun from her purse. They drove south on US 1 for a little over an hour to Tavernier, a quaint village in the northern Keys. They had rented a small cottage on the bayside of the village, which was a few hundred yards off the highway and in in the middle of a palm-tree forest. Their cabin and their parking spot were not visible from the highway.

They went into the cottage and tied Ann to a dining table chair. They kept her hands tied but gave her Brad's mobile phone. They wasted no time talking.

"Ann, I want you to call Steve and tell him you are with us. Tell him to wire $5 million to our Idaho account. He has the wire instructions from our prior dealings. We do not want to hurt you. We just want what is fairly ours for the time I spent with him and the promises he made to me," said Karen.

Ann did as she was ordered and made the call.

"Dad, I am being held hostage by Brad and Karen. They feel you owe them $5 million for the time Karen spent with you and for the money you made them lose with your risk taking," Ann said.

"Let me speak to Karen," Steve said.

"Tell Steve he needs to speak to me," answered Brad, who was listening to the call by standing near Ann.

"Tell Brad to get away from the phone unless he wants to go to jail in the next five minutes," said Steve.

Ann handed the phone to Karen.

"Karen, I will make you one and only one offer. You let Ann walk out the front door right now, and there will be no kidnapping charges. You guys just went for a ride to the Keys to enjoy the breeze," said Steve.

"For the time you spent with me, I will buy you a two-bedroom house in your hometown and furnish it to your taste. I will send you $1,000 per month for two years unless I learn you are scamming someone else. After two years, you are on your own, and I never want to see or hear from you again," said Steve.

"By the way, Ann and I know all about the scam you were pulling, and we have for months. Ann saw you making love when you thought we were both away from the ranch house. You were going to scam me for all I am worth. I think you even planned to kill me after I married you. I am disgusted that I was taken in by you, but I did have some fun, and you have my only offer," said Steve.

"Steve, I wanted to marry you! It was Brad who wanted to do the scam, not me. Don't blame me for Brad's behavior and plan," said Karen.

"Karen, you are pathetic, and I have no doubt you are just as greedy as Brad," scorned Steve.

"We expected both of you bums to act in an evil way when you ran out of money. I gave Ann a pair of sandals with a tracking device in the soles, and we were never more than a mile behind you guys. You have only two choices: take my offer or go to jail," said Steve.

"Steve, please don't do this. I love you, and we can still live together and be happy. I will send Brad away," she pleaded.

"Karen, listen to me carefully. I am outside with two armed bodyguards, and the cottage is surrounded. If you don't take my offer immediately and let Ann walk out of the cottage, we will take you to the local police station and file kidnapping charges. You will go to jail for a long time. I think you understand that Ann knows her way around the criminal justice system," he said.

Karen untied Ann and let her walk out of the cottage. Steve and the detectives put Ann in the car and left Tavernier for Miami. Steve did not go into the cabin or say a single word to Brad or Karen before leaving the Keys.

He did not speak to Karen or Brad ever again. As promised, he bought her a house in a remote community near her childhood farm; and for several years, he sent her enough money to buy food and some basics but not much else. He gave Brad nothing.

Karen and Brad separated when they returned to Idaho, and Karen would likely live out her life in modest surroundings with a massive regret for losing the life that could have been with Steve had she been an honest partner.

A couple of months after the kidnapping, Ann invited her mother to experience the ranch life for a few weeks. Marie agreed to join Ann and Steve for a two-week visit.

The visit gave Marie and Steve time to get reacquainted; and the last we heard, they planned to spend more time together at the five-hundred-acre ranch and in New York City.

# A FAMILY TALE

*Rejoice with your family in the beautiful land of life.* Albert Einstein

# Perez Family Tree

### Brothers Born in Cuba

Miguel Perez    Born 1854, died 1920, age 66
Immigrated to Brazil in 1874 to work on the Manaus rubber plantations.
Luis Perez      Born 1855, died 1914, age 59
Immigrated to the USA in 1875 to work in the Key West cigar factories.

### Born in Brazil, Descendants of Miguel

| Gabriel | Born 1910, died 1970, age 60, businessman |
| Arthur | Born 1940, died 2000, age 60, businessman |
| Daniel | Born 1980, businessman |
| Gustavo | Born 2000, businessman |

### Born in Key West, Descendants of Luis

| Ricardo | Born 1905, died 1965, age 60, fisherman in Key West |
| Nelson | Born 1940, died 1982, age 42, fisherman in Key West |
| Rafael | Born 1980, fisherman in Key West |
| Marco | Born 2000, Islamorada fishing guide |

# PROLOGUE

I T WAS LATE in the afternoon on a cool April day. The twenty-five-foot Contender eased its way to a reef just a few miles offshore from Tavernier Creek Marina in the Florida Keys. The captain, Marco Perez, was at the helm; and today he was fishing alone.

Marco was a fishing guide who usually took clients with him, but tonight he was on a trip to catch fish for sale. He needed some extra cash and needed it right away.

He was going to his favorite reef to fish for "flag" yellowtail snapper. The average yellowtail is around twelve to sixteen inches, but they call the bigger yellowtails, eighteen to twenty inches and over three pounds, a flag yellowtail.

Marco could sell his fish to countless mom-and-pop restaurants offering fresh yellowtail entrees on their menus. A single yellowtail fish is an excellent main course served in multiple ways: fried, blackened, pan-roasted, ceviche, pan-grilled, onion-crusted, potato-crusted, and many more customized styles. The local chefs compete for the most flavorful combinations of toppings, sides, and presentation. It is a big market!

Marco found his secret spot in seventy-five feet of water and carefully anchored a few yards away to avoid any damage to the fragile coral reef. He was delighted to discover there was a medium-to-strong current flowing from south to north. He hoped that he might also catch some mutton snapper, grouper, and mangrove snapper. Seeing the ideal current, Marco was confident he could make some good money tonight and perhaps take away some pressure from his current financial stress.

He put out blocks of chum, made from ground fish, and let it drift back into the current. He had a couple of beers while he waited for the yellowtail snapper to be attracted to the chum line. Forty-five minutes later, he began fishing; and within two hours, he had over seventy-five yellowtail snapper of varying sizes. Some were smaller than twelve inches, and many were true flag class. He was a lucky man and was about to pull up the anchor and go home.

Suddenly, a marine patrol officer appeared out of nowhere. He asked for permission to board Marco's boat. He boarded the Contender; and when he looked into Marco's fish box, he saw multiple violations. Yellowtail snapper must be longer than twelve inches in length, and the maximum limit is ten per day per person. Marco had sixty-five too many fish, and some were too small. The officer was furious.

Marco had been fined $1,000 once before for a similar violation; and if an angler gets a second violation, it is a more serious offense. The second violation carries a $500 fine and sixty days in jail. The law also provides for the confiscations of the boat and all fishing equipment, including the boat trailer.

This was the same officer who had cited Marco before, and he was disgusted with Marco's behavior and Marco's total disregard for the well-known regulations. In the officer's opinion, Marco was nothing but an out-of-control poacher, and he planned to throw the book at him and enforce the maximum penalties. A district attorney in the Keys hated poachers like Marco, and Marco knew his case would be assigned to that tough-ass DA.

Marco was already broke, and now he was totally busted.

# CHAPTER 1

# The Florida Family Begins

"**I** AM HERE to work," said Luis Miguel Perez. Luis arrived from Cuba in 1875, and he was expecting to work as one of the two thousand cigar makers in Key West. By 1876, the Cuban cigar makers in Key West were producing sixty-two million cigars a year, and it was easy to leave Cuba and work in this small city at the southern tip of Florida. These cigar companies imported the tobacco from Cuba, rolled them in Key West, and avoided the US customs duties.

By the middle of the 1880s, over one-third of the Key West population was Cuban. They created restaurants with new flavors, pharmacies, laundries, bars, and other businesses and went to doctors who they knew from Cuba. They kept their native culture while in their new homeland. Luis married a Cuban woman, and they had two children. Luis and his wife both died in 1914, the same year World War I began. One of Luis's children stayed in Key West, and one went to Brazil to live with his uncle Miguel. The son who stayed was named Ricardo, and he worked his entire life in Key West on the commercial fishing boats. He got married and had one child named Nelson, who died at forty-two in a boating accident while fishing for swordfish.

After World War I and the disaster of the great depression, a rise of worldwide cigarette usage replaced the cigar industry. The Key West cigar industry was devastated and essentially died. The Cuban game bolita (a numbers game of chance) survived for a while; but eventually, even it disappeared. The opportunity for substantial foreign employment disappeared, and the Cuban population was reduced.

The Cuban Revolution further reduced the Key West population. When Castro took power in 1959, legal travel between the island and the USA stopped. However, in 1980, as many decided to flee Castro's strict hand and a weak economy, Key West became a first stop for exiles fleeing Cuba. Once again, the town was flooded with people seeking new opportunities. To this day, almost 20 percent of the Key West population is Spanish speaking. The significant influence of these industrious workers is still present.

In 1980, Rafael Perez was born; and like his father, Nelson, he worked on the commercial fishing boats out of Key West, pursuing all kinds of fish and shrimp. Rafael also worked for a few commercial boats that sometimes boosted their income by smuggling drugs. The fishing boats would meet the huge mother ships, far out at sea; and they would offload drugs for the dealers in Key West.

Rafael and Marie had a son in 2000, and he and his wife named the baby Marco Luis Perez. Marco, as he was called, went to Key West High School and worked part-time with his father on the commercial fishing fleet. He learned the water, the tides, and the best locations for the different species they would target at specific times of the year. Marco was an intelligent, hard worker both at school and at work; but he never planned to attend college.

Marco was proud of his Cuban heritage and often told his classmates that his great-grandfather had come to America almost 150 years ago. He decided he would marry a Cuban woman when he had enough money. Marco's parents continued to live in Key West. His father still worked on commercial fishing boats, and his friends were mainly fishermen like himself. His mother worked in a seafood restaurant as a waitress.

When Marco graduated from high school, he moved to Islamorada to work on charter boats that catered to rich people who could afford to pay $1,000 or more for a day of fishing. He started as a mate whose job was to prepare the bait, put it on the hooks, watch the lines for a bite, and often set the hook for the inexperienced anglers. He learned how to fish, where to fish, and when to fish for the different types of fish that thrived in the waters near Islamorada.

Most importantly, Marco learned how to please the wealthy anglers willing to pay big money to catch fish. Marco was charming, accommodating, and efficient when he was not drinking. Unfortunately, he was driven by the desire to make lots of easy money; and he would never forget the drug trafficking connections, which he had observed while working with his father.

He worked on the charter boats, based at Jim and Jane's Marina, for five years before he saved enough money to buy a fifteen-year-old Contender fishing boat. It had two rebuilt outboard Yamaha engines, and the hull was in perfect condition. He found a used trailer that was pulled behind his old Bronco. He passed the test for his guide license; and in several months, he was in business.

His six-pack guide license permitted him to have a maximum of six clients onboard at any time, which was more than enough for most charters. He was now one of many guides in the famous Keys, and he was sure that he would become one of the greatest and most prosperous. Marco was ambitious and wanted to have more beautiful things than his parents had provided during his childhood. He was twenty-four years old and ready to make his mark.

Marisol Maldonado was the full-time bartender at the Sunset Bar. The bar drew locals and tourists who wanted to watch the sunset over the bay and drink the night away to reggae music. Marisol knew how to make the best tropical drinks, and she had the face and body to keep the customers entertained while they drank up the booze. She had tattoos on each arm with the images of sailfish and marlin. She wore short shorts and a top that barely supported her ample breasts. Marisol married twice but had no children, and she was an incredible flirt.

Marisol's parents were Marielitos, who were part of the mass exodus from Cuba in 1980, known as the Mariel boatlift. Their economy had tanked; and the mass emigration continued for almost six months, during which over 125,000 fled Cuba in 1,700 boats, many of them makeshift contraptions.

Castro also opened his jails and mental institutions, and some Marielitos were criminals. Marisol's father had been in one of the notoriously dangerous prisons for committing various petty crimes. Her mother's parents were doctors, and she had hoped for a solid college education upon high school graduation. Marisol's parents met in a refugee camp where they were detained for two months while being processed. Her father lied about his criminal past and was released without any difficulty. They moved to Key West for the Cuban culture, and they fit in perfectly from day one.

Marco was awestruck the first time he saw Tracy preparing drinks. He sat at the bar to be near and watched her for two hours before she asked him for his name, which he happily gave to her. She smiled; and without any more hesitation, he asked her to go for a bite of food after the bar closed. They had been a couple since that night two years ago.

Marisol was living with Marco in a single-wide trailer in an oceanside RV park. They paid $800 per month in rent, which included the utilities. His guide business was doing okay, and he typically had two or three clients per week at $600 per day in the busy season. He had expenses for boat insurance, engine repairs, gas and oil, and bait. His net take-home was usually around $1,000 per week. Plus, he had to pay for help with his website and commissions when one of his clients came from a marina or bar that recommended him. They both had car insurance to pay, and Marisol had a car payment of $400 per month. She earned good money in tips at the Sunset Bar, and together they were getting by with the two incomes. They were not lazy, and they were willing to work long hours and felt sure they would be okay.

# CHAPTER 2

# Marisol and Her Situation

MARISOL HAD BEEN in a three-year intimate relationship with one of the owners of Sunset Bar when she met Marco. She decided to live with Marco, but she never planned to give up her fun with Bob. Bob was a 40 percent owner of the bar; and his job was to keep the vibe of the bar alive with the authentic furniture, fixtures, music, and bartenders.

His partner, Tom, handled the finances and bought the food, booze, and other supplies. They opened the bar together six years ago; and after a slow start, it had become a profitable enterprise. They were both twenty-six years old, and they were having a ball meeting joyful people and loving the Keys lifestyle. They frequently wore only a T-shirt, shorts, and flip-flops or no shoes. They lived in a modest two-bedroom apartment above the bar, which made it easy for Marisol and Bob to conduct their relationship in secret. Of course, Tom knew everything, but the secret was safe with him.

Marco was unaware of her affair, and he would have been upset to find out. She and Bob were careful and made sure Marco was fishing when they went upstairs. To be sure he was on the water, Marisol would call Marco on his mobile and ask how the day was going and who he was fishing with. If he did not have a client, she and Bob postponed any intimate contact. The affair was a little risky, but Marisol also checked Marco's reservation book every morning before she went to work at three o'clock in the afternoon and worked until 1:00 a.m.

Marisol was afraid of Marco's temper when he got angry. Marco was a big man who stood over six feet and weighed 180 pounds. His jobs had required heavy physical work, and he had powerful rocklike muscles. He was a handsome man with weathered skin from working outdoors, and he stepped into any room with confidence. His eyes were set deeply into his brow, and their soft blue color contrasted with his overly serious nature; if you met Marco in a bar, you would not want to get in a fight with such a powerful, tough-looking guy.

Marco had been in many fights over the years. It was not easy working around the fishermen who spent long hours at hard labor, letting out the nets, pulling in the nets, removing the fish, and doing it again and again. Tempers often flared on the boats; and when they finished work and went to a bar, there were many fights. These were macho men who took pride in their toughness, and Marco had learned the hard way how to fight back. Marco rarely started a fight, but he was often the winner because of his strength and determination.

Marco had warned Marisol about cheating on him. He knew she was a flirt and had experienced time with many men. However, he believed that when she met him, her chasing around had stopped. Marco did not see Bob as a threat to his relationship because Marisol complained about how difficult Bob could be as a boss. Bob and Marisol had kept their secret for over two years by being careful.

Marisol and Bob not only enjoyed sex they also liked drugs when they went upstairs. They probably had three encounters each month, and Bob provided various drugs: marijuana, prescription opioids, heroin, fentanyl, and cocaine. They both needed to work after their rendezvous, so they kept the usage low and did not do the same drug repeatedly. Bob told Marisol that if they changed drugs each time they met, the chances of developing a habit would be exceptionally low. They just wanted to get high and relish their sex to the max.

About three months ago, Marisol started taking home a little of each drug Bob brought to their meetings. She shared the extra with Marco, who also liked to get high. She told Marco she bought the drugs from Tom with some of her tip money when she had an extra good night. She said that Tom was dealing on the side in a small way and that Bob did not know about it. That was not true, but she felt it would take away any suspicion about how she was getting the drugs.

The summer was coming soon, and it would be a slow season for the restaurant and Marco's guide business. In the summer, it was too hot in the Keys for many people, and the number of tourists dropped dramatically from June to September. Their income would decline, and it would be harder to afford a move to the new place that Marisol had discovered. Marisol was pushing Marco to get out of the trailer and into a small rental house on the Florida Bay side of the island. She loved the water, and the beautiful sunsets and the RV park had no view of anything and no swimming pool to cool off in the hot weather. The new rent would be $1,800 per month or almost double their current amount.

Marco wanted to please Marisol, but his guide business did not generate enough money even during busy times; and with summer coming, he could not afford to move. To get some extra cash, Marco was selling fish of all kinds to the restaurants, and he consistently broke the rules and regulations in effect for the ocean and bay. He usually left the dock near sunset and would fish all night if necessary to "load the boat" with fish of any size and any species. He felt it was idiotic for the government to impose rules on the open water of an ocean. Why wasn't the ocean free to anyone to do anything? The damn government had their nose in his business, and they could go to hell.

The first time he got caught, he paid the $1,000 fine because it did not make a dent in his business with the restaurants. This time was different because they took away his boat and equipment, and he could no longer make money as a guide. The idea that he would spend sixty days in jail was infuriating to him, and he was an angry man when he arrived at the bar to tell Marisol what happened.

He knew Marisol would be furious because she had her heart set on the new house on the bay. He had no intention of causing trouble when he entered the bar to find Marisol.

# CHAPTER 3

# The Bar Scene

WHEN MARCO ARRIVED at the bar, Marisol was making a Cuba Libre cocktail, which is rum and Coke with a dash of lime juice. The rum is usually a light rum such as Bacardi, and it is a favorite of many islanders. Marisol had a secret ingredient that made her locally famous for her special drink. She could hardly keep up with the demand for these cocktails.

The bar was jumping with patrons, the reggae band was terrific, and their music was loud and pulsating. The vibe was just as the owners hoped they would achieve, and the fifty people in the bar were having a great time. The lights were low, and a few couples were kissing and hugging in the dim light. It was a Keys evening, and many of the blue-collar workers hoped it would never end. Tomorrow they would go to work at physically tough jobs, but tonight they were somewhere on an island of happiness.

However, Marco was not one of the happy patrons. He moved to the bar and pushed between two men sitting on the barstools having a conversation. He did not say "Excuse me" or "May I order a drink?" or anything polite. He just shoved the men aside and yelled at Marisol for a drink. Marisol had been so busy she had not seen Marco arrive. She smiled at him and said she would be there to serve him shortly.

Marco yelled back that he wanted his drink right now and did not want to wait for others who came before him. Marisol smiled, trying to make light of his rudeness; and she shook her bottom and went back to work. The two men were getting upset with Marco, and one asked him nicely to be more polite and wait for his turn.

Without any warning, Marco hit the man who spoke to him with a tremendous blow to the jaw. The man toppled from the barstool and dropped to the floor. His friend stood up to say something, but Marco walloped him above his right eye; and with another blow, he hit his left temple. Both men were on the floor, and Marco yelled at Marisol to give him his damn drink.

Tom came running over to stop Marco and calm the crowd who ceased having fun and was looking at the two men on the floor. Brawling was not the vibe Tom and Bob wanted in their friendly bar, and it could severely hurt their business. Tom asked Marco to leave, but Marco insisted on getting his drink. Marisol was furious at Marco and would not give him a drink. Marco picked up one of the beers on the bar and threw it at her, and it hit her hard in the stomach.

As soon as Marco tossed the beer, Tom took his pistol from his back pocket, put in up against Marco's back, and ordered him out of the bar. Marco did not fight against a gun pressed to his body. Marco's body was shaking with anger at everything and everybody, and he saw his hard work and dreams crashing around him. He had tried hard to be a responsible citizen and look at how it had turned out. At that moment, Marco decided he would become an outlaw when he got out of jail.

Once outside, Tom kept the gun on Marco while Bob called 911. The police arrived almost immediately, Tom told them what happened, and they arrested Marco for assault. They took Marco to the local jail, and he stayed there until a judge determined what to do with him.

When they let him out, Marco decided he was leaving the country with or without Marisol. He just needed to find his passport, and he would be gone.

Marisol was crying so hard she could not work. Bob took her upstairs, and they shared a joint. She could not believe Marco's behavior, and she did not know what to do. Marisol was afraid to help him get out of jail because he seemed totally out of control, and she had no idea what had set him off. She asked Bob if she could take a few days off from work and go home to see her parents, who lived in Miami. She needed her mother to hold her and tell her everything would be okay.

Bob told her to take a week off, and he would cover for her. He had been a bartender for years, and he could do her job for a week with no problem. Bob also suggested that she dump Marco and just hang with him for a while. She could live upstairs with him until things were straightened out, and she did not need to go back to Marco and potentially get hurt. If Marco asked where she was, Bob promised not to tell Marco anything.

They did not think Marco would come back to hurt Tom because he had pulled a gun on him, but they were not sure what he would do when they let him out of jail to await a court date. Marco could be violent, and they would both need to be vigilant and watch out for trouble.

Marco was released from jail after being formally charged with assault, and his father posted a $1,000 bond. Marco was now facing two serious charges: the fishing violation and an assault charge. He found a pro bono attorney who advised him to calm down and wait for his court date to be determined. The attorney saw no way for Marco to avoid spending time in jail for his two charges. He also told Marco he would likely face a civil suit for his attack on the two men in the bar.

Marco was still angry, and his left eye was twitching badly. His eye had always twitched when he was angry, and his friends and associates were wary around him when they saw this tic appear. He felt the system was rigged against him, and that unfair rules and regulations had destroyed his future. He decided to go to Key West with his father for a few days and try to get control of his anger. He needed to think clearly to figure something out.

His father, Rafael, now forty-four years old, had never been arrested; but he had worked with more than one boat captain who was jailed for drug dealing and smuggling. Rafael was disappointed with Marco, but he and Marie made room for him in their small rental house. Marie tried to take his mind off his troubles by feeding him his favorite foods and talking of his childhood friends and family.

A few years back, when US citizens could travel to Cuba without so many restrictions, Rafael, Marie, and Marco had applied for and received their passports. They had tentatively made plans for a trip to visit some distant relatives in Cuba and Brazil. Nelson, Rafael's father, had mentioned these cousins on numerous occasions. The trip never materialized, but their passports were still valid.

After discussing his options with his family, Marco decided to travel to Brazil as soon as possible. The USA and Brazil had an extradition treaty; but for such minor offenses, Marco and Rafael agreed it would be an unlikely action to be taken by the Keys authorities. Marco made airline reservations from Miami to Manaus, Brazil.

Rafael had the address of a distant relative in an old letter his father had received in 1979 from a cousin named Arthur Perez. Some of the original Perez family had gone to Brazil to live in the 1890s, and they kept in touch occasionally with their relatives in Key West. Marco did not care if he found a distant family or not, but Manaus seemed remote enough to start a new life without too many questions. Of course, Marco was not supposed to leave the Keys much less the United States, but they had not yet taken his passport, and he was going as soon as possible.

He decided to visit Marisol one last time before he went away. He called her phone, but there was no answer. He called the Sunset Bar, and there was no answer. He called Tom and then Bob, but nobody would answer his phone calls. He called the landline at the trailer, but there was no answer. Everyone in Islamorada had refused to take his calls. His eye started twitching as his anger built again to full force. What was wrong with the world? He decided to leave without saying good-bye, and Marisol could just go to hell.

While thinking of his decision to leave the USA, Marco wondered if he could ever control his anger and improve his life.

# CHAPTER 4

# Manaus, Brazil

THE ONLY THING his Key West family could afford to give Marco was $500 and a copy of the old letter with the name and address of a likely long-dead relative. Marco's father was not happy he would lose the $1,000 bond he had posted; but still, he wished his son a good life. Marco kissed his mother good-bye, thanked his father, and prepared to leave the USA, angry with the government for mistreating a hardworking man just trying to survive.

Two days later, he boarded a LATAM Airlines nonstop flight from Miami to Manaus. The trip took around twelve hours, and suddenly he was in a Brazilian-Portuguese-speaking country. Marco was fluent in Spanish; but on the plane ride, he learned that Brazilian Portuguese is not the same as Spanish.

He had a long conversation with the passenger in the seat next to him, and he learned that something like only 30 percent of the words matched between both languages. He would need to work hard, but he was confident he would be able to communicate until he could properly learn the new language.

Marco had no problem getting through the customs checkpoint. He had only a carry-on bag with a few clothes, and he went searching for work before even looking for a place to stay. He believed he could instantly find work on a boat of some kind, and he would ask his new employer for a cheap place to stay. He did not want to spend the $500 until he had no other choice because he wanted to use it to eventually start some small business. He began looking for any job that had to do with fishing or guiding.

Marco made his first stop at the Manaus Fish Market to see what kind of fish were being caught and to get a feel for the fishing activity in the area. When he got there, he was amazed to see that the Manaus Fish Market was teeming with fish for sale. The market had countless small vendor stalls and a bustling quantity of shoppers.

It covered many acres of land and was one of the largest fish markets in Brazil. Marco was stunned at how many different types of fish were displayed. He assumed correctly there must be a large commercial fishing fleet in Manaus and a substantial population.

Next, he went to the port on the river to check out the commercial and sport fishing activities. Many cruise ships also visited the port, and it was a busy place filled with passenger ferries and vendors trying to sell trinkets and tours to the tourists.

Just as he had hoped, numerous sportfishing guides serviced clients, hoping to catch the large beautiful, hard-fighting peacock bass and a multitude of other sporting species. The Amazon River is the largest river in the world; and it is home to some incredible and edible freshwater fish like the peacock bass, pirarucu, tambaqui, matrinxã, and the tough-looking piranha. Marco was highly qualified to work on either the commercial fishing boats or the sportfishing boats.

He searched for some successful-looking guides and was surprised to find several that looked like first-class operations. He approached a man who seemed to be around forty years old and asked if he was the owner. The man said he owned two guide operations that specialized in peacock bass fishing. One of his boats was called *Peacock Fly*, and the other was named *Reel Peacock*. He said they offered both traditional reel fishing and fly-fishing trips.

Marco told him he was new in town and was looking for work as a mate or captain on a sportfishing boat. The man asked Marco to have a seat, and they talked for several hours while Marco told him about his experiences in Key West and Islamorada. The owner was named Enzo; and after a while, he offered to buy Marco a drink at a nearby bar.

After many drinks and a Brazilian dinner, Enzo offered to give Marco a chance to work as a mate on the *Reel Peacock*. He and Marco worked out a trial wage, and Marco asked where he could sleep for little money. Marco had explained to Enzo that he lost his assets in a difficult divorce and that he needed to work immediately and had little money to pay for a place to stay. Enzo suggested Marco might stay with the new mate on the *Peacock Fly*, who had also just arrived in Manaus. Enzo introduced Marco to Mike, and he agreed to let him stay in his room until Marco could earn enough to have his own place.

Marco did not care how awful the room might be or that his wages were small. He would scope out the opportunities in Manaus and find a profitable way to spend some time before looking for his relatives. Marco was a hard worker and willing to cut corners to make more money. He did not want to come begging if, by any chance, his remote cousins still existed in this place.

# CHAPTER 5

# Learning to Guide on the Amazon River

THE AMAZON RIVER Basin is home to over three thousand species of freshwater fish. Manaus is a particularly productive fishing area because it lies at the "meeting of the waters" where two rivers come together: Rio Solimoes (light in color) and Rio Negro (muddy dark brown). Every visiting angler wants to catch the plentiful and beautiful peacock bass. These fish can weigh over twenty-five pounds and are known worldwide for an incredible fight on light tackle.

Marco learned that the best time to fish the river is in the dry season, which changes from region to region. In the Manaus region, the dry season is June to October; and that is the time the river is low upon its banks. In the wet season, the water goes far above the banks into the trees and bushes; and it is hard to find the fish. The peacock bass is just one of many hard-fighting fish like the traira and arowana. The Manaus region was a destination for anglers from all over the world, and they had plenty of money to spend for a day or two of fast action.

Enzo observed Marco's hard work and superior knowledge of how to catch fish, but he was most impressed with Marco's ability to make the clients feel special and to encourage them to give big tips at the end of their trips. After six months, Enzo made Marco the captain of the *Reel Peacock*.

Marco also had contacts from anglers who had fished the Keys, and he invited them to a week of fantastic fishing in the Amazon waters. He did not attract many USA anglers; but the ones who came were happy to spend large amounts of money on fishing, drinking, and a nice hotel. Marco arranged to get a commission from all the establishments that hosted his anglers. Marco wanted to be a player, and guiding was not going to hit it big unless he could add some spice.

When the cruise ships docked at Manaus, there was big business in boat tours, nature and wildlife tours, and even boat rentals for the tourists not interested in fishing. Thousands of passengers each week disembarked at Manaus, and they wanted to see the famous river and the beauty of the region by water. As soon as he could get enough money, he was planning to buy a boat with room for twenty passengers who wanted a day or a half-day tour of the area. He saw so much opportunity that his mind just exploded with money-making ideas.

Marco had moved out of the room he was sharing with Mike and now had his own room in a low-rent neighborhood two miles from downtown. He was quick to observe the drugs flowing like water throughout his community. He made a few small purchases of marijuana and a one-time buy of cocaine. He wanted to see how the deals were done and who was making the face-to-face transactions. He knew if he got involved, he would need to start at the low-street level and work his way up the chain to real money. He was not bothered by the moral considerations of dealing drugs.

Marco spent time at a bar near his new home filled with seedy characters and hard men. Marco had been in a couple of fights solely to get a reputation as a tough guy with a no-back-down persona.

He met Al one evening after a hard night of drinking. Al knew where they could find some cute girls, and Marco followed him to another bar with many young women looking for a good time. They had a fun night of dancing and romancing; and from that night on, they became the best of friends.

Al had been in Manaus for ten years, and he worked in the Manaus Fish Market as a seller of fish. He bought the fish from suppliers all over the Amazon Basin, and he knew hundreds of productive fishermen. He also knew some who were bringing drugs down the countless rivers and streams from Colombia, Peru, and Bolivia. There were thousands of miles of wilderness between Manaus and those three countries. No government could patrol all that vast area, and the drug dealers had almost free rein in Manaus and the suburbs of the city.

Marco wanted to know why Al did not get involved in buying and selling the drugs since he knew where to buy them. Al told him that a few strong, powerful drug lords controlled the market; and anyone who tried to start a small business would be killed within the first week. The homicide rate in Manaus was enormous, and shootings and stabbings were occurring daily. There were days when the homicides exceeded twenty killings in the area. The homicide rate in Manaus was four times as great as Sao Paulo, which was itself considered a violent city by global standards.

Marco decided to stick with the fishing business; and during the next two years, he expanded his business to include three guide boats and two tour boats. He was becoming a known personality on the fishing docks and was regarded as smart, tough, and honest. He moved to a better neighborhood but remained close to Al, and they continued to party together. Marco had always liked the sexy bartenders, and he found one to live with him while she worked at a tourist-focused bar. Merci was not as cute as Marisol, but she was loyal to him, and they had a good time together. They did recreational drugs but never got involved in selling or dealing in any way.

Marco decided it was time to look for his relatives and introduce himself as a small but successful businessman. He had no idea who they were or how meeting them would change his life.

# CHAPTER 6

# The Relatives

EL TIGRE WAS the most famous drug lord in Brazil. He had one of the most remarkable backgrounds of any known drug lord before he went to the dark side. He was in the British Army, a member of MI6, and a DEA agent for the USA. He became a wealthy man with huge assets and influence over most of Brazil. He had never been arrested, although warrants for his arrest were often issued and the federal police conducted a country-wide search several times. In 1965, with help from his cartel, he simply disappeared with no trace. He remains, to this day, an invisible powerhouse in the illegal drug business. The mention of his name among rouge drug traffickers sends a chill because of his unrelenting violence against any unwanted intruders into his extensive network.

Marco had heard of El Tigre on many occasions when people gossiped at bars about the Manaus drug trade. He knew that anyone associated with El Tigre had the power to kill at will to preserve their influence and power. Marco decided not to do anything that could remotely imply he was involved with drug trafficking. His caution was particularly important because many boat owners were involved in moving the drug through the Amazon wilderness to the cities of Manaus, Belem, Rio, and Sao Paulo. His guide business, which now consisted of five boats, could be a perfect front.

If anyone in the drug business suspected Marco of moving drugs without their approval, he was sure they would kill him within moments. These men did not ask questions; they simply acted without fear of local law enforcement. The police, judges, and federal agents were paid generously to let the drugs flow. There was an excellent opportunity for Marco in Manaus if he did not get sideways to the cartel leaders or soldiers.

He kept away from most bars where the locals and tourists went for drugs. When a tourist asked Marco if he knew a place to get drugs, he always said he knew nothing about drugs or where to get them. Marco was super careful not to trust anyone when the subject of drugs was mentioned to him. He knew the gang members were constantly looking for anyone thinking of getting involved in the lucrative business without approval from the cartel. In the years since Marco had been in Manaus, he had read about more than five hundred drug-related murders. The drug trade was the most significant potential obstacle to Marco's business and safety. But he could not get the possibility of vast wealth out of his head; and with the right plans and connections, he might get involved.

Marco took the old letter sent to his father in 1979 out of his desk drawer and looked at the name and address of the sender. It was from Arthur, and he had bragged that the Perez family was thriving in Brazil, and he invited his cousin Rafael to visit. The letter was over forty years old, and Marco did not expect to find anyone at the old address when he decided to visit.

Two years ago, Marco bought a used motorcycle for traveling around the city and nearby countryside. He had a map of the area, and he was familiar with many roads and neighborhoods in Manaus. But as he looked for the address, he had never ventured this far from the city, and he was afraid he had made a wrong turn or gotten lost. Finally, he stopped at a large gate with the address in raised bronze letters.

Marco could not believe his eyes when he saw the spectacular estate with several homes that looked like palaces on the grounds that covered more than ten acres. The trees, bushes, and plants were carefully manicured; and the houses sparkled with the look of money. Marco was about to walk away when he saw a bronze plaque below the address, which read Daniel and Gustavo Perez.

He decided to visit another day when he was better dressed. He rechecked the address to make sure he was in the right place. Good lord! He could not see the entire property, and he would later learn that the estate was the former home of a German rubber baron and that it covered over three thousand acres.

Marco went to an upscale men's store and bought an attractive set of casual clothes. He asked the clerk to help him dress like a prosperous young Brazilian businessman. He bought a nice pair of well-tailored black slacks that were neither baggy nor tight, an expensive white shirt, and an attractive leather belt with a matching pair of black shoes. The clerk told Marco to leave only two buttons open on the dress shirt because showing chest hair is not appropriate in most Brazilian business meetings. He did not buy a hat but got his haircut by a stylist who assured him that he was giving Marco the cut of a prosperous young man.

This time, when he walked up to the iron gate and asked to enter, he looked like a well-dressed, Portuguese-speaking, handsome, and fit thirty-year-old man with an American accent. He was ready to meet his wealthy relatives.

# CHAPTER 7

# The Reception

A UNIFORMED GUARD met Marco at the gate, who asked the purpose of his visit. Marco handed the guard the old letter and said he was a distant relative of the family and had come to introduce himself. He also gave his name to the guard and waited while a call was placed and answered. The guard waved him through the gate, and Marco walked up the long gravel road looking at his surroundings with awe. He had never been around such opulence and was utterly amazed at the grounds, the statues, and other sculptures that covered the extensive green lawns.

He walked up six marble steps to an elaborately carved wooden door and pressed the doorbell. A small man opened the door and greeted him in the elegant dress of a manservant with status. He was ushered into a massive living room with incredible art and furnishing.

Marco was greeted by a tall man who looked to be his father's age and had a familiar face and eyes that Marco recognized as those of his grandfather Nelson. He introduced himself as Daniel Perez. They shook hands, and the family relationship began to unfold.

"I am here to work," said Marco using the greeting his great-great-great-grandfather had used in 1875 when he immigrated to the United States. For generations, that had been a motto passed down with pride. It was a repeated declaration and defined the hardworking Perez family. They were proud of generation after generation working endlessly to provide for their families and to walk proudly among their community. Marco hoped the Brazilian family would know of that motto, and he was right.

"Where did you learn that comment?" asked Daniel.

"From all of my family for years. It is a phrase we use with pride because it came from our family patriarch, Luis Miguel Perez, when he first came to America," said Marco.

"My great-great-grandfather is the brother of Luis. His name was Miguel Nelson Perez, and he came to Brazil before Luis left for America. Our family has been in Brazil for more than 150 years," said Daniel.

"It is my pleasure to make your acquaintance," Marco said in accented Portuguese.

"What are you doing in Manaus?" asked Daniel.

"I had a bad experience in Key West and decided to leave for Brazil in hopes of eventually meeting some family that my father had mentioned," said Marco.

"How long have you been here?" asked Daniel.

"Almost three years. I did not want to introduce myself to you until I had achieved some minor success as a small businessman in the fishing and guiding world," said Marco.

"I had no idea of who my family might be in Manaus. I was not even confident anyone would be at the address in the old letter. I did not look up your address until last week, and I was surprised at your beautiful grounds and homes. We did not achieve such financial success in America. We were workers on fishing boats for many generations and provided very few material things for our wives and children," said Marco, somewhat embarrassed.

"I wanted to speak with you and tell you of our family connection, and I have no purpose except to say hello and let you know I am in town," continued Marco.

"Are you looking for work?" asked Daniel.

"Not really. I just used our family motto in hopes that your family would recognize I am truly a distant relative. I own five boats used for guided fishing and tours. I am always looking for more opportunities, but things are okay," said Marco.

"I can tell by looking at you that you are one of us. You have the eyes, the chin, and the ears. You look like my son, Gustavo. I am happy you came by to say hello. We will stay in touch," said Daniel as he rose to show Marco to the door.

Marco left, feeling somewhat rejected after such a short meeting with Daniel; and he wondered if Gustavo was his age. He was sure that he had not given the impression of a poor relative asking for a job. His opening statement had been a good idea and was pleased that the Manaus Perez family used the same phrase. He hoped that single motto would create a small family bond. Still, he did not understand why he was dismissed so quickly.

The next day, Daniel sent five soldiers to secretly find out everything they could about Marco Perez, an owner of fishing and touring boats. His soldiers bought a day trip on each of Marco's boats during the next month. They went drinking with Marco after a day on the water; and they talked with him about women, drugs, and money.

Marco expected his cousin would check him out, and he was always on his best behavior. He had no idea which of his new clients were working for Daniel, so he treated everyone with the highest respect and showed no interest in drugs or prostitutes.

For a while, Marco forgot about Daniel because his boats were filled with clients, and the peacock fishing action was outstanding. The cruise ships were full of passengers eager to see and experience the Amazon environment on a boat. He had made connections with the tour managers on the ships to recommend him, and in turn, he gave them some benefits when they came ashore.

He was making good money, and he had enough to buy another boat that came with a captain and mate. He put the new boat to work immediately. He was expanding his business, his relationship with his barmaid was excellent, and he had no trouble of any kind. For the first time in his life, things were working out well for Marco. He just needed to control his temper, not engage in any improper activities, and be patient as he developed his first successful business.

# CHAPTER 8

# An Invitation for Lunch

MARCO WAS PREPARING to leave the dock with a full-day fishing charter when he was handed a beige envelope with his name in bold engraved gold writing. He looked at the man who delivered it for an explanation, but the man only said he was told to present the envelope to Marco in person. Marco excused himself for a moment and moved away from the boat to look in the envelope.

It was a formal invitation from Daniel printed in gold lettering to join him and his family for lunch the coming Sunday at 2:00 p.m. Casual dress was suggested, and a handwritten note by Daniel said, "Please come. You will meet more of the family."

It was the dry season, and Marco could not handle all the business offered to him. If he had four more boats with crews, he would still turn away eager tourists and anglers with money to spend. However, he knew the demand for fishing would not continue past September when the river began to rise, and the fish dispersed into the brush and trees.

He was thinking of following the low water with two fishing boats to several other regions to determine if there was a viable business away from his home base. He might need to covert the fishing boats to tour boats because the demand from the cruises did not stop based on the season. However, the small fishing boats could not carry enough passengers to be efficient. He was not sure what to do about his seasonal business and the drop in revenue during the wet season.

Marco arrived at Daniel's estate ten minutes after 2:00 p.m. and was ushered onto a large patio that overlooked an Olympic-sized swimming pool with two children splashing and laughing. There were three adults seated at a cloth-covered table with room for four diners.

"Hi, I am Gustavo, and this is my wife, Lily. My father told me about your recent visit, and I wanted to meet you myself," said a tall man with dark curly hair.

"I am glad to meet you and Lily," replied Marco.

"This is my wife, Maria," said Daniel.

"I am pleased to meet you, Maria," said Marco.

"Those two youngsters in the pool are my children, Jose and Mary," said Lily.

Servants delivered drinks along with a light lunch. The table conversation was focused on the weather, the changing river water, the crazy tourists from the cruise ships, and the growing population in Manaus. After lunch and the gentle conversation, the women excused themselves to go into the pool with the children. Maria was lovely with long black hair and a lithe body, but Marco did not look at her even one time.

When the women were in the pool, Gustavo asked Marco to tell them about his family life in the Florida Keys. Marco told him the truth about everything the family had done from the arrival of Luis down to his father and mother. He told them about his work on the commercial fishing boats and his guiding business, and he even included his trouble with the law. He saw no reason to lie because he reasoned that if they wanted to find out about him, it would be easy enough to do the research.

Marco told them how he had slowly built a growing business in Manaus because he understood how to please clients and how to catch any kind of fish that swam in the water. He did not brag, but he was slow and confident in his telling. They could tell he had an entrepreneur's view of making money.

Marco did not ask them what they did for a living because he had mentioned their name to his friend Al one night when they were drinking, and Al immediately asked how Marco knew their name. Al told Marco that the name Perez in Manaus was the same as saying the name El Tigre.

Al said that Daniel was the head of the Manaus drug cartel, and Gustavo was being groomed as his replacement. That explained the big houses, fancy grounds, and security personnel. Marco was smart enough to let them tell him whatever they wanted without asking.

"Do you need any help with financing your operation?" asked Gustavo as he carefully picked at the skin around his fingernails.

"Not really, it is still small, but I generate enough revenue to cover my expenses, and I make around $5,000 per month profit. I live modestly with a fun girlfriend, and I am saving money each month. I have never made more money, and it seems like I can expand slowly and continue to grow by investing my savings in new boats and equipment," said Marco.

"Would you like to expand faster and make more money right away?" asked Daniel.

"I do worry about my fishing business slowing down during the wet season. If I had more money, I could buy more and larger tour boats, and they would be unusually profitable because I already have good connections with the tour managers from three of the cruise ships," Marco responded.

"We just sold some land near Belem, and it generated some extra cash for us that we are looking to invest in a local company," said Gustavo.

"I have never borrowed any money except one time to buy a car. I do not know how business deals are properly structured, and I am afraid of going into debt. I am probably better off to just grow from my savings," said Marco.

"We were not thinking of a loan but a partnership. We have been searching for an opportunity to invest in the boat tour operations for a couple of years. You are part of the Perez family, and we want to join you in this potentially lucrative business. We can provide the money, and you will manage the operation as you are doing right now. We will only take a 40 percent share of the business so that you can keep control," suggested Daniel.

Marco thanked them for lunch and the business proposal and left with his head spinning. What was this all about? They did not need any more money, and the boat tour business could never be as profitable as their drug dealings.

They must have some angle, and he should take his time in deciding what to do. Their offer could be the break of a lifetime, but would it involve doing things that could get him in trouble again? He knew very little about his relatives, except that they were powerful drug dealers. He needed to be smarter than ever to make the right decision, and he had nobody he could talk to about the offer.

# CHAPTER 9

# Daniel's Reflections

DANIEL WAS ALONE in his study; and today, he was thinking about the past and the Perez family's time in Brazil. He remembered the names Miguel; Sergio; Alonzo; Gabriel; his father, Arthur; and his son, Gustavo. So many names, so many memories, and so many deaths. Daniel was not a religious man, and he resisted the constant pushing of his wife to attend church and for him to show more interest in her Catholic religion. He had been responsible for death on so many occasions that he found it hard to be a church-going man. His right thumb was bouncing slightly as it often did when he was in a thoughtful mood.

His forefathers had been brave, industrious, and unforgiving businesspeople. They had forged an empire out of the Amazon Basin, which is the wildest, wettest, meanest, harshest, toughest geography in the world. The basin is a large area with tall trees that often block the sunlight from hitting the soil, and the ground is damp in most places. Rivers and streams are everywhere, and the abundance of plants and animals is astonishing.

Daniel knew that over fifteen hundred different animals live in the forests, including large colonies of bats and rodents. Some of the larger animals were killers like the jaguar, puma, and ocelot, while others are just interesting to watch, such as the capybara and tapirs.

Snakes live on the solid ground, in treetops, and the shallow water. Some of these snakes are poisonous, and some are large constrictors like the anacondas and boas. Large macaws and other parrots make colorful flights through the trees and on the riverbanks. The diversity of wildlife and plant life is unmatched anywhere on earth. Unfortunately, these animals and birds are often victims of poachers who have sold them to dealers who export them all over the globe.

The Brazilians are a mixed race of people who were descendants of the Portuguese explorers, immigrants from many European and Asian countries, and the indigenous tribes throughout the country. There are more uncivilized indigenous people living in the Amazon jungles than anywhere, and Daniel remembered fondly how many of them are friends of the Perez family. These poor ancient, wild people had been part of the secret that led to the tremendous fortune accumulated by his family. He worried about the impact civilization and the drug trade was having on the lives of his friends and helpers, but he did not plan to cease his smuggling activities using their assistance.

Miguel Perez came to Brazil in 1874 and worked as a common laborer on one of the most extensive rubber plantations throughout the boom years from 1879 to 1912. The rubber industry made Manaus one of the wealthiest cities in South America in the 1800s, and they needed immigrants and local natives to work long hours to tap rubber out of the trees. Daniel could remember family stories about one baron who started his plantation with forty thousand local indigenous people and Indians; and several years later, all but five thousand had perished. Harsh treatment and yellow fever took the lives of many workers.

The plantation owners treated their workers terribly; and there was no legal protection against slavery, brutality, killings, and beatings. The dead were often thrown into mass graves. Miguel was a clever man and moved up steadily in the ranks of the plantation workers. After five years, he was appointed the supervisor of two thousand daily laborers because his production numbers were higher than any other. He appeared to be a hard taskmaster, and the owner rewarded him with extra money and better food.

Without the knowledge of any other supervisors or managers, Miguel gave extra rations to his workers and treated the natives with respect and dignity. He had the vision that a strong relationship with the millions of poor people who lived in terrible conditions throughout the Amazon Basin could be profitable in the future.

The Indians and indigenous people admired this white man who treated them well, and they remembered his kindness when the boom was over. He had not yet traded in illegal products, but he had made the right contacts.

Miguel visited the baron's villa on a few occasions in the wealthy Manaus neighborhood of Adrianopolis, and he vowed one day he would have a nicer one. Miguel did not live long enough to achieve his dream, but Daniel was the owner of an old plantation with a villa that would have made his father proud.

The rubber barons were extremely rich, and they competed to see who could build the biggest villas and have the nicest of everything. They built a magnificent opera house to imitate the fancy ones in Europe. They displayed ostentatious behavior like watering their horses with champagne. The barons were mostly German and incredibly competitive in showing their wealth.

Unfortunately, the seeds from the rubber trees were stolen, taken by thieves to Southeast Asia, and planted in their rich soil and perfect climate. When the Asian rubber trees were mature and producing, the demand for Manaus rubber declined; and the area lost its monopoly on rubber.

Manaus could not compete with the low Asian prices. A few years later, the city fell into a state of poverty; and it has never really recovered. The city has continued to grow even without the rubber business; and today it has over two million citizens, many of whom live in poverty. Many also love illegal drugs.

# CHAPTER 10

# Miguel, Aliza, and Javaro

ALIZA WAS TWENTY-THREE years old when she married Miguel in 1908. Her parents had also come from Cuba around the same time as Miguel, and they hoped to work on the rubber plantations. Her father eventually worked for Miguel, and she met Miguel one weekend at a small festival to celebrate some Cuban holiday.

Miguel and Aliza saw each other only occasionally before dating, but they married one year to the day after their first meeting. Miguel was fifty-four when they married, and he was twenty-one years Aliza's senior. Their child, Gabriel, would be born two years later.

Aliza was unusually smart, soft-spoken, and attractive in a mousy sort of way. She wore her hair short, used glasses for reading, and had a habit of pushing them up on her forehead when tired. Aliza had worked in a local sewing factory from the time she was fifteen until she married Miguel. She had no boyfriends before meeting Miguel, and she had given most of her money to her mother to help pay for their living expenses. She helped with all household chores and never complained.

She was devoted to her parents and had only one time-consuming activity, which was to read everything she could find to buy or borrow from the poorly stocked library. Aliza was astonishingly well educated for someone who had dropped out of school in the tenth grade. Had she ever taken an IQ test, she would have scored over 150.

By the time he married, Miguel had been a supervisor for fifteen years; and they were lucky to live in a small three-room house provided by the German baron, who owned the plantation. Their home was more comfortable than the thousands of people who worked for the baron.

Most workers lived in shacks made of tree limbs, tarpaper, broken pieces of wood, tires, brush, pieces of tin, large leaves, and anything else that would help stop the rain, wind, and heat. The native workers were almost naked and always hungry. The baron provided only the cheapest and barest food of broth, bread, and potatoes. The heat and mosquitoes would often take a heavy toll on the weakened men and women, and many died from malnutrition and yellow fever. Some men would go into the woods to hunt for meat, but they soon depleted the nearby jungle of most edible animals. It was an inhuman environment but profitable for the baron.

Miguel was not inhuman; and it troubled him that such indifference, hatred, and disrespect for an entire race of people was not right. He was in no position to change the attitudes of the mainly German owners, but he could find ways to make the lives of some workers a little better if he was careful. Miguel started by devising a reward system for improved production. Initially, his workers thought it was a trick, but soon he started giving them some extra food for the same output.

Miguel bought food with his own money and left it off the property for them to find. He could not make a difference to all the workers, but he helped as many as he could. The word of his generosity spread amongst the workers, and his reputation grew.

He met Javaro one day as he was hiding a supply of food behind a thicket of heavy weeds. Javaro was a large man with dark skin and black curly hair. Miguel did not hear him approach, and he was standing only three feet behind when Miguel turned to get more food from his truck. The presence of such a large silent man startled Miguel so much that he fell back against a tree so hard that he almost broke an arm.

"Hi, my name in Javaro, and I have come to help you. Do not be afraid because I am a friend." He laughed.

Javaro was probably twenty-five years old, and his naked chest rippled with well-defined muscles. He was the leader of a small tribe of local people. Over the next few years, his leadership skills would elevate him to the chief of a few thousand indigenous people who worked for Miguel.

Brazil had over two hundred tribes of indigenous people with a total population of over one-quarter million. Most tribes have a unique culture, but the one thing they all have in common is the desire to be untouched by modern society. Many tribes in the Amazon Basin share a similar language, and the men are skilled navigators of the mysterious waterways.

Miguel was ambitious, and he was continually thinking and hoping to find ways to make more money. He had seen the way the barons lived, and he wanted that kind of life for his family. Miguel had seen the disgusting way Javaro's people were treated, the daily toll of their poverty, the horrible misery in which many lived; and he wanted to help them. Miguel and Javaro became friends, and that friendship lasted until Miguel's death and beyond.

Miguel had a pressing idea that he had been contemplating for years, but he never had the opportunity to implement it. He had heard stories of enormous wealth being created by drug dealers in the big Brazilian cities of Sao Paulo, Rio de Janeiro, Brasilia, and others.

He was intrigued when he learned the drugs were coming from Peru and Colombia on overland routes. Those routes were long, and shipments were vulnerable to arrest by the federal police or robbery by other drug lords. He thought he had a better idea.

One day, Miguel and Aliza invited Javaro to meet in their small cottage on the grounds of the last operating rubber plantation in Manaus. Miguel told both of them he wanted to discuss a life-changing idea. It was an urgent meeting because the previous day, the baron announced he was closing the estate and returning to Germany. Miguel and all the workers would be without employment in a few weeks.

Miguel, Aliza, and Javaro spent hours discussing his idea of potential opportunities for smuggling drugs and other products through the vast waterways and rivers of the Amazon Basin. The extensive network of waterways and tributaries reached all the way into the interiors of Peru and Colombia. The indigenous people of the basin used these waterways daily and had an intimate knowledge of the best routes to travel to many locations. Javaro surveyed his people and confirmed that none of the current drug lords were using these waterways.

If they could devise a plan to bring the drugs directly from Peru or Colombia to Manaus, Miguel believed they could make a fortune. The knowledge of Javaro's people was the key to this idea. Miguel told

Javaro that any profits they made from their smuggling business would be split evenly between his family and Javaro. They would be fifty-fifty partners.

Javaro was eager to try the idea because he wanted the money to buy food, implements, and clothing for his hungry villagers and their neighbors across the basin. Javaro had never dreamed he would have such an opportunity to help himself and his people. Javaro was a charismatic leader, with his large stature and a broad smile. He was a kind man, but if necessary, he could use harsh discipline to keep his people in line. He was married and treated his wife with respect. When he gave his word, he kept it.

Miguel had been frugal with the money he earned from the baron, and he had enough saved for an initial purchase of drugs if they could find a seller. They were about to begin their venture together when Miguel was sickened with malaria and died two weeks later.

Before he died, Miguel asked Javaro to work with Aliza until Gabriel was old enough to take over the management of their planned enterprise. Gabriel was only ten years old when Miguel died in 1920.

Aliza also promised both Miguel and Javaro she would work diligently to maintain a friendly and helpful relationship with the indigenous people that were soon to be unemployed.

In was a decision that would change countless lives when Javaro agreed to work with Miguel's family. Almost a hundred years later, his descendants were still working with the Perez family without the knowledge of any law enforcement agencies.

Women were not accepted in the Brazilian business world of that time; but Aliza was clever, and when needed, she would dress like a man. She had a slim figure, short hair, and a husky voice that could be trained to sound manly. Aliza put her intelligence to work and reviewed countless maps of the Amazon region. She and Javaro were searching for ideas when an opportunity finally arrived.

A local drug distributor had the same idea about bringing marijuana and cocaine products through the remote waterways from Leticia to Manaus. His name was Pedro, and he approached Javaro to help him do it. Pedro explained why Leticia to Manaus was the key to his smuggling idea. Javaro was skeptical of any stranger wanting to do business with an indigenous person, but he listened carefully and saw this as a similar idea to the one Miguel had proposed. Maybe it validated the concept. Javaro thanked Pedro for considering him but declined the offer.

Javaro knew he would never be accepted as a businessman in Brazil because of the rampant bigotry and racism against his people; but he hoped that if he worked secretly with Miguel's family, they could make plenty of money to share.

Javaro decided to take Pedro's idea of Leticia to Manaus back to Aliza.

# CHAPTER 11

# Learning the Drug Trade

L ETICIA WAS A city on the tri-corner border of Peru, Colombia, and Brazil. It was the perfect location as a distribution point for drugs headed to Manaus, Belem, and other populated cities in Brazil plus Suriname and French Guiana. The drugs came from Peru and Colombia, and Leticia was overflowing with illegal products waiting for distribution.

In Leticia, there were countless marijuana, cocaine, and diamond dealers looking to make deals with reliable distributors. It is seven hundred miles through the Amazon jungles from Leticia to Manaus. The trip was almost impossible to make safely without extensive knowledge of the remote wilderness rivers. The drug dealers in Leticia were desperate for an organization that could make the trip successfully and often.

Javaro took Aliza to Leticia on a circuitous thirty-day trip through the mysterious waterways. Several main waterways used by ferries and other commercial vessels take four days, but that was not the route taken by Javaro. Law enforcement agents aware of the illegal drug and diamond trade patrolled those popular routes. The police were almost certain to stop a boat carrying illicit drugs unless they received a substantial bribe. However, the agents did not patrol the many small rivers and streams that were tributaries away from the public routes.

Aliza was dressed as a man when they finally arrived in Leticia. She met with a dozen drug-dealing men to discuss the arrangements of becoming a smuggler for them. The drug dealers said they had many people who wanted to work with them, and many rejected her quickly because Aliza had no reputation. She asked Javaro what she was doing wrong, and he shyly told her that she needed to make gigantic promises to get their attention.

"Tell them you can produce more demand that anyone who has ever taken products from Leticia to Manaus," suggested Javaro.

She took his advice and changed her approach.

"I can use more of your product in one year than anyone in Manaus," boasted Aliza.

"How can you do what you are promising?" asked a tough-looking young dealer.

"How do I know you can provide the volume of products that I need?" she answered aggressively.

"I have solid contacts with producers in both Peru and Colombia, and they can ramp up their production quickly if the demand increases," he said.

"What is your name?" Aliza asked the dealer.

"My name is Davi," he said.

"Davi, I am looking for a source of products and a relationship that will last for centuries. If you work with me, our children and grandchildren will mention our names with awe," she said, looking this young man in the eye.

"Will you have a drink with me?" he asked.

They had a drink or two and made the deal of a lifetime for both families. She gave him all the money she had, and he supplied her with a massive load of marijuana and a kilo of cocaine. She left with the product, and Javaro took Aliza and the products safely to Manaus.

On the way home, she needed to stop for a bathroom break in one of the most remote areas in the Amazon Basin. Javaro had taken them far from any public route, and enormous trees and jungle sounds surrounded the small river they were traveling. Javaro found a small island with solid ground, and she took care of her bathroom needs. As she was returning to the boat, a rare white eagle landed only three feet from her head on the branch of an overhanging tree. The eagle seemed to smile at her for a moment and then abruptly flew away. She took this event as a positive omen and decided to call her products "Aguila

Blanca" or "White Eagle". That label would one day become the most famous illegal drug name in Brazil.

When she and Javaro needed food or water, they stopped at the tiny indigenous villages located in the most remote parts of the basin. Javaro introduced Aliza to the leaders of the small communities and told them to respect her and her family. Javaro left supplies like metal knives, axes, pots, pans, strong bows, and arrows. He promised more helpful things if they would help the Perez family and kill any other drug dealers moving though the area. A network of small loyal communities in the heart of the jungle was being built one village at a time.

When she finally arrived back to Manaus, she asked Pedro to prepare for a large quantity of drugs and asked how much he could distribute. He told her he was only limited by the sourcing quantity, not by the demand; and he could handle any volume she could bring to him. She asked him to prepare his organization for a plentiful supply that would be delivered twice each month. Pedro never knew that Javaro was working with Aliza or the Perez family.

Pedro paid Aliza her for the first delivery, and she split the profits fifty-fifty with Javaro. He thanked her and ran to his family to spread the good news. The village held a celebration and spent the money on desperately needed things.

Javaro continued to pass the word to the close and distant tribes of his people that the Perez family was trustworthy. He asked that his family and all indigenous people help them now and for years to come. The dynasty of the family started in 1921 by a strong woman. Out of admiration for the courage and leadership of Aliza, the Perez family always treated their women with the utmost respect and gave them responsible positions in the operation of the business.

It was a marvel that a young widow could have started this vast enterprise while traveling the hostile back rivers of the jungle, dressed as a man, all alone in Leticia with only an uneducated indigenous Indian guide and no business experience. She was a blessed saint!

# CHAPTER 12

# Gabriel Perez Matures

B ORN IN 1910, Gabriel was a beautiful child and grew into a handsome man. Aliza sent him to the best schools in Sao Paulo from the time he was eleven until he graduated from the university. When in lower school and high school, Gabriel lived in the school housing. When he attended the university, Aliza bought him a house nearby because the university had no housing on campus. He was a serious student in the school of engineering and international affairs and graduated with honors in 1931.

He loved to party and had many girlfriends during his time in Sao Paulo, but he never got in any trouble because he knew his mother would not tolerate misbehavior. Gabriel came home to Manaus every time Aliza would allow, and he stayed committed to learning the family business.

During the summers, he traveled with Javaro and his team of smugglers to Leticia; he learned the names and faces of their contacts, he learned the Manaus contacts, and he learned how to negotiate at both ends of the drug dealings. He met the network of indigenous natives in the jungle waterways and made sure to pay them respect and provide the things they needed.

When he came home to stay and take a more active role in the business, he was an educated man with intimate knowledge of the family business. He planned to help his mother expand the successful drug-dealing venture to include even more products and more extensive distribution. His greatest strength was his calm demeanor and utter ruthlessness when he felt it was necessary.

However, they had a problem that needed to be solved before any expansion could occur. The quantity and frequency of the drug shipments coming on their boats to Manaus were so large they were becoming visible to the law enforcement agencies and to competing drug dealers. Aliza and Gabriel needed a piece of property with extensive acreage that extended into the jungle and abutted some of the rivers and streams used to transport the drugs. If they could find such a property, the drugs could be offloaded and stored on their land until delivered to the distributor's warehouses.

Global and local circumstances helped their situation. The rubber boom had been over for almost twenty years, and the American economy was just entering the depression stage, which was starting to have a global impact. Foreign investors acquired several of the large plantations after the boom collapsed, hoping to use the land for developing industrial parks or for residential communities. Usually, those development plans failed. With the depression hurting businesses everywhere, the foreign investors wanted to sell the old plantations for almost any price.

Gabriel found a plantation that fit the bill perfectly. The property not only had three thousand acres of rubber trees that had been unattended for years but also included an abandoned villa that had once been the envy of the other barons and their wives. Thick jungle surrounded the property, and it was virtually impenetrable from either side. The far end of the property could only be approached by four-wheel vehicles that could drive through ankle-deep mud and water. Three small rivers passed within a few yards at varying points along the back edge of the vast property. They had found the ideal place to receive their shipments, store them, protect them, and distribute them with no one having easy access to steal their products or raid their property.

Gabriel made a fair deal and paid cash to the Argentine speculator, who was relieved to find a buyer under these severe global conditions. In six months, they began using the property to receive shipments and store them for distribution.

Gabriel, who had an engineering degree, used Javaro and his followers to build a secret compound at the back of the estate. They constructed housing for fifty men and built two large warehouses using corrugated steel. He brought in generators to provide power to the warehouses; and for the social hall, he created for the workers to use on their off-hours. He painted the tops of the buildings with green camouflage colors and draped green camouflage fabric over their sides. The structures might not be entirely hidden, but it would take an aircraft with a specific mission to find them.

He asked Javaro to hire fifty men to work full-time on the plantation. They would live comfortably on the property and, they would be divided into two teams of equal size. Twenty-five armed men would always guard the property riding in off-road trucks, with walkie-talkies for communication. The other twenty-five men would work the warehouses, receiving, unloading, storing, and shipping the drugs and diamonds.

Gabriel researched the value of rubber trees for lumber. To his surprise, rubberwood is often compared to highly regarded teak wood. He discovered that it was effectively used for woodworking, flooring, and other expensive furniture products. He had a genius idea that protected the family's drug enterprise for years.

As a front for his drug-dealing activities, he bought three more cheap run-down plantations and soon owned over ten thousand acres of rubber trees. He and Aliza were now in the legitimate business of harvesting rubber trees for lumber.

He hired one of Javaro's sons to manage the lumber business and to use as many of his people as possible to cut down the trees and transport them to the port for shipment to a large lumber mill in Belem. He wanted the lumber business to continue for years; so when the trees were removed, new ones were planted. He would always have a reason for so much activity on his plantations. He did not care if it was profitable; he just wanted to help Javaro's people and create a distraction.

Aliza and Javaro disappeared on a trip to Leticia in 1935. It seemed impossible that anything could happen to them after all their years of traveling the wilderness rivers, but their bodies were never found. Gabriel had asked his mother not to keep going to Leticia because she was nearly fifty years old, and she should stay in the comfortable office they owned in downtown Manaus. Aliza had always loved the outdoors and was not content to work in the office. She insisted that she work on the boats or around the plantation compound.

Javaro's son was named Kaiapo; and he surmised that a jaguar must have attacked one of the two travelers, knocked that person in the water, and the other person tried to help, fell in the water, and either drowned or was eaten by the vicious piranha. He said some of the villagers had recently seen a mating pair of jaguars, along the route, who might have been hunting for meat.

Gabriel held a private ceremony for Aliza and made a headstone for her in a hilly and shady section of land several hundred yards beyond the villa. This plot of land would become the Perez family cemetery where generations would be buried. His mother's death devastated Gabriel, and he did not return to work for one month. Gabriel never used drugs, but he did drink rum on occasion. The passing of his mother was one of those occasions, and he stayed alone in an alcoholic stupor for two weeks. When he pulled himself together, he promised that the Perez family would be more careful about going into the wilderness without firearms.

Gabriel was twenty-five years old and in charge of a growing enterprise, and he needed a son to help him.

# CHAPTER 13

# The Beginning of Arthur's Influence

ARTHUR WAS BORN in 1940, four years after Gabriel married Sophia. She had an easy natural birth, and most of Arthur's life would be one of ease. He did not need to create the business; he did not even need to keep it going. His father, Gabriel, maintained total control of the company until he died in 1970.

Arthur was one of those people who felt entitled from birth. He had nannies, personal attendants, and sometimes even cooks who worked just for his special meals. He would not become as smart as his father or as brutal, but he would grow into a man who was physically strong and mentally attuned to his surroundings. He could instinctively understand what another person wanted or needed.

Gabriel had little time for Arthur because he was intensely focused on the business, which was having severe problems that required his full-time attention for years. The law and the competition were causing the family operation a lot of trouble, and it needed a tough man to deal with the constant attacks from both.

Sophia was an attractive but unsophisticated woman with little training to raise a child in a wealthy family. She hired as many helpers as she could find to help her raise their only child. She asked her mother to live with them, but her mother was afraid of the Perez family, who she said had a reputation as people who might be dangerous.

Sophia had been raised and educated in Manaus. She graduated from high school and attended a two-year college studying art and music. Sophia met Gabriel at her college when he was being recognized for donating a new science laboratory. She went up to him to thank him for the contribution, and he was immediately attracted to her. She was nineteen when they married, and Gabriel was twenty-seven. They had a beautiful honeymoon in Europe for four weeks; and three years later, Arthur was born.

In 1934, Gabriel and Aliza had begun the restoration of the old villa. They hired artisans from Europe to assist in making it a showplace. By 1940, it had returned to its magnificent beauty and elegance of the past. By the time Arthur had reached the age of ten, there was no more exquisite mansion in all of Manaus. Also, Gabriel built a smaller but equally grand second villa a few hundred yards away from the main house to be used by Arthur and his family when the time arrived.

Despite his troubles, Gabriel entertained the townspeople with gala affairs at his villa; and Sophia was a beautiful sight, always dressed in the recent Paris fashions. The people of Manaus suspected the Perez family might be involved in drugs, but they also saw the nonstop timber moving to the port. Most citizens had decided to simply enjoy the fun while attending the fancy events at the Perez villa and let someone else worry about the source of their money.

When Arthur was born, the world was transfixed on the global conflict happening in Europe and the Pacific. World War II would last for several more years, but the family enterprise did not suffer too much thanks to Gabriel. Although there was a national draft, few of the Brazilian men needed to go to war; and Manaus remained more normal than most places in the world.

When he was eleven, just like his father before him, Arthur went to boarding school in Sao Paulo. Unlike his father, he was a goof-off and caused a lot of trouble by complaining about the lack of everything he received from his attendants at home. His mother went to Sao Paulo several times to plead for more tolerance by the school and to discipline Arthur.

Throughout middle school, high school, and the university, Arthur was a mild troublemaker and a disappointment to his father. When he graduated from college, Gabriel did not want him in the business because he knew nothing about their operation, and he was an immature twenty-one-year-old playboy.

Years earlier, Gabriel had attended the university with a classmate now a lieutenant colonel in the Brazilian army. He asked him for a favor, and it was granted. Two months after graduation, Arthur was drafted into the army as a private. There was not a widespread draft, but some rules were left over from the war days, and the colonel pretended that Manaus had not sent their share of men to the draft. Arthur was drafted along with twenty other young men from Manaus to make up for their lack of wartime service.

The army was a shock for Arthur, and he rebelled for a while until he saw that his family could not influence the military or their actions. He was an intuitive young man and decided if he could not get the attention he expected by being a Perez, he would get it by being a great soldier. He applied himself to every assignment and stopped complaining about things. He was the first to volunteer for anything the officers asked. The colonel heard about this change and the dedication Arthur was making to his assignments. He asked to have Arthur transferred to his command. He watched Arthur from a distance for ten months before asking him to be his attaché. A few months later, the colonel gave Arthur a direct commission as a second lieutenant.

Arthur was a natural with weapons, and he competed in every shooting contest the command sanctioned. He gained a reputation for his skills with pistols and rifles, but his most remarkable shooting came from the use of long-range sniper rifles. He could hit targets at over one thousand yards and made shots that were not believed possible before him.

Before his discharge after four years in the army, he had broken over twenty-five world shooting records. He went home a captain, with a perfect record and a commendation from his colonel. The army had changed him from a pampered baby into a seasoned soldier and an adult ready to help his father. His people-reading skills would reward the business as his influence expanded.

# CHAPTER 14

# Gabriel and Arthur Encounter Trouble

THE FAMILY ENTERPRISE was prospering in 1965 under the leadership of Gabriel.

Brazil did not send troops to Vietnam during the prolonged conflict, but somehow the war did increase the use of drugs in America, and Brazilian drug dealers looked thoughtfully at the US market for the first time. Once again, there were serious problems that needed resolution before the Perez family could undertake any expansion.

When Arthur returned to Manaus from the army, his father was delighted. Gabriel was told by his friend the colonel that Arthur had evolved into an excellent soldier and a fine gentleman. There was plenty of work to be done, and another capable set of hands could not have arrived at a better time.

A drug dealer called El Tigre was becoming well-known all over Brazil. He had not yet made his way into Manaus, but Gabriel heard the rumors that El Tigre and his men were planning a tour of the Amazon Basin soon. Their trip to Manaus was upsetting to Gabriel because he had no connections to El Tigre or his organization.

Gabriel had never had serious competition from any other drug dealer. He had asked Kaiapo to kill a few small-time dealers on two different occasions, but they had been more of an annoyance than a serious threat to the family business. Gabriel knew that this crazy, powerful man could disrupt his business. He needed Arthur to help him devise a plan to confront or embrace El Tigre on his visit.

El Tigre had military training and connections with the US DEA and the British intelligence organization. Gabriel had no links to any government anywhere, including Brazil. Gabriel had always made it a point to deal only with illegal personalities and had never paid a government official or law enforcement person a bribe. The strength of the Perez family business was the indigenous people and their loyalty, plus the trust Gabriel had in Pedro's family.

Trouble was coming, and the father and son decided they needed a comprehensive study of their operations: what were their strengths, and where were weaknesses? Gabriel and Arthur looked over maps of the area. They did a profile analysis of the Manaus political leaders. They assessed the power and loyalty of the dealers they used to send drugs out of Manaus to the buyer destinations. They decided the primary weakness was their Manaus distributor. If Pedro's family chose to work with El Tigre, the Perez operation would have no pipeline out of Manaus for their products.

They had been working with Pedro's family since 1920 or almost fifty years. Gabriel took Arthur with him to visit the eldest son of Pedro, Mario, who was currently running the operation. Mario was happy to accept an appointment with Gabriel and Arthur.

Pedro had died five years ago, but Gabriel was an extraordinarily loyal person, and he did not want to disrespect the relationship his father and mother had created, so he never looked for another dealer.

"Hello, Mario. This is my son, Arthur," said Gabriel.

"I am delighted to meet you, Arthur. I heard you just got out of the damn army," said Mario, smiling in a friendly manner.

"Yes, I was in for four years after attending the University in Sao Paulo," answered Arthur.

"What was it like to be in such a controlled environment?" asked Mario.

"I actually enjoyed my last two years. The army has so many resources that almost anything you can envision you can try if the superiors have confidence in your abilities," Arthur answered.

"Well, it is good to know you are back and ready to participate in the business," Mario said.

"Mario, we are here on the most serious business you and I have ever discussed," said Gabriel.

"Please tell me what is on your mind," Mario answered.

"We believe the El Tigre is on the way to Manaus to disrupt our business together," said Gabriel.

"That is true. I have a meeting with El Tigre next Monday. He asked for a meeting, and I was afraid to offend him. He has a ruthless reputation, so I decided to hear what he has to say," explained Mario.

"Why did you not call me?" Gabriel asked angrily.

"Why should I make you worry? We will meet, and I will tell you what he wanted. There is no way I would stop working with the Perez family after fifty years of successful business and family friendship. Do not concern yourself. I will tell him our relationship is unbreakable," promised Mario.

Gabriel and Arthur left the meeting with grave concerns. Mario had not confided in them or warned them of El Tigre's visit. If they had not discovered the information through their own network, they would have been blindsided. They no longer completely trusted Mario and his organization.

They decided they would try to make direct connections with dealers in Belem. If they could ship from their plantation directly to the dealers in Belem, they would not need Mario's organization.

The next morning, they took a plane trip to Belem and quickly located the dealers they knew were receiving the drugs from Mario. They talked to them about direct shipments, but they did not get the positive reception they had expected.

They met with the largest dealer in Belem, who was shipping the drugs to other cities in Brazil, Suriname, and French Guinea. He said that he had recently made arrangements with El Tigre that if anything ever happened to Mario and the Manaus supply, they would deal with him.

Gabriel asked if they would deal directly with him, and the dealer said no. Arthur explained that it would be more profitable to the dealer if Arthur sent his drugs straight to the dealer because there would not be a middleman. The dealer said he and his organization were afraid of El Tigre and would not want to cross him for any reason. Nothing Gabriel or Arthur said persuaded him to change his mind.

They returned to Manaus discouraged, and they went back to Gabriel's villa for dinner and discussion. Sophia was included in the conversation but did not speak. She had a sharp mind and had developed a good business sense. She would listen and talk with Gabriel after Arthur had returned to his villa.

"Arthur, we have a really bad situation here. Mario is not to be trusted, and the dealers in Belem are afraid to do business with us because El Tigre is so violent and strong," said Gabriel.

"Dad, we have something none of them have. We have the supply coming out of Leticia. Even if Mario folds and the dealers in Belem work with El Tigre, we are still the ones with the supply. I do not believe that El Tigre can frighten our indigenous friends, and I think Kaiapo will tell them he does not understand what drug dealing even means," said Arthur.

"Perhaps you are right, but I have another idea," said Gabriel.

"What are you thinking?" asked Arthur.

"I think we should invite El Tigre to our villa for a party. We can invite half the town and put on a real gala affair. We can do a little more research and find out his exact itinerary and plan the party for the second night of his visit," said Gabriel.

"We will pretend to have just discovered his presence and say it would be our honor to have him as one of our guests at the gala affair we have scheduled to honor our current mayor," continued Gabriel.

"I would like to impress him with our affluence and, after dinner, have a chat with him alone. We could ask what he is doing in Manaus and if there is any way we could help him," said Gabriel.

"I am sure he will know in advance that we are the primary suppliers from Leticia. We will just make it easy for him to meet with us," said Gabriel as he continued.

"What do you think he will say to our invitation? If he accepts, do you think he will want to do business with us?" asked Arthur.

"He will accept. I want you in the meeting with us until I tell you to ask our manservant for more wine. That will be a clue that I think El Tigre is going to try to ruin our business, and I want you to kill him. Your answer to me will be 'Of course, Dad' but explain that you are needed next door to be with your mistress who is having a baby," said Gabriel.

"What do you mean?" asked Arthur astonished at his father's comments.

"He is a violent man, and if he has decided not to work with us, he will kill us. We must kill him before he has a chance to do that. Get your long rifle and position yourself on top of your villa. You should have a clear shot as he leaves my house," said Gabriel.

"What if things are going okay during the meeting? What if he wants to work with us because of our supply?" asked Arthur.

"I think he would have contacted us for a meeting if he intended for us to have a role in his plans," said Gabriel.

"I want you to meet with Kaiapo and find out if everything is solid with our relationship. Several months ago, I heard that his brother is dissatisfied with something and is trying to make other arrangements with some new parties. Now, I think I understand who those other parties might be," said Gabriel, remembering a story he had discounted.

"We could lose our advantage if El Tigre can make a deal with Kaiapo's tribe and persuade them to work with both the Perez family and a strong organization like his. If they agreed, it would not be long before El Tigre would shut us out, and our business would be over," said Gabriel.

"I will meet with Kaiapo in the morning. If his brother is causing a problem, we will need a plan to neutralize his actions and still keep Kaiapo and his tribe as our friends and business partners," said Arthur.

Father and son finished their discussion, and Arthur went across the lawn to his villa. He did have a pregnant mistress who he intended to marry. The baby she was delivering during this crisis with El Tigre would be named Daniel.

# CHAPTER 15

# El Tigre

ARTHUR PAID AN early morning visit to Kaipo, and they ate a simple breakfast of rice and toast with butter. Arthur had spent many leisurely hours with Kaiapo, who was just a few years older than he. Arthur always enjoyed shooting and hunting, and Kaiapo was eager to be a partner in those activities. They were friends and business partners who had made numerous smuggling trips together through the wilderness rivers.

Kaiapo, like his father, was a large man with dark skin and black curly hair. Javaro had instructed Kaiapo repeatedly to work with only the Perez family and to remain loyal to their children no matter what other offers might appear attractive. Kaiapo had loved his father completely, and he had promised him he would never abandon the Perez family; nothing could change that.

"Kaiapo, I have heard that your brother is unhappy with our family about something, and he is looking to find another partner," said Arthur.

"He is not unhappy with you. He is unhappy with me. He thinks he should have a greater role in our operations. He also wants you guys to pay a larger share of the profits," said Kaiapo.

"We heard he has reached out to El Tigre's men in Sao Paulo, and they are coming to visit him next week," said Arthur.

"I am sorry to hear that but let me assure you that he will not be here next week to meet with them. He will be visiting some of our relatives far away from Manaus, or he will be dead and buried," promised Kaiapo.

"Thank you, my friend," said Arthur solemnly.

"Dad, one problem is solved. Kaiapo's brother will not be available to meet with El Tigre," said Arthur upon returning to his father's villa.

"Good, now take the invitation for El Tigre to Mario so he can give it to him at their meeting. Also, extend an invitation to Mario as well," said Gabriel.

The days passed quickly as Gabriel and Sophia planned their party. One hundred invitations were hand-delivered, plenty of alcohol was ordered, the caterers were hired, and three bands were selected. There would be one band inside, one on the patio, and one roaming among the manicured lawns.

Sophia selected a gorgeous black gown with sequins that highlighted her trim figure. She was an experienced hostess and looked forward to the ball. The villa and grounds were undoubtedly one of the most beautiful estates in Manaus.

On the night of the gala, many guests had been partying for several hours before El Tigre finally arrived with only one associate. The associate had a military bearing, and it was apparent that he was carrying a weapon in a shoulder holster under his coat, but Gabriel said nothing. The Perez family greeted El Tigre with warm smiles and firm, friendly handshakes.

El Tigre, like his associate, had the movement and body carriage of a soldier. His posture was impeccable, and his clothes were obviously tailored and fit him well. But he was a dangerous-looking man because of his dark penetrating eyes and his jutting jaw. He did not smile. Neither was he effusive, but he was polite.

Arthur's intuition told him to be wary of this man. They were all surprised at how haggard and tired the drug king appeared. Something was wrong, and this evening could be the most critical meeting since Aliza started their business all alone in Leticia.

The bands created a festive mood, and the partygoers flowed back and forth between the interior and the softly lit grounds. Dinner was a sumptuous buffet, and everyone enjoyed it. One of the bands started playing dance music, and the happy guests jammed the marble dance floor.

"El Tigre, could we offer you a drink of brandy in our library?" asked Gabriel.

"I would enjoy that very much." El Tigre nodded.

"Please stay outside by the door," El Tigre said to his associate, and then he asked Arthur to lock the door.

Gabriel was surprised by this unusual request, but he nodded to Arthur to lock the door as El Tigre walked in and took a seat.

"Before either of you say anything to me, I want to tell you a story," said El Tigre.

"I want you to help me disappear! The federal police plan to arrest me next week on an extensive list of drug trafficking charges. I made this trip especially to see the two of you," explained El Tigre.

"Everyone thinks I have come to Manaus to take over your operation, but I have come to share my cartel with you, fifty-fifty. I want to go into partnership with your family. I will share the details of my operation with you," he said, startling Gabriel and Arthur.

"I don't believe you! This must be some kind of trick," said Arthur quickly.

"Listen to me, I have no children, I am seventy years old, and I do not want to die in some dirty Brazilian prison. Of all the smaller drug-smuggling operations in Brazil, I have decided that your family is the most capable of running my organization after I disappear," he explained.

"How would this idea possibly work?" asked Gabriel.

"I want your indigenous friends to hide me in a small remote village in the heart of the Amazon Basin, where I can never be found. I know the federal police will search for me when they hear I have disappeared, but I am sure you can find a place that I cannot be discovered," he continued to explain.

"One of you—and you alone—will visit me and keep me informed of any issues that arise anywhere throughout my vast network. When you need my help, I will give you the instructions with a code as I have for years. The members of my organization know how the code system works. The leaders have a codebook that confirms the orders are coming directly from me. Orders without a proper code are not followed, and the person giving those fake orders is executed. That is how I have managed to control such a large organization for so many years," El Tigre said with pride.

"We can rule side by side for years to come. You can add to the organization with my help, and we will become the largest cartel in the world. There are many more places where we can export our products if we can be clever in creating an effective supply chain," said El Tigre.

"What will you do with your share of the money? How can you enjoy living in such a manner? It does not make sense," said Arthur, shaking his head in disbelief.

"During my younger days, I had exciting experiences in remote and dangerous places around the world. It was the happiest time of my life. I have yearned for years to leave the pressure of my organization and live a basic life. Now with my imminent arrest, the time is perfect for me to disappear and live simply," he responded.

"What should we do with your money, if we agree?" asked Arthur.

"Put my share in a safe place, and maybe one day when the search for me has stopped, I might go back to England to die in comfort." He smiled.

"When do you plan to disappear?" asked Arthur.

"I want to vanish tonight. I have a plan that will make the authorities suspect I was killed seventy-five miles from here on the road to Belem."

"What do you have planned?" asked Arthur.

"I will make a scene by appearing to be happy but drunk and loud. I want everyone to see me leaving your villa. I will leave with my driver and my associate, who is outside the door. We will drive a few miles from your property. My car will stop briefly, and you will arrange for the leader of your indigenous people to pick me up in his vehicle. He will drive me to the boat he has prepared to take me to my new home," said El Tigre.

"What will you do with your car?" said Gabriel.

"My driver will continue with my associate, and they will take the road to Belem that we would normally take for me to return to my routine affairs. Fifty miles from Manaus, my associate will cut the throat of the driver and abandon my car on a dirt road several miles off the highway. My associate is well trained in jungle warfare and will find his way out through the jungle until he can secretly return to Sao Paulo," said El Tigre.

"It will appear that I was abducted on my way home. There should be no suspicion that I was captured or killed by anyone associated with your family," he continued.

"El Tigre, this is a startling request. Please give us some time to discuss this in private. Why don't you and your associate enjoy some brandy in this room, and we will go into my private study to have a family meeting?" said Gabriel.

"That is a logical request. Please ask my associate to join me," agreed El Tigre.

"We will not be too long," said Arthur.

"Remember, your family name will carry my endorsement for many years. It is Arthur I want to become the apparent head of the cartel. We need a young energetic leader to keep the organization in line. Of course, Gabriel will continue to be the real family member in charge until he chooses to give the reins over to Arthur," said El Tigre as he got up to pour another brandy.

Gabriel and Arthur located Sophia, and they held a meeting in a private study. The meeting lasted for an hour. When it was over, the Perez family decided to accept the offer of El Tigre. Arthur called Kaiapo and told him about the plans. Kaiapo went into action immediately, and things worked exactly as planned.

Overnight, the Perez family became the largest and most powerful drug cartel in Brazil.

# CHAPTER 16

# From 1965 to the Present Day

THE RUMORS WERE rampant in all of Brazil concerning the disappearance of El Tigre. Many said he was dead; and some said that he fled to Israel, where he had a sister. Others speculated that he went back home to England or that some powerful cartel was holding him. The federal police conducted extensive search parties all over the area where they found the car. They kept federal agents in Manaus for months hoping to find some clues, but nothing was uncovered. No one ever considered that he had chosen to live out his life in the remote Amazon jungle.

The country prepared for violent disturbances as the different dealers and small cartels were expected to go to war to decide who would take over for El Tigre. To the surprise of the citizens and the police, there was little fighting. There were over fifty deaths among the drug dealers, but that was small compared to the expected number.

El Tigre did everything he said he would and more. He sent the word to all his soldiers not to tolerate any intrusion into their territory and to recognize the Perez family as if it were him personally. Those few soldiers who thought they might be able to assume more power were tortured and killed immediately.

Most drug dealers who had their own territories did not try to expand when they heard that the Perez family was in charge. Arthur quickly gained a reputation among the cartels for zero tolerance of disloyalty or any attempted efforts to take any of his territories or business of any kind.

The business flourished under the guidance of the four men: Gabriel, Arthur, Kaiapo, and El Tigre. Gabriel died in 1980 at age seventy from a stroke while riding one of his favorite horses. He was buried beside the headstone of his mother, who was the one that started it all.

El Tigre never made it back to England because he also died in 1980 at eighty-five while fishing for peacock bass on a sunny afternoon. As requested, his body was tossed into a nearby river for the piranha to enjoy. He had no desire to have a monument created in his memory. The federal police never found him, and he never asked to leave the village. He lived with an indigenous woman for fifteen happy years, but they never had any children.

By 1980, Arthur was forty years old and in control of perhaps the largest illegal enterprise in the Western Hemisphere. Arthur's son, Daniel, born in 1965, was fifteen when his uncle died, and he was still too young to help his father. Daniel, like his father and grandfather, was sent to San Paulo for his education.

Daniel was more like Gabriel than Arthur; he was diligent and polite. He studied supply chain management and operations research. Daniel must have gotten his high intellect from his grandmother, Aliza. He knew the key to their future was the development of sophisticated supply routes using the latest technology and equipment. Arthur trained him from an early age to behave modestly and call no attention to himself. Without his knowledge, Daniel was looked over by three full-time bodyguards while getting his education.

Upon graduation from Sao Paulo University, Daniel was accepted to MIT in Boston, Massachusetts. He earned his MBA in information technology and returned to Manaus in 1990, well educated in the skills needed to help his father grow the business.

Father and son made a great team. Arthur knew the supply and distribution routes in great detail, and he knew many of their key players. Both he and Daniel had a good relationship with two of Kaiapo's sons. Kaiapo died in 1982, and their supply routes were so busy that Kaiapo had trained two of his sons in the wilderness routes and connections in Leticia.

Daniel enlarged the size of their trucks and boats and included small aircraft as both carriers and lookouts. He installed the Internet in many of his crucial distribution points and warehouses. He started the extensive use of mobile phones and hired IT professionals to write secret apps just for their operations.

Unfortunately, Arthur died in 2000, the same year that Gustavo was born. Daniel missed his father, Kaiapo, El Tigre, and his mother, Sophia. They had been among the smartest people he ever knew, and they had loved him. Now, he would show the same love and attention to his son, Gustavo.

The family needed to address several significant issues in 2020: (1) extremely violent, uncontrollable Brazilian gangs were becoming more interested in the drug trade; (2) Daniel had expanded their routes south to Brasilia, but they were often robbed; (3) they needed more overall supply, and they were looking for a secure route with dealer contacts in Bolivia.

Daniel felt they needed another set of family hands that could be trusted, and suddenly Marco Perez appeared. They wanted to learn more about him, and a partnership in the boating trade was a way to do it. His knowledge of boating and the water could become helpful in finding a safe route to Bolivia. If they used him for that assignment, it would be a dangerous mission but enormously profitable when accomplished.

Bolivia was not yet known as a major drug-producing country, and the law enforcement pressure was minimal. Daniel had recently taken a flight to La Paz where he met with several small-time drug dealers. The region around La Paz was undeveloped, and growers of the coca plant were steadily increasing their supply for delivery to the secret laboratories that processed it into the product Daniel wanted. Daniel would organize the dealers more effectively if he could find a reliable unpatrolled water route from La Paz to Manaus.

Daniel and Gus took a half-day tour on one of Marco's tour boats. They also enjoyed a half day of peacock fishing with him as the guide. To complete their initial assessment of the business, they also took a trip with his most well-financed competitor. After spending a few days learning more about the boating activity happening at the port, they invited Marco to Daniel's villa for dinner.

# CHAPTER 17

# Decisions

MARCO WAS CHANGING from a risk-taking, don't-give-a-damn young man into a more mature and organized person. He was surprised at how quickly he had built a legitimate business. Marco had broken no regulations, like those silly fishing regs in Islamorada that had caused him to flee for Manaus. As he looked back, he could not believe that in one single day of fishing and fighting, he had caused such a change in his life. In the Keys, they were ready to throw him in jail. But, in Manaus, he had become a moderately successful businessman with good prospects to become even more successful in the fishing and guiding business.

He decided that he was afraid of Daniel and Gus. They were toying with him for some purpose he did not understand. They were renowned drug dealers with more money than anyone in Manaus, and now they pretended to want to partner with him. He was pretty sure they only wanted to take over his business and use his boats for some drug-dealing purpose. He decided not to make any partnership deal with them and went back to thinking about how to grow his business.

Marco was going about his daily routine when the invitation was hand-delivered to him. He took the envelope, but he did not open it until he got home that night. He had rented a new apartment with two bedrooms, two baths, a beautiful kitchen with granite tabletops, and a den he used as an office. His girlfriend was pleased with the upgrade from their other smaller home.

Barmaids had always been Marco's favorite type of women. He loved their movements when filling drinks, and he loved the way they controlled the customers. He was excited to watch them with their skimpy shorts and flimsy tops. He enjoyed watching the other men ogle his girlfriends while knowing they were coming home with him. The tattoos his current girlfriend had in sensual places with sexy comments turned him on. He had been with this woman for almost two years, and he thought she was a good confidante. He told her everything about his business; and when he had a problem, she helped him with solutions.

"Merci, what do you know about the Perez family that lives outside of town?" he asked as he sipped bourbon in his den.

"I was born in Manaus, and now I am twenty-five years old, and I have heard about that family my entire life. I would not ever talk to them, go near their estate, or even mention their name out loud. They might be the most dangerous people in Brazil," she said.

"Wow! What have you heard that makes you think like that?" Marco asked.

"Because people who mix with them die a terrible death," Merci answered forcefully.

"Is that just rumors, or do you know anyone hurt by that family?" asked Marco in a gentle voice.

"Yes, I know someone who was hurt by them. The Perez family killed my cousin after he bought drugs from a new guy in town selling drugs on the streets of Manaus. The Perez soldiers warned my cousin that the cheaper drugs he was buying were not pure, nor was he buying from the right source. He ignored the warning he received from those two goons carrying pistols," she said.

"Two days later, he was shot in the back of the head, then hanged from a downtown street lamp to make sure the local people got the message. His tongue was removed, and his eyes were missing. The new drug dealer was hanged beside him with his head tied to his hands," she said.

"How do you know the Perez family had anything to do with that killing?" Marco asked.

"Because around the torso of each man was the picture of a white eagle," she said.

"I don't think the current Perez men are like that. How would you like to come with me to the Perez estate for dinner and see for yourself?" asked Marco.

"You know those bastards?" she asked.

"Yes, they are my distant relatives, and they want to do business with me. So far, they seem very cultured and want to be helpful to me. They have invited me to dinner, and I would like for you to come with me and be an observer of everything. I do not know what to do, and I need someone to talk with about their offer," said Marco.

"Marco, you must be crazy! You will get us killed if I go with you!" She yelled.

"Why would they kill us?" Marco asked.

"If you offend them by refusing their offer, I think they will kill you," she said.

"Will you come with me?" he asked nicely.

"Absolutely not. I am so scared that I am moving out tonight. I have enjoyed being with you, and we have had a lot of fun, but you are going to get yourself killed, and I do not want to die with you," she said as she went to her room and started packing.

Marco was startled with her reaction. It as plain as day that Merci was scared out of her mind with fear of the Perez family. Marco decided to visit his friend Al to talk about the offer from Daniel and Gus.

Al was having a few drinks with his friends; but when Marco asked to see him in private, he left his buddies and joined Marco in a booth.

"Al, do you remember that I asked you about the Perez family a while back?" Marco inquired.

"Yes, and I told you not to even mention that name around here," Al said.

"Al, I have an offer from them to be a partner in an expanded boat touring and fishing business. They will provide unlimited capital, and I will control the company. They only want 40 percent, which leaves me completely in control. I can buy more boats, new boats, and bigger boats," said Marco.

"Why would they pick you?" Al asked.

"They said they believe in family. I am a distant relative, and they think the boat business I own can be expanded and make both of us a lot of money," explained Marco.

"Marco, you cannot be foolish to think that the richest, most powerful drug dealers in Brazil need to get in business with you." Al laughed.

"I have received a dinner invitation to discuss their offer. Would you come with me to listen and help me know how to respond?" asked Marco.

"Not on your life! I am nothing but a seller of fish. Thanks for telling me your story, but I am going back to my simple friends, and I will have a drink or two before going home to my safe little room," Al said as he left the booth.

Marco wanted to go, but he was afraid to go alone. He needed someone else to hear the discussion and help him make a decision.

"Merci, I will buy you a new cocktail dress if you come with me to the dinner tomorrow night," said Marco as he looked across the long bar as Merci was making drinks for a busy crowd.

"How nice?" she asked.

"You pick it out. I don't give a damn what it costs. I need you with me," Marco pleaded.

"I will let you know tomorrow after I go shopping. Now leave me alone and let me do my job. I am super busy," Merci said and turned away to keep making drinks.

"Marco, I got my dress. It is the most beautiful dress I have ever owned. I decided that I will go with you. If I am to die, this is the dress to die in," she said solemnly but with a twinkle in her eye.

# CHAPTER 18

# A Deal You Can't Refuse

MARCO AND MERCI arrived at the Perez estate in Marco's new Mitsubishi SUV. They were stopped at the gate until a phone call cleared them for admittance.

"Oh my god! This place is even more dramatic than anything in the stories I have heard. Marco, I am scared I will make a bad impression," said Merci as they made their way up the long driveway.

"You are a beautiful girl. You are my girl. We are going to this dinner party as a fun-loving, happy couple. Do not be nervous and do not be silly. This is no different than being nice to a rich customer who sits at your bar and demands a drink," said Marco.

The brothers and their wives welcomed Marco and Merci at their front door. The wives were dressed beautifully; but Merci held her own with her new dress, haircut, and professional makeup. A small table for six was prepared on the back patio, and they chatted casually as they walked through the massive interior of the mansion. When they arrived at the patio, they could hear the gentle sounds of a small band playing softly at the far edge of the courtyard.

"I am so glad you could join us tonight," said Gus.

"Merci and I have been excited to join you. Thanks for inviting us," smiled Marco.

Marco was impressed at how easy the wives made it for Merci to be included in their conversations, and they seemed to treat her with respect. Merci was happier than ever in her life. These were not mean people. They were gorgeous and friendly. The rumors about them must not be accurate.

Marco was enjoying the conversation about peacock fishing and the trip they had taken together a few weeks ago. It was after a pleasant and delicious dinner that the women took Merci into the parlor with them to play some board games and talk about women things.

When the men were alone, the two brothers began speaking to Marco in solemn tones.

"Marco, we need your help. We still want to fund the expansion of your boating enterprise, but we have a more exciting proposal for you to consider," said Daniel.

Gus brought a set of detailed maps to the table. They were the most accurate view of the Amazon wilderness Marco had ever seen.

They identified waterways, tributaries, islands, and even the vague outlines of remote indigenous villages unknown to exist and never exposed to any modern person.

"We paid thousands of dollars for these maps, and we want you to look at them carefully," said Gus.

"Can you envision a river route from Manaus to La Paz? I want you to study the maps carefully for as long as you like, but then I want you to draw the route you would take," said Daniel.

Daniel and Gus walked over to the portable bar and fixed themselves a drink. They chatted while Marco looked over the maps and studied every detail carefully.

"I would need more time to exam every river, stream, and tributary, and I need to learn more about the rising and falling of the river during different seasons. But at first glance, this is the route I would take," said Marco as he handed them a map with a black route drawn on top of the largest map.

"How long would it take to navigate your route with one ton of product on board a small boat with two ninety-horsepower engines?" asked Gus.

"It would depend on many factors, not the least of which is food, water, gas, and oil supplies," replied Marco.

"If you had all the supplies you need, how long would it take?" insisted Gus.

"My first guess would be two months," said Marco.

"We want you to find that route for us. We are impressed with your boating experience and your ability to please your clients. We will provide you with a trusted indigenous guide to be in your boat and a supply boat to follow you throughout your journey," said Daniel.

"I am not sure I could be successful, and I do not think I can leave my current business for over a month. It might even be more than that if I got delayed for any reason. My clients would become impatient and choose my competitors, and my hard work might be lost," said Marco, trying to find a way to say no.

"Marco, we will guarantee no loss of business for your Manaus operation," said Gus.

"I appreciate the offer, but I think I will just slowly try to grow my little business. You gentlemen are far above me in success, and I am proud that the Perez family has done so well in Brazil, but I do not think I can do what you want me to do," said Marco.

"How much money will you make in profit this year if all goes well?" asked Daniel.

"I will probably clear $150,000 after expenses. I will put $50,000 into savings and buy some more boats and hire some additional workers with the extra $100,000. That is the most money anyone in my family has ever earned," bragged Marco.

"We will pay you $10 million to find a dependable route and then train the indigenous people to make the trip," said Gus.

"Are you crazy? That is more money than I can ever make in my boating business. That is a ridiculous offer. Why don't you use your indigenous people to find the route and save yourself the money?" asked Marco.

"Our family has never let our indigenous partners be the ones to establish our routes and contacts. They are reliable to deliver the products every time, on time, after the supply network has been established," replied Daniel.

"I cannot absorb such an offer and such a challenge in one night. Let me have a few days. You can visit me anytime if you wish so that I can ask you more questions. Can I take the maps with me?" asked Marco as he rose to leave.

"Of you course you can. However, please do not show the maps to anyone, including your girlfriend. Do not speak with anyone about this discussion. Marco, listen to me carefully. If you show these maps to someone or talk of this idea with anyone, we will kill them," said Daniel firmly.

Marco left with the maps and a twitching left eye. For the first time, it was not out of anger but out of stress. The discussion with Daniel and Gus had filled him with two different emotions: greed and fear.

# CHAPTER 19

# Researching a Dangerous Trip

MARCO WONDERED IF the $10 million discussions to travel to and from La Paz was an offer or a command. For sure, he was afraid to anger Daniel and Gus by refusing to make the trip; but he was also interested in the enormous payoff. Marco had never imagined that he could have so much money. So, he decided to research the part of the Amazon he would be traveling.

Marco read a book by Candice Millard called *The River of Doubt*. It was a detailed story about the 1913–1914 expedition of Theodore Roosevelt, who traveled over one thousand miles through the jungles of the Amazon looking for a lost river the natives called the River of Doubt. It was an incredibly difficult journey of courage and perseverance, and the book highlighted the dangers and survival skills necessary to make such a trip.

Roosevelt hired Brazil's most famous explorer Candido Rondon, who, in 1913, had spent more time in the Amazon Basin than any non-indigenous person. Even with Rondon's extraordinary skills, the trip encountered many impossibly dangerous and deadly situations. Roosevelt's journey was somewhat farther south in the jungle than Marco would be traveling, but the issues would be similar. To his advantage, Marco would have more technology than had been unavailable to the Roosevelt team.

As Marco read and reread the book and other limited research about the interior of the Amazon from Manaus to La Paz, he was not confident that he could accomplish such a trip. He would need to prepare carefully and be lucky.

He used the latest technology to discover a remote route, including Google Maps with overlays of the region. He would have no Internet on the trip, so he made copies of everything he could find. Most of the way he had envisioned was not visible on the Google tools because the growth of the trees covered the rivers, streams, and small tributaries. However, many of the more extensive waterways were visible; and he calculated there would be smaller navigable waterways near them. He also noticed the location of the tallest trees, which would generally indicate deeper water and a broader stream.

He calculated they could make an average of fifteen miles per day. Some days would be less when the brush clearing was difficult, but there would be days when they found large tributaries and could make fifty miles in a day. He estimated the distance to be one thousand miles, so he figured that the trip would take around seventy days.

The things to consider were overwhelming, and organizing supplies for as much as two months in the wilderness might be impossible. They would need food, cooking and eating utensils, gas, and oil for more than a thousand miles, weapons and ammunition, medical supplies, tents, sleeping bags, and many other vital supplies.

They would also need reliable and sturdy equipment for clearing the unused waterways of overhanging trees, obstacles in the water such as rocks and dead limbs, and trees growing in the water and blocking any passage. For the clearing work, Marco decided he would need at least ten eighteen-inch gas-powered chainsaws, twenty eighteen-inch machetes made with a rust-resistant coating, and ten manual bow saws. These tools would probably be put to hard use every hour of every day.

If he made the trip, what kind of boat would he use? How many people would he need? He would need one or more vessels large enough to carry the supplies and passengers and to navigate some potentially rough waterways. But it had to be small enough to travel through the shallow water, overhanging branches, and dense underbrush of the lesser rivers. He was also worried about the rapids but hoped to avoid them by using the smaller tributaries.

He decided he would use two twenty-three-foot-long, wide-beamed, shallow-draft boats from the boatbuilder *Intruder*. These boats could travel in water as shallow as ten inches but still had the stability if needed for the rough waterways, and the storage was considerable for such a small boat. He would use only one ninety-horsepower four-stroke motor for both speed and efficiency on each boat. Each Intruder would also tow an aluminum boat four feet wide and ten feet long. He would carry one extra motor for backup.

They would need five people to make the trip: two in the front of the lead boat to clear the way, one driver in the lead boat, and two in the rear boat with one in the bow and one driver. The worker in the back boat would rotate places with workers in the first boat. This rotation would give him three men to clear the brush each day. They would need a lot of food.

He would ask Daniel to contact his friends in the army to get five hundred MREs (meals ready to eat) that were simple to heat up, and they were nutritious. He would need to keep the workers well-fed and healthy to clear the path through the dense jungle. They would also pack canned goods and dried food and start with some fresh meat. Maybe they could kill some animals along the way to supplement their food supply.

He calculated that they needed four hundred gallons of gas and the oil to accompany it. Each boat had a fifty-gallon tank, so they would need to carry six fifty-gallon bladders in the towboats. The four boats would be heavily loaded when they began the trip, but he felt they were the right choices for the trip.

Two days after the dinner, Marco was still puzzling over the trip when Gus came to visit him at the fishing dock. He asked Marco to take him to the same peacock fishing location they had fished before. He wanted to show something to Marco. Gus had a solemn face and said nothing during the trip.

When they arrived at Marco's favorite spot, they saw a boat anchored in the middle of the area where the lures were usually cast. In the boat were three dead bodies, all with their throats cut. One body was Merci, and the other two were her work associates.

"We told you not to share the maps or your Google overlays with anyone. Merci saw your maps while you were sleeping or working. She shared some of the contents with two of her fellow workers. One of our soldiers heard them talking about a trip you might be planning," said Gus.

"Damn you! That is beyond cruel. She was an innocent person," yelled Marco.

"We told you once. We have a family rule, and it is to give only one warning, no more. We told you this trip must be kept secret. You did not take proper precautions, and you are responsible for the deaths of those three people, not me. You should learn to listen," snapped Gus.

"Gus, I no longer trust that you guys have my best interest in mind. I think you are forcing me to do something good for you but not necessarily good for me," said Marco.

"This is business. We have made you an exceptionally generous offer. We will keep your boat business intact, and you will have $10 million in your bank account when you return with the drugs," said Gus.

"There is no reason for you to be afraid of us. You will not be harmed upon your return. We can continue together in the tour boat business, and you will be a rich man," explained Gus.

"Gus, this trip is going to be difficult. I have done the research, and I don't think I am qualified to find a route through the wilderness using unknown rivers and tributaries. The federal police patrol the main large rivers like the Madeira and Puras, and those waterways cannot be used safely for drug smuggling," said Marco.

"We know that the main routes are not acceptable for our business. That is why we need you," replied Gus.

"I cannot do this alone. I need help," said Marco, giving up on saying no to the offer.

"We will send Kaiapo with you. He knows some of the remote waterways, and he has tribal influence with his indigenous people part of the way," said Gus.

"I will need four people besides me. The amount of supplies will be huge, and the work to clear our path will be incredibly hard. I need three strong men plus Kaiapo. I think I have decided upon the best boats to use for the trip, and I already have the ones I need," said Marco.

"Then start your trip," urged Gus.

"It is not that simple. I will need your help to purchase these supplies, and Daniel will need to get a large order of MREs from his army buddies," explained Marco as he gave the list of supplies he had prepared to Gus.

"I am glad you are so prepared. You have been thinking clearly about the trip, and I am impressed. We expect you to leave in two weeks," said Gus.

"Gus, I will go in two weeks and try to accomplish what you have asked me to do. But I want to change the method and timing of the payment to me. I want you to wire $5 million to my parents before I leave. You can pay me the other $5 million when we have arrived in La Paz, and I have successfully created a remote route. I will give you a detailed map that you and your team can use for years. On the way back, I will assist Kaiapo in using the map to make sure he can train his people. Then I will have my own money to celebrate when we return to Manaus," said Marco

"I will need to discuss this with Daniel," said Gus.

"I will continue my planning for the trip because I hope you will agree to this minor change," said Marco.

Two days later, Gus told Marco that the new payment terms were acceptable. He had given the list of supplies to Daniel; and Daniel was buying the items requested, including the MREs.

Marco called his parents, and they gave him the bank routing information from a blank check. He gave the information to Gus and asked his parents to let him know when they saw a large deposit in their bank account.

Marco usually called his parents twice a year to give them an update on his life. He had often told them of his success in the boating business and offered to pay for them to visit. So far, he had not convinced them to travel.

On this call, he told them he was being paid a large amount of money to take a trip through the Amazon jungle. He thought it would be a safe trip, but he wanted them to have the money in case he did not return. He said they could spend the money on anything they wanted:

a new house, a new car, a vacation, help his sisters, or any other thing they might have dreamed about.

Daniel wired the money. Marco's parents called, confirmed the deposit, and they all had a long conversation with his mother crying about the possible danger.

Marco would be ready for the expedition to leave in two weeks, but at the same time, he was working on a plan to punish Gus and Daniel for killing Merci. They had destroyed his desire to be a part of their life after this trip.

# CHAPTER 20

# The Trip Begins

AN ENORMOUS QUANTITY of supplies was purchased and loaded into the four boats. The boats were sitting low in the water with more weight than recommended, but Marco hoped they would be stable enough in the small remote waterways they planned to use for the beginning of the trip. As the trip progressed and the load emptied, the boats would become more stable for use in rough water if they needed to move out of the dense jungle.

Marco, Jaluca, and Tupari were in the lead boat with Kaiapo driving the rear boat and Ajani in the bow. Daniel had given Marco the most efficient and trusted workers familiar with his operation. They left from the back of the Perez estate, where the loading and unloading of products arrived from Leticia. Daniel did not want to build another complex of warehouses and residences. He wanted both delivery routes to end at the same place.

For the first one hundred miles, the jungle was familiar to Kaiapo. They stopped briefly at a couple of villages for Kaiapo to visit with the elders, leave a few supplies, and keep their friendship. But soon, Kaiapo was in unfamiliar waters.

So far, the rivers had been easy to clear, and their progress was better than Marco expected.

Marco had large spools of white twine; and when they entered a waterway leading in a new direction, he would tie a small piece of the string to a tree trunk three feet above the waterline. He put it on the trees as infrequently as possible to avoid strangers using it as a route marker. Marco also made a detailed paper map as he traveled. On the map, he noted the places where he had left the string indicating the points of critical directional changes.

Marco was also using a GPS with a tracking feature that recorded where they had traveled. All of the tools combined should make it a snap to follow the new route.

The air was thick with mosquitoes; and despite the nets covering their entire bodies, they were often bitten. The mosquitoes were just waiting to attack when they needed to relieve themselves or when preparing camp and eating. The mosquito nets were hot and sticky. The jungle was so dense that no sunlight penetrated through the trees to land on the damp soil near the river, and it was so humid that it almost felt like you were drinking water with each breath. It was physically miserable.

The men were not complaining, but the work to clear the way was exhausting and nonstop. Around every bend and when entering almost every new tributary, they found thick limbs and underbrush to remove. They were making less than five miles on some days, and Marco felt they had fallen behind schedule.

The boats had mileage indicators; and after two weeks of fourteen-hour days, they were less than one-fourth of the way.

Although they were moving slowly, things had gone remarkably well. There were so many choices and so many tributaries and small rivers that they were surprised at how easy it had been to stay headed in a southwesterly direction. They mapped and marked the route and were pleased with their ability to keep moving in the right direction.

Over the next two weeks, the rivers became broader and deeper, and the effort to clear the path was much less. It was also the dry season, and the river was lower than it would be in the wet season, which meant the tree limbs were not as close to the water. This route would be harder to travel when the water was high.

They had made up the lost time, and they were moving slowly down a new river without thick foliage. The men in the lead boat were resting, and Marco was almost napping when Kaiapo felt a sharp sting hit his leg. At first, he thought it was a wasp or some other large insect; but when he looked down at his leg, he saw a dart.

G. ALAN BROOKS

"Marco hit the gas as hard as you can! Men with blowguns are attacking us with poisoned darts!" Kaiapo yelled at Marco and the other men.

Marco and Kaiapo both gunned their motors, and all five of the men flattened themselves as low into the boats as possible. The darts hit the side of both boats but struck no one again. Although it only took several minutes for the boats to travel away from the attackers, they continued to move as fast as possible for three hours. Kaiapo did not know the people who had made the attack.

When they stopped to camp for the night, Kaiapo was in great pain. His leg was swollen to twice the usual size, and he was shaking with chills and a fever. Marco did not know how to treat a poisoned dart injury, but Kaiapo said to cut the wound and let it bleed. Then get some leeches and put them into the open cut so they would suck the poison from the dart.

Leeches were everywhere in this jungle since they love freshwater pools and sluggish streams. In fact, the most gigantic leeches in the world are in the Amazon Basin. A net pulled along the shallow bottom will almost always find a few leeches and sometimes hundreds. Marco quickly cut the wound with his pocketknife and then picked up two lively ones from a dozen black leeches that Jaluca had collected. Marco put them into the wounds, and they immediately started eating and sucking. Kaiapo said they were uncomfortable but not unbearable.

They spent two days in the camp watching Kaiapo, giving him lots of water, placing wet towels on his head, and putting new leeches into the wound every four hours. Kaiapo was a big healthy man, and the dart was probably designed to kill small animals. The amount of poison was not enough to kill a large man, but it made Kaiapo sick for three days. They left after two days, with Kaiapo still feeling bad but improving. They could not afford to waste any more time. They were now almost five weeks into the trip, and the diminishing quantity of supplies and gas was starting to worry Marco.

Marco had not included a stop in Porto Velho when he planned the trip. But when looking at his maps, Marco realized that they might be within one hundred miles of the city with a population of almost five hundred thousand people. Porto Velho is on the Madeira River, which is the longest tributary in the Amazon. It is over two thousand miles long, and it is probably the most active waterway in the Basin.

Now he decided that since they had nothing illegal on the boats, they should visit the city and get more supplies, including gas and oil. They would avoid this city when loaded with drugs, but now it seemed like a smart place to briefly visit.

Six days later, they found the city of Porto Velho and purchased the supplies they needed to continue toward La Paz. Using the main waterways, it was probably only five or six hundred miles to La Paz; but using the remote tributaries, it might take another five or six weeks. They now had plenty of supplies and left Porto Velho confident they would finish the trip in under two months. Not bad for a trio of inexperienced Manaus explorers.

# CHAPTER 21

# The Trip Back to Manaus

THEY ARRIVED IN La Paz forty days after leaving Porto Velho and immediately called Daniel to let him know they were in the location as planned. Daniel and Gus got in their private airplane and arrived in La Paz six hours later. Marco, Kaiapo, and Jaluca took rooms in a cheap hotel and slept while waiting for the father and son to arrive.

Gus and Daniel arrived at the motel and awakened the sleeping men to get an explanation of what they had discovered. Marco showed them his impressive map drawings with the string notations and other graphics.

"My god! Marco, you and Kaiapo have done a remarkable job of finding a remote route. This map and this route will make us millions of dollars in profit," said Daniel.

"Our $10 million deal with you was a bargain. Thank you for this incredible accomplishment," whispered Gus as he took Marco aside so no one else could hear his voice.

"Don't forget to wire the additional $5 million money to my account this afternoon," said Marco quietly.

"Marco, we are proud to have you in the Perez family. I am sure we will accomplish many great things together. I have already made the transaction we discussed," smiled Daniel.

"All of you guys should be in the history books for such an achievement. But for now, let's keep it a secret." Daniel laughed.

Everyone was in a festive mood when they went to a restaurant with a bar. The food and wine kept coming until all were completely satisfied and half drunk. They toasted one another repeatedly. Afterward, the five explorers went back to the motel; and each took a room. Kaiapo and his team slept through the night like dead men.

Marco left his room and got online at a local coffee shop. He checked his bank account and saw that $5 million was deposited that afternoon. He then wired the entire $5 million to his parents' account in Key West. His parents, who had always been poor, would now have $10 million of the Manaus Perez's ill-gotten money. That made him laugh out loud. He had finally been a good son.

Early the next morning, they all met for breakfast. Marco reviewed the return trip and what they needed to make it back without stopping at Porto Velho. He now needed to implement the plan he had made with Jose.

"I have been thinking about the return trip. We want to make sure we can return successfully using the map I created. We should not involve any more people at this point. I think the five of us can make it, but we will need another boat loaded with the drugs to make the trip," recommended Marco.

"Why don't we take another Intruder? I will drive the boat loaded with our marijuana and cocaine," said Gus.

"Daniel, have you arranged for our products yet? How much room do we need?" Marco asked.

"Yes, and we can buy as much as we want. The dealers here are full of products, and it is a buyers' market. We can make a huge profit if we load up heavily on the cocaine," said Daniel.

"Then I agree with Gus that we need a fourth boat to carry most of the drugs," said Marco.

"We can put some under the floorboards of all the boats and then put the balance in the boat I will be driving," said Gus greedily.

The next day, they bought another Intruder. The dealers brought the drugs to the water's edge, where the boats were tied up. They loaded as much product as they could safely put in each boat.

When they finished packing, Daniel had purchased $18 million of cocaine and marijuana. The dealers were ecstatic to know the Perez family had made a route through the Amazon to Manaus. It would mean much more business for them.

Daniel told each supplier that anyone who spoke of this new route or used the Perez name would be executed immediately along with all their family members. Daniel insisted that this new arrangement must be kept secret; there would be no more warnings.

Just before leaving La Paz, Marco made a secret call of his own to Manaus.

In the dark of night, the three Intruder boats towing the two aluminum jon boats left La Paz with plenty of supplies and a load of illegal drugs worth $50 million on the street. It was an exciting time for Daniel and Gus to see another supply chain adding to their already profitable enterprise. Daniel called the airport and arranged for his flight home.

The sequence of the boat caravan consisted of Marco and Jaluca in the lead, next came Gus and Tupari with the heavily loaded drug boat, then Kaiapo and Ajani. Kaiapo had almost recovered from the poison dart, but he still had migraine headaches that almost disabled him.

They made good progress for ten days. It was a much faster trip now that the limbs and obstacles had been removed. Marco saw they were getting close to the spot where the dart attack had occurred. They were probably six to seven hundred miles from La Paz and two hundred miles north of Porto Velho. Marco figured this was about as remote and primitive as the Amazon could get.

"A few miles ahead is where we were attacked before by the darts. I think we should camp here for the night and prepare for another attack. We can make some shields out of the used gas cans. Let's cut them into pieces so that we can hold in front of us if we are attacked," advised Marco.

"I think that is an excellent idea," said Gus.

They made camp and set up their cooking pots around a fire. Jaluca was the cook most of the time, but tonight Marco had volunteered to cook a small deer he had killed earlier in the day as it was watering on the river's edge. Kaiapo and Jaluca knew how to skin the deer and cut it into deliciously edible parts.

They had an abundant supply of dried and canned goods, such as beans and rice, which they heated and served with the deer. Everyone was enjoying their meal, and Marco was cleaning the rifle he had used to kill the deer.

Before anyone could react, Marco shot each man in the chest with his automatic rifle.

"Gus, you bastard! You killed something of great value to me when you killed Merci. You are nothing but a piece of garbage! I hope you burn in hell," said Marco as he glared into the dying blue eyes of Gus.

Kaiapo tried to speak, but he never got the words to come, and Jaluca and the other two men were dead before they hit the ground. Marco took the money from their pockets and tossed each body into the river to be eaten by whatever wanted a meal.

He felt no remorse for killing those drug-dealing, ruthless bums.

Now, Marco was all alone in the most remote part of the Amazon. Nobody on earth knew his whereabouts or what he had done.

Marco had to consider carefully his next choice that would determine how to live the rest of his life.

1. He could stay in the jungle and try to live with the primitive people who shot the darts. Since childhood, he had dreamed about living life with a primitive tribe.
2. He could return to Manaus with the drugs and work with the Perez family widows. It would only take him another ten days to reach Manaus, and he had plenty of supplies. He could tell a good story about how the group got separated, and perhaps the others are still lost. They might never show up, but it would not be his fault. He could become enormously wealthy as the new Perez family head.
3. He could take the drugs on Gus's boat to Porto Velho, sell them, disappear for a while, and then go back to the Keys and live well with part of the money he sent to his parents, plus the drug money. Selling the drugs would risk being caught, but it would give him a lot more money.
4. He could leave everything in the jungle and go back to Porto Velho or on to Manus. He could tell the sad story of his lost companions. Fly home and enjoy life in the Keys. He would

ask his parent to give him back the second $5 million, and he was sure they would.

Marco was so tired that soon he fell into a deep sleep and started dreaming. At first, he had slept without dreaming; but after a while, he had a nightmare.

In his nightmare, he saw Daniel coming down the waterways to kill him and everyone nearby. Daniel was using the map, and his guide was using binoculars to scan for the white string. They were moving at an incredible pace in some kind of speedboat, and they would be in the village at any moment. They were heavily armed, and he knew they would ask no questions before killing him and the entire village. He ran toward his boat to get some weapons, but it was too late because Daniel was standing next to him with a machine gun. Marco suddenly awoke in a heavy sweat; but when he realized where he was, he smiled.

Marco knew Daniel would never kill anyone again.

# CHAPTER 22

# The End of the Daniel

DANIEL HAD EMPLOYED Jose for fifteen years, first as a bodyguard and later as his most trusted driver. Jose was loyal and had been with his boss on several occasions when he saw Daniel and his soldiers commit extreme brutality. Still, he never said anything or showed any emotion.

When Daniel and Gus bought a private airplane, it was Jose who took them to the airport; and he was always there to pick them up upon their return. He never had any other passengers in the car but the father or son.

A year ago, Marco met Jose when he and Merci were having a drink at a dimly lit bar in a run-down section of Manaus. It was the neighborhood where Merci was raised, and she loved to go to her old haunts. A large man in a nice suit approached their table and sat down.

"Marco, I would like for you to meet my brother, Jose," Merci said.

They shook hands and had one drink before Jose left the bar. Marco never saw Jose again until the day he brought Daniel and Gus to the port for the trips they took on Marco's boats. It was then Marco realized Merci's brother worked for the Perez family. Marco never told Merci what he had seen because he was sure she did not know that Jose worked for them.

After Gus killed Merci, Marco found Jose's phone number on her cell phone. He invited Jose for a drink. Marco told Jose about the mutilated bodies that Gus had forced him to see. He said the reason Merci and her friends had been killed was to keep his upcoming trip through the Amazon a secret.

Jose was furious! Merci was the one thing in his life he had loved the most. Jose was so angry that he crushed a beer glass in his hands and needed to stop the bleeding with his handkerchief.

"Jose, would you be willing to kill Daniel if you could escape and flee to a safe place?" asked Marco, taking a chance that Jose would not stay loyal to Daniel.

"I would be happy to kill him with my bare hands!" growled Jose.

"Great, let's take down this evil family," said Marco.

Marco told Jose he had a plan that would end the Perez drug cartel and destroy their family. Marco explained why he was taking the trip to La Paz with Kaiapo and Jaluca.

He told Jose that when his team arrived in La Paz, he had to call Daniel and let him know they had made a successful trip. Then, Daniel and Gus would fly to La Paz to buy the drugs. As usual, Daniel would ask Jose to drive him and Gus to the airport. Jose would then be ordered to pick them up when they returned.

Marco told Jose he would make sure Gus joined the team on their return trip to Manaus. He knew that Daniel would want to smuggle as much as possible; and to do so, they would need Gus to drive the fourth boat.

"I will call you before we leave La Paz to let you know for sure that Gus is driving the drug-laden fourth boat," explained Marco.

"If Gus gets in that boat, I promise you that he will never live to see Manaus again. I will kill him in the jungle, and then you will kill Daniel when you pick him up at the airport," said Marco as he outlined his plan.

Jose gave Marco his bank information, and the next morning Marco wired $150,000 for Jose's retirement in the far south of Brazil.

"As soon as you kill him, drop his body into the jungle and take a flight to Rio Grande, which is an old city near Uruguay, far away from everything. The Perez cartel will be in a frantic turmoil when they discover that Gus, Daniel, Kaiapo, and Jaluca are all missing. They will never think of looking for you, and even if they thought about it, there would be no one to organize a search. The fighting for control of the cartel will be bloody and chaotic," said Marco.

"I will shoot him in the stomach to make him suffer, then cut his throat as he did to my dear sister, and finally, I will toss him to the caimans. No one will ever find him," pledged Jose. A little over a month later, Jose would do just as he had promised.

Marco and Jose, two unimportant people, had destroyed the most powerful drug cartel in Brazil. Marco was confident that Jose had kept his promise; so he laughed at his nightmare, got out of the hammock, and went to the hearth to stare into the flickering fire. What sweet revenge!

The Manaus Perez family's corrupt success story was over, but the Key West Perez family was just beginning to enjoy their fortune. How great was that?

# CHAPTER 23

# Marco's Choice

AFTER MARCO'S NIGHTMARE about Daniel and the remembrance of Gus and Daniel killing Merci, he decided that he wanted nothing more to do with the Perez family in Brazil. He despised the entire family so much he could never be happy working with any of them. Marco knew that the widows were involved in every significant decision, and they were just as corrupt as the men. He ruled out, going back to Manaus to work with them.

He genuinely wanted to experiment with living in a primitive village, but the fear that he would be killed while trying to meet with the tribe stopped that idea. The uncontacted people who lived nearby had wanted to kill them with their poisoned darts. They might do the same to him if he approached them with the idea of living in their village. It was just too dangerous, and he was still too young to die.

He knew that the federal police were active in Porto Velho; and if he got caught with the enormous drug boat, he would go to jail for a long time. He might even be killed while trying to sell such a large amount of drugs. He knew no drug dealers, and he would be taking a giant risk to trust anyone with such a load. He thought about taking a smaller part of the shipment to sell, but even if caught with a small amount, he would be put in a filthy jail or prison and probably die in that place.

He spent two days thinking about his choices. He ran the possibilities over and over in his mind and concluded that he should be satisfied with the $10 million already safely in Key West. His parents would give him back as much as he asked for, and he decided that he would leave them the original $5 million minus what they had already spent. He would have $5 million to start up a new guiding business, which should be plenty of money to buy new boats, equipment, and create a fancy website.

He once again estimated that he was two hundred miles north of Porto Velho. In one of the Intruders, without the towboat, he could make the trip in two days. He did not need to clear any limbs or underbrush from his path, and he was confident he knew the route. He only needed to fill the boat with gas and food to last for two days of fast travel.

Having made his decision, Marco put all of the drugs into one boat and set the other boats adrift into the current of the river. He found a small creek that led into the jungle a few hundred yards off the main river. In the little stream, Marco covered the drugs with waterproof tarps and tied the boat loosely against a large tree. He left plenty of loose rope to give the boat room to lift with the rising water of the wet season.

If he ever needed money desperately, he could return and take the risk of selling the drugs. He felt the drugs would be safe and not deteriorate for a few years. He would have time to decide if he needed to return before they became worthless. He hoped he would never return, but it was a backup plan.

He left for Porto Velho in one Intruder boat, confident with his decision. Now he just needed to get out of Brazil without being stopped or killed by the Perez cartel organization. He had his passport in his pocket.

Despite what he told Jose, they were a powerful organization with many loyal soldiers.

# CHAPTER 24

# Going Home

MARCO MADE IT to Porto Velho with no difficulty. He assumed his best approach would be to find a small hotel several miles west of the city. He found a dilapidated riverside motel eight miles from downtown.

His ultimate plan was to go to Cusco, Peru, by way of the Madeira and Madre de Dios rivers. It was over nine hundred miles to Cusco using the two rivers.

He needed a faster boat because the rivers were the safest means of travel until he was safe. He could not risk a plane trip from Porto Velho. If any Perez soldiers were looking for him because Daniel had disappeared, they would be looking in Porto Velho and La Paz. He did not think they would look in Peru.

He should be safe on the water in an old speedboat. He would look like an average guy cruising the river for the thrill of a fast ride.

Once he was in Cusco, he would hide for one month and then fly to Lima and catch a plane to Miami. He wanted to avoid any more time in Brazil.

After checking in at the riverside motel, he looked in the ragged phone book for marinas. He called several boat dealers before he found a fifteen-year-old Formula for sale. The engine had just been overhauled, and the twenty-three-foot boat would run at least forty miles per hour for long distances. He arranged for a demo the next day and went to sleep.

On the demo run, the Formula performed well; and he traded the Intruder plus $4,000 for his new ride. He left the marina and was soon cruising the Madeira River at almost fifty miles per hour. He ran the boat for fifteen hours, which put him nearly two-thirds of the way to Cusco.

He had put three MREs on the Formula, and he spent the night on the boat and did not risk checking into a motel. He had a mosquito net, and the Formula had a small cabin. It would be hot, but he could bear it without complaint.

Early the next morning, he continued his journey to Cusco. He quickly sold the boat for $2,000 and found an old hotel in the heart of downtown. It was a dingy old town, with crowds of bustling people; and he found a comfortable room with a window air conditioner.

He went to a used clothing store and disposed of his jungle clothes and bought used clothing to dress like the men he had seen walking the streets. He shaved his beard, had his hair cut short, and dyed his hair red. He bought a new pair of reflective sunglasses and put a stone in his shoe to cause a limp. He had a good disguise he would use for four weeks.

He did not think the Perez organization would reach this far, but he took no chances. The newspaper headlines were carrying the story of Daniel's disappearance and the absence of Gus. There was speculation that a drug war was happening, and the Brazil federal police prepared for a bloodbath.

He went to a local restaurant and bar for some food and drink. The conversation throughout the establishment was all about the missing heads of the Perez cartel. At the bar, one man was talking loudly about the horrible revenge the cartel would take on anyone responsible for hurting the Perez father and son.

It worried Marco that even in Peru, the cartel was known and feared. He would lay low for a while before attempting a flight home.

Marco ate at only two or three restaurants close to the hotel. He stayed off the street and spoke to no one. It was not a fun time, but he read and watched TV. The time passed slowly; but after four weeks, he boarded a plane to Lima and then Miami.

He made the flight to Lima and then to Miami without any trouble. When he walked off the plane in Miami, he had no luggage. He took a cab to a Ford dealership and bought a used Explorer. He drove directly to Key West and surprised his mother and father.

They celebrated his arrival for several days. He asked for them to return $5 million of the $10 million he had sent. They were happy he left them half of the money. They hugged him as he said good-bye, and then Marco drove up to Islamorada. He rented a cottage on the bay for one month and visited all the marinas within twenty miles of Islamorada.

He talked to many locals about who were the best fishing guides, he looked at the websites for hundreds of guides, and he visited with the management of numerous marinas to choose his new business location.

He decided to base his operation out of Jim and Jane's Marina. They had room for both of his boats, and their location had easy access to the Atlantic Ocean and Florida Bay.

He bought a 2016 Boston Whaler Outrage fully equipped for $650,000. It had every electronic device he needed for offshore fishing and many comforts for six clients, including an onboard grill, an air-conditioned cabin, and a comfortable head. He named his new boat the Perez Prize.

He also bought a Hell's Bay Marquesa flats skiff for $60,000, which is one of the best shallow-water boats ever built.

He hired a captain for each boat and paid a first-class web designer to create an impressive web presence. He paid the designer to put him on all social media channels and paid her to keep a blog updated with exciting fishing photos and facts about his operation. In two years, he became one of the most successful guide operations in the area.

He hired a top-flight attorney and got the fishing violations, and the assault charge dismissed with some fines and community service. The law was off his back.

He found another sexy barmaid to live with him, bought her a bar of her own, and still had over $4 million in the bank to cover his Florida Keys lifestyle.

You can usually find Marco hanging out at the marina or the Perez Sunset Bar at mile-marker 90 on the Overseas Highway.

After a few drinks and after watching the sunset over Florida Bay, he often ruminates about that $50 million pile of drugs he left in the jungle. Marco fantasizes about what he could do with $50 million! After two more drinks, he thinks he just might go back.

# Check Out This Different Ending!

"Gus, you bastard! You killed something of great value to me when you killed Merci. You are nothing but a piece of garbage! I hope you burn in hell," said Marco as he glared into the dying blue eyes of Gus. Kaiapo tried to speak, but he never got the words to come, and Jaluca and the other two men were dead before they hit the ground. He took the money from their pockets and tossed each body into the river to be eaten by whatever wanted a meal.

He felt no remorse for killing those drug-dealing, ruthless bums.

Now, Marco was all alone in the most remote part of the Amazon. Nobody on earth knew his whereabouts or what he had done.

# CHAPTER 25

# Finding a Home in the Amazon

UNKNOWN TO THE others, just before the dart attack began, Marco had seen a young brown girl running through the jungle.

He thought of her often since he had watched her run and then stop to look at him. She looked exactly like the picture he had hung in his Key West bedroom, and he believed that she had smiled at him.

Marco had been interested in the primitive tribes of Brazil before he met the Manaus Perez family. His senior English thesis was on the indigenous people of the Amazon. When he was sixteen, he had seen a picture in *National Geographic* of a beautiful young brown girl with a trim figure and long black hair leaning against a dark-green tree in a remote Amazon village. He cut it out and put it on his bedroom wall, and he dreamed of her for years. When he came to Manaus, he checked out as many books from the library as he could find on primitive people. He began to wonder if he could live in the jungle with some of these people.

He was happy to learn that Brazil was home to the most uncontacted people anywhere. Marco read that there could be as many as one hundred primitive groups who had never had contact with the modern world still living in the Amazon Basin. The rubber boom drove some tribes near Manaus from their original homes, and they fled into the jungles of the northern Amazon Basin. Others ran from loggers and ranchers all over the basin who were destroying the forests around their villages.

When he first had the idea to kill Gus, Kaiapo, and Jaluca, he was going to shoot them closer to Porto Velho and then sell the drugs for whatever he could get. With the $5 million in his bank, plus the drug money, he would be a rich man. After he killed them, he would vanish down the Madeira River and live quietly for a few months before flying back to Key West. With his money, he would buy a beautiful sports fishing boat for the ocean and a Hell's Bay skiff for the backcountry. He would be a successful fishing guide and have everything he had wanted, except the girl of his dreams.

He had not decided to live in the jungle until he saw the girl, and that changed his plans.

He suspected that this tribe was too far from any city to have been displaced by mining, ranching, or logging. Maybe they had seen white people before, and perhaps they even used some everyday household items, but they clearly wanted to be left alone. They would not have used the blowguns if they were looking to meet outsiders.

Perhaps he really could live in the jungle as El Tigre had done happily and peacefully. It was an old dream with new possibilities.

He changed his plans and decided to kill the men and keep all the supplies and drugs. He would have many supplies to help the primitive people, and he had enough gas to return to Porto Velho if he or they needed anything. He had so much cocaine to sell in Porto Velho or to use himself that he or his new village would never deplete it. His problem was how to be accepted by the people of the tribe and to find the girl.

He had given some thought to the best approach. He left the boats hidden in the jungle underbrush near their current campsite. Since the dart attack had come from the edge of the river, he surmised there must be some solid ground near the attack site. Maybe they heard the boats approaching and shot right from their village. They might have never seen a boat with a motor before. Perhaps they had never seen a white man. It did not matter; he was going to meet them.

He took off all his clothes, including his shoes, despite the mosquitoes and leeches. He would keep only his pistol in case things went to hell, and he needed to escape. He began walking toward the village when he saw a small brown man with a blowgun.

Marco was not sure what to do, but he had read about a scientist who found a remote village and acted foolishly when he first encountered the tribe. The scientist was met with laughter, not hostility; and Marco had always been amazed that his antics worked.

The small brown man had short black hair that looked like it had been cut with a bowl over his head. He had two white paint slashes under his eyes, and he was naked except for a small piece of loincloth.

Marco dropped the pistol and raised his hands and laughed hysterically. The man lowered his blowgun and waved more small brown men forward.

Marco kept laughing and jumping up and down. They looked at him with amused expressions, and then they laughed and jumped up and down. He yelled at the top of his lungs, and they yelled at the top of their lungs. He sat on the ground, and they sat on the ground. The foolish behavior was working.

He was surprised at how quickly they became friendly and not hostile. Maybe curiosity replaced their initial fright. What could he do now? He rubbed his stomach and moved his hand to his mouth like he was eating something. They copied his movements again.

He wanted to be taken to their village but did not know how to ask or pantomime that idea. He decided to lie down on the ground and close his eyes like he was taking a nap. This time, they seemed to understand and walked away.

He arose from the ground and followed them. They kept looking back but did not appear to have any aggressive ideas. The damn mosquitoes were driving him crazy, but he gritted his teeth and promised himself not to act as if they were hurting him. He pulled two leeches off his right leg.

When he entered the small village, he saw a large communal house with hammocks strung from the rafters. It looked like the structure was old, and he guessed that the village had been here for a long time.

In the middle of the communal house was a large cooking hearth where the families shared their food. He knew these structures were called malocas. He saw a few more men and perhaps twenty women. It looked like the community consisted of around fifty people. It was not unusual for primitive societies to be small because of the difficulty in feeding a large group, but he was surprised there were not many young men.

The men he had been following sat down by a small fire outside the maloca. The one who appeared to be the leader pointed to a pot of something cooking on the fire. Marco did not know how to eat anything because he saw no plates or utensils. Suddenly an older woman dipped a metal dish plate into the pot and handed the food to him with an old metal knife. He used the knife to put the food into his mouth. He had no idea what it was, but he would eat it if it killed him.

It was late in the day when one of the men took Marco by the hand and gave him a few items: a small loincloth, some oil to repel the mosquitoes, and a hammock in the maloca. There was no need for any other personal possessions; the community provided everything else except for blowguns, which they were not going to give him yet. It looked like ten hammocks were unused in the maloca.

He had dropped his pistol into a bush as they were entering the village open space, but he hoped he would never need it. One of his hidden boats had numerous weapons and a considerable supply of ammo if he needed them to protect himself or the tiny village.

Marco applied the oil; and almost immediately, the mosquitoes stopped biting. Bites covered his body, but the oil helped calm the itching and burning. As he lay in the hammock, he knew there were two things to accomplish quickly: he must find a way to be acceptable to the community, and he must locate the girl.

# CHAPTER 26

# Becoming Part of the Community

MARCO WAS LOOKING into the fire when one of the women came to begin the morning meal. She wore only a small waistcloth, an armband, and an anklet made of fiber. She had fish and large root vegetables overflowing in a straw basket.

She sliced the fish into bite-sized chunks and did the same with the vegetables. When she had enough food for the villagers to have a small breakfast, she dropped everything into a black cook pot. She hummed as she worked, and she smiled at Marco but did not speak.

Soon thirty people filled the hearth. Each had their plate but no eating utensils. They used a wooden dipper to fill their plates and ate with their hands. Once again, Marco was amazed there were only two young men at the breakfast table. Where were the young people—and the girl?

Marco spoke softly in English and got no response. He did the same in Spanish and got no answer; and when he finally spoke Portuguese, one of the older men smiled and said hello.

In April of 1500, the Portuguese landed in Brazil; and their presence was dominant until the early 1800s. They controlled the entire country and penetrated the interiors of the country, encountering many ancient indigenous people. Perhaps this man had ancestors who had been exposed to the Portuguese explorers, or maybe he had been in another village with more modern exposure.

After he said hello, he began speaking in a halting manner. "Why are you in our village?" he asked.

"I want to live here," said Marco.

"I do not believe you. What do you really want? No white man wants to live like us, and we do not want to live like the white people who have destroyed our country. We want to live as our ancestors did twenty thousand years ago," he said.

"I do want to live like you. I do not want to live like the white people you describe," Marco replied.

"How long do you want to live with us?" he asked.

"I want to live in this village for the rest of my life. I never plan to return to modern life," said Marco.

"We do not trust you, but I will speak to the village council and give you an answer. My name is Nawi," he said.

Marco looked for the girl again, but she was not to be seen. He went to his hammock and stayed there for the entire day. He did not want to do anything to offend the small community, so he waited for an answer.

In the afternoon, Nawi came to his hammock and asked him to go to the communal hearth. When he arrived, fifteen middle-aged men were waiting for him.

"They want to ask you some questions," said Nawi.

"I will be pleased to answer them. Please give them my respects before we begin," Marco asked.

Nawi did as Marco asked, and the men nodded.

Nawi interpreted the following conversation:

> "Nawi said you want to live here. Is that true?" said the leader of the men.
>
> "That is true," answered Marco.
>
> "What can you bring to our village except another mouth to feed?" asked another man.
>
> "I have many supplies hidden in the jungle. Food, axes, machetes, fishing equipment, guns, and boats," Marco replied.
>
> There was a discussion among the men before any more questions were addressed to Marco.
>
> "Show us what you have," said another elder.
>
> Marco was not so eager to show them everything he had hidden. He had been careful to hide each boat separately and one mile apart before he had walked

toward the village. If they discovered everything he had brought to the camp, he had been afraid they might kill him and be done with him.

He decided to show them the boat with the food supplies and metal implements to see their reaction.

"These are the supplies I thought you might need," Marco said as he pulled back the tarp.

They looked at one another in total shock. They had never seen so many things before, and they did not recognize what most cans and packages contained.

"In these cans, there is good food. In these packages, there is more food. Look at these tools," Marco explained as he showed them the axes, pots, and pans.

Then, he took his knife and opened a can of beans, and asked everyone to take a bite. They did as he asked and smiled as he pointed to fifty more cans. Then he opened a package of dried beef and did the same routine. They tasted the meat; and once again, they smiled with glee when looking at another plentiful supply.

He offered to move the boat closer to the village so the women could see the supplies. He asked the men to get in the boat. They got in with some fear because they had never seen a boat with an engine before.

All of the village people were on the shore when they arrived. The men quickly tossed the canned goods and packaged meals to the ground. They left many things on the boat; but for lunch, they had beans and dried beef.

"You have brought happiness to our community, but what would you do for us after the supplies are gone?" asked one man.

"I know how to catch fish and to kill animals for food," Marco answered.

"How would you kill animals?" asked another man.

"I could learn to use a blowgun, or I could use my guns," said Marco.

"We are not familiar with guns," said the leader.

"Let me show you," Marco said as he took a rifle from among the supplies.

"Put a can over there by the green tree," said Marco.

Once a man placed the can by the tree and returned to his side, Marco shot the rifle and hit the can. The group was silent. They were stunned by what they had just observed.

"Do that again," ordered the leader.

Marco did it again; and for good measure, as the can was rolling from the first shot, he hit it twice more.

"What do you call that thing you have in your hand?" asked Nawi.

"This is called a rifle, and it can also shoot for long distances," explained Marco.

"Can it penetrate a man?" asked Nawi.

"Yes, it can penetrate and kill a man," said Marco.

"We have an enemy tribe who have taken our young people. They came last week and took both young men and women. We are too small and weak to fight them," said Nawi.

"I can recover your people if you will accept me," Marco boasted, hoping he was not crazy to say such a thing.

The next night, they made a raid on the enemy village, which was only three miles away. It was a simple raid, and nothing much happened. Marco went into the tiny village, shooting his rifle in the air, and the villagers fled when they saw the white man with the gun. There was no killing and no drama. The prisoners were taken from the small house where they were housed, and they all returned home.

Later that day, there was a celebration with the women putting colorful paint over their bodies and dancing in circles to rhythmic drumbeats.

The next day, the council said Marco could stay if he liked, and they gave him one of the Portuguese names for thunder: Estrondo.

As he had hoped, the girl was in the group of rescued young people. She was as beautiful as he remembered. She was eighteen years old, and he chose her to be his mate. Her name was Nawie, which meant the daughter of Nawi.

Estrondo and Nawie lived together for twenty years and had two boys and a girl. Estrondo was an excellent supplier of food for the village, and he became a respected member of the tribe. He never became the leader, but the council often sought his advice.

He traveled back to Porto Velho one time after ten years in the village to get more food supplies. He was disgusted at the scene of modern Brazil and vowed never to go again, and he never did.

He was killed when he fell all alone into a tiger trap that the enemy village had set years ago. The wooden spikes pierced his body in four painful and deadly places. As he lay dying in a remote jungle in the Amazon, Marco saw in the clouds the image of a brown-skinned girl leaning against a green tree. He died, pleased with his life.

Nawie is still living, and her children are proud when they hear the wondrous stories about their father.

# WE CAN DO IT!

*Fall seven times and get up eight.*

—Japanese proverb

# PROLOGUE

# December 2019

I T WAS RAINING cats and dogs. The skies were black and heavy with wind and water; and after two days of torrential rain, there did not appear to be any break in the weather.

The twelve inches of rain that had already accumulated in the vegetable fields of the Florida Redlands was unusual for late December, and the massive amount of water was killing the crops in the fields. Destruction by the floodwater was occurring over a wide area and killing many kinds of vegetables, including beans, sweet corn, squash, tomatoes, eggplants, melons, okra, and others. If it kept raining, there was no telling how much damage this farming community would suffer.

The Redlands, just southwest of Miami, is the breadbasket of Florida and many other Southern states. December is a critical time for the farmers ready to harvest their crops for the holiday season and on into the winter.

Every member of this rural community knows that farming is a tough life. So much is uncontrollable, blistering sun, unpredictable rain, grasshoppers or other flying insects, blight or other diseases, flocks of crows, and other destructive birds, and of course the banks (oh yes, the banks). But this rain was unexpected and unrelenting, and it felt like an omen to many.

On the morning of the third day, Mario Moretti and his brother Carlo were in the kitchen drinking coffee and looking at the sky while waiting for the rain to stop so they could go to their jobs.

Anna, Mario's wife, was getting dressed for her work as a loan officer at the Wells Fargo bank in Homestead. Eight years old, John was ready to go to the bus stop.

"If it rains another four inches today, there will be no crops to harvest. That will be a disaster for many people in this community," said Mario.

"I agree. This flooding will undoubtedly impact the farmers I buy from, and I don't know if many of them can survive such a total loss. It will also hurt my performance as a buyer. I have been paid bonuses for increasing the amount of tomatoes and other produce my company can sell to the restaurants and cruise lines," said Carlo.

"I don't know if my boss at the tractor dealership can survive either. He gave loans for the equipment to so many of the farmers. If they can't pay, I don't know what he will do. He has only a small credit line remaining to pay the manufacturers," said Mario.

"Mario, it is scary as hell how many people will be affected by this flood. Many may lose their livelihoods," said Carlo.

It continued to rain steadily for the next twenty-four hours; and when the downpour finally stopped, it had destroyed 80 percent of the crops in the Redlands.

# CHAPTER 1

# A Catskills Childhood

MARIO AND CARLO Moretti were raised in a small Italian family fifteen miles west of Kingston, New York.

Kingston is located on the Hudson River, about a hundred miles north of New York. It has had a colorful history since 1614 when Dutch traders set up a trading post on the river. It played an essential role in the Revolutionary War and was New York's first capital city in 1777. During the war, in a major offensive, the British burned Kingston to the ground. Despite its early importance, Kingston did not develop into a significant cosmopolitan area, and today the population is slightly less than twenty-five thousand.

The Morettis lived on a ten-acre farm in a wooden home built in the early 1900s. It had two bedrooms, a kitchen, a living room, one bathroom, and a small front porch. Mario and Carlo shared a bedroom with two bunk beds.

In the summer months, with no air-conditioning, Rosa was often on their small front porch. She loved to look at and listen to the little creek that meandered in front of their property. The front porch was her favorite hangout, in her rocking chair, shelling peas or preparing other vegetables for dinner when she returned home from work. She was a payroll clerk for a Kingston construction company, and her $18,000 annual salary was critical to keep the family finances afloat.

Years ago, Alberto had attended a vocational training program and worked for three years as an apprentice to receive his plumbing certification. He had an excellent understanding of household plumbing pipe layouts and the related aspects of sewage removal, including septic tanks. He never wanted to work for anyone or any company; and he was happy with his loyal customer base and his income, which averaged $30,000 annually.

Alberto loved to spend time in the two-acre garden when coming home from his job as a freelance plumber. He planted tomatoes, bok choy, radishes, melons, beans, corn, and some assorted mushrooms. The garden was his pride and joy; and from May to November, he was obsessed with making sure his vegetables grew successfully. It certainly helped supplement the family food supply.

Alberto and Rosa bought the house and the property in 1975 for $75,000. They often joked about the $75K in '75, and Alberto always thought he had made a great deal. The property had been overgrown with trees and brush, but he knew how to clear the land and make it beautiful. Their combined income of almost $50,000 was plenty of money to live in their house and maintain two vehicles in good condition.

Their boys were born in 1980 and 1982. The second bedroom accommodated the kids nicely, and they had plenty of room to run and play outside. Alberto set up a basketball hoop and made a regulation half-court of poured concrete. Alberto was a remarkable handyman who could fix anything, and he taught the boys to be the same.

The boys grew up athletic, and they started shooting baskets at four years old. By the time they were in middle school, they were among the best players in Kingston. Both played varsity and were popular kids throughout their school experience. Each boy went to J. Rosado Bailey Middle School and Kingston High School. They both like sports and girls more than academics.

When Mario finished high school, he went to Ulster County Community College in Stone Ridge. He lived at home and helped his father in the plumbing business. He took some farm management courses and completed one year at the college before taking a job with the largest farm in the area.

The farm was over two thousand acres and was the region's largest producer of corn used for producing ethanol. Mario got a job as a tractor driver; and he quickly learned the numerous responsibilities of plowing, planting, weeding, fertilizing, spraying, and harvesting. Any tractor driver will tell you it is also necessary to learn how to fix minor equipment problems if you want to keep your job. Going back to the maintenance shed time after time is a sure way to get fired. Mario became a skilled mechanic on most of the farm equipment.

Alberto had a shed behind the house filled with tools of all kinds, and he taught the boys a lot about the implements used on a farm. Besides learning about gardening, they learned how to turn a forest into productive land. The property may have been overgrown in 1975; but by 2000, Alberto and the boys had completely cleared the other six acres with hand tools, a small tractor, and hard labor. Their pastures were green and lush.

Alberto waited until Mario was twelve, and Carlo was ten to use the weekends for land clearing. The boys were tough, respectful, and hardworking. Neither ever complained about the work; if their father could do it, they could do it. One night when they were teenagers, the two of them made a pledge. They promised each other that no matter what life tossed their way, their attitude would be to stick together and believe, "We can do it!"

After the land was cleared, Alberto bought three cows, including a milk cow. They not only raised some beef, but they had a steady stream of fresh milk. Rosa loved milking the cow and making all kinds of fresh baked goods and butter.

Carlo pretty much followed in Mario's footsteps. He was a star basketball player who loved to party. Carlo and Mario shared an old Plymouth station wagon, and they used it to drive anywhere there was a party going on. Carlo also graduated from Kingston High, but he went to a vocational training school to study vegetable farming and crop management. He loved the land and wanted to be a farmer someday. Carlo went to work for the Kingston Farmers Market and helped receive and sort the produce from the farmers and present it to the shoppers. He enjoyed his work and was considered a fine person and a good worker.

Mario and Carlo purchased a used Winnebago towable RV together, and they parked it under the shade trees next to the creek on the west side of the ten acres. It had room for both of them and the privacy they needed for their girlfriends to visit. Carlo still used his room in the house once in a while.

In 2010, they were a happy family living simply but comfortably when tragedy struck. Alberto and Rosa were killed by a drunk driver while they were returning from a grocery shopping trip to Kingston. The drunk driver, in a lumber truck, hit their small car head-on; and Alberto and Rosa both died instantly.

After the funeral, the boys did not want to live on their homestead anymore. They talked about different places to live, and one day Mario saw an article describing year-round farming opportunities in the Florida Redlands. They had always hated the harsh winters and the absence of much farm work during the cold weather. The idea of living in a warm climate that could be farmed all year excited them, plus they would have steady jobs all twelve months.

They looked on the Internet for real estate and found a listing for five acres with no house in the middle of the Redlands. The photos showed that the entire property was overgrown with weeds and underbrush, and it contained straggly trees from an unattended small orchard. They had cleared land before, and they could do it again if it saved money to buy a poorly maintained property. They had the Winnebago and a pickup truck they could use to pull it to Florida. They could live in the RV until they decided what to do for a permanent place.

They asked the real estate agent about the need for farmworkers in the Redlands, and he said skilled men were in high demand. They sold the home where they were raised for $250,000 and paid the same amount for the five acres in the Redlands.

They were starting a new life with no debt and no obligations. Each had around $25,000 in savings, and they were optimistic they would find work quickly.

"We can do it!" They both shouted together and smiled as they headed for Florida.

# CHAPTER 2

# Trip to Florida

"CARLO, WE HAVE almost fifteen hundred miles to travel. Pulling this thirty-five-foot Winnebago is going to take us four or five days to reach the Redlands. I think we should pick up I-87 in Kingston and stay on the major highways all the way," said Mario as they pulled away from their childhood home.

"I agree. We can pull off at the rest stations on the interstates and sleep in the RV. We can cook our meals some of the time, but we can eat at the restaurants or fast food joints when we want," said Carlo.

"We don't have any specific time we need to arrive, but I am anxious to find a job as soon as we get there," said Mario.

"Me too, but I don't want to speed. Let's try to stay five miles per hour under the speed limit. I can't afford another ticket." Carlo laughed.

"Yeah, that last bender you tied-on cost you a bundle. How long did the law keep you in jail?" asked Mario.

"I stayed in for two days, but the worst thing was the DUI charge. That cost me $1,100 in fines and $3,000 for a damn lawyer. Plus, they suspended my license for six months," sighed Carlo.

"I will drive most of the way, and you only need to drive when I am too tired," said Mario as he stopped to fill up the gas tank near the entry to I-87 in Kingston.

"Let's try to make it to the outskirts of Philadelphia tonight. It is a couple of hundred miles, and let's get set up early and make sure everything is working A-okay," said Mario.

"That sounds good to me," said Carlo.

The brothers were close in many ways. They loved each other, had each other's back, and wanted to live near each other. However, Mario was far more responsible and steady. Carlo loved to party too much and often mixed alcohol with pot and even more potent stuff. They had argued often over Carlo's trouble and disregard for the rules and regulations of life.

Mario was an alert and competent driver. They made their way down I-87 to I-287, then to the Garden State Parkway, and finally to I-95, which they would take to Miami. As planned, they found a rest stop near Philadelphia and stopped for the night.

They had sold their trucks and kept their father's 2008 F250 Fx4 Super Duty Ford truck. Alberto kept the truck in perfect condition, and it was powerful enough to pull the RV without straining. But the RV needed new tires. They had not changed the tires since they bought it, and it had been sitting in the yard for five years. The brothers checked the tires on both the pickup and the RV.

"I don't know if those RV tires are going to make it. I hate to stop and waste time having them changed, but if they blow on the interstate, it will be hard work for us to change a tire," pondered Mario.

"I am not afraid of hard work. Let's try to make it. I hate to spend the money on the tires because when we get to the Redlands, we are just going to park the RV. Who knows how long we will leave it on the new property, and the tires won't matter," said Carlo.

They examined the one spare tire for the RV and inspected the jack to make sure it was working okay. After some discussion, they decided to buy another spare in case they blew two tires simultaneously. When they filled up at the next Shell station, they bought a used spare and tossed it into the back of the pickup. With two spares and a working jack, they felt they could handle any blowout situation.

"Our goal for tonight is Richmond, Virginia. We should get there midafternoon. I would like to find a food market along the way and buy some ground meat, potatoes, and veggies. I feel like grilling out for dinner," said Mario as they began their journey for the second day.

"I am for that, but don't forget a case of beer." Mario laughed.

They found a rest area south of Richmond, with a restroom, vending machines, and long parking spaces, which was perfect for their rig. There were picnic tables and a couple of outdoor grills. They had picked up the needed supplies, including the beer.

"Let's use that grill next to the picnic table by the large tree," suggested Carlo.

"Looks like a good spot to me," said Mario.

They moved everything they needed to the picnic table, and Mario put the charcoal in the old outside grill. He cleaned the cooking surface by heating the coals and then using olive oil, a knife for scraping, and napkins to remove the rust and old meat particles. Mario was always meticulous about making his eating area a clean place. No matter how rough the camping or hunting trips, he kept his eating utensils, plates, and grill sanitized. Carlo, on the other hand, could care less about things being perfectly clean.

They were enjoying a cold beer and laughing with pleasure. They had the coals perfect, the meat sizzling, the potatoes heating up in their aluminum wraps, and the veggies about to be placed on the grill when a loud voice caused them both to jump.

"You cannot drink a beer in this public rest area!" said a man in a wife-beater shirt, with a beard and Southern accent.

"We didn't know that, but if you want to join us for a beer, you can be our guest." Carlo smiled.

"You must be a wiseass, huh?" asked Wifebeater.

"Hey, man, we are just cooking dinner and not looking for trouble. We will put the beer away. Sorry we troubled you," said Mario.

"It is too late. I have already seen you, and now I will report you to the police or just maybe kick your ass!" he yelled.

"What the hell is wrong with you?" asked Carlo.

"I saw your New York license plates. You damn Yankees think you can come through here and do anything you want. You must think you are Ulysses S. Grant," Wifebeater snarled.

"What is your problem? We are just cooking dinner and not making any attempt to create trouble. Please, if we have offended you, I am sorry. Would you like a hamburger?" offered Mario.

"I wouldn't eat with a damn Yankee no matter what," said Wifebeater.

"Okay then. You have been obnoxious, but we offered you a beer and a burger. You refused both, but now I gotta give you a Yankee knuckle sandwich," said Carlo as he hit the man in his left eye with a powerful blow.

The man fell to his knees. He got up slowly and pulled a switchblade knife from his back pocket. Without any comment, Mario hit him across the face with the long fork he was using to turn the vegetables. The man tried to rise again, and Carlo kicked him in the groin with his work boot. The man tried once more to attack Carlo, but Mario hit him in the head. This time, the man did not rise.

"Dammit! Let's pack up and leave," said Mario.

"Not before I try to find out who this idiot is and where he is from. He sounded like some white supremacist or something," said Carlo.

Carlo took the man's wallet from his back pocket. He was Buford Stratton from Murphy, North Carolina. One of his ID cards was for membership in the Aryan Brotherhood, and another was for his membership in the Klan.

"Good lord! How did we happen along at the same moment as this fool?" said Mario.

"I don't know, but I am going to keep my pistol in my pocket until we get to Miami," said Carlo.

They never finished their grilling and left as soon as they could toss things into the RV. They felt no remorse for leaving Buford lying on the ground because they knew he was alive, and they believed that he had been a danger to them. They did not stop for the night, and they were on full alert for trouble.

# CHAPTER 3

# Continuing their Trip

MARIO PLANNED HIS next overnight stop to be at a rest area near the exit on I-95 to Charleston, South Carolina. It was too far out of the way to visit Charleston, but the exit made a reasonable target destination. They kept the rig at fifty miles per hour to save the tires too much stress and to avoid any speeding tickets. I-95 was not as busy as it can be, and they made good progress without any incidents.

"I wonder if that guy will try to follow us. He knows we are heading South, and he can recognize our rig easily. He seemed crazy enough that he might try to track us down," said Mario.

"I have my pistol in the center console, but I will also get one of our shotguns. I still have some buckshot in my hunting jacket from our last deer hunting trip. I'll put it up front with us," said Carlo as he reached behind the seat of the pickup for his hunting jacket and shotgun.

"Do you think he will report the fight to the police?" asked Carlo.

"He might, but I think he is one of those country folks who probably have a police record and does not want any involvement with the law. I noticed he had tattoos all over his body, and maybe he got some of them in prison. In any event, he did not look like a law-abiding citizen." Mario laughed.

They were near the Lumberton, North Carolina, exit when a tire on the right rear of the RV blew out. Not only did they feel it, but they also heard the pop from inside the cab of the truck. The camper had two wheels on each side, but only one had blown. It was around 2:00 a.m., and the moon was the only light in the sky.

The RV was heavy and fully loaded, and it might weigh close to nine thousand pounds. Mario slowly pulled the rig over to the right side of the expressway. He pulled it far enough away from the travel lane to avoid getting hit by passing cars. He put on his hazard lights, and they gave plenty of warning to passing vehicles that a disabled vehicle was on the roadside.

Unfortunately, the emergency lane was not wide enough to keep the flat tire on the pavement. The expressway didn't have lights, so they used a lantern from the RV to cast light on the blown tire.

It was challenging to stabilize the jack on the rocky, grassy area. After clearing some rocks away, leveling the ground with a shovel, and placing a board on the ground, they made a flat area for the jack. The hydraulic jack was designed to help lift the trailer, and it gave some support to the manual effort. They had just removed the blown tire when bullets hit the ground around them.

Mario flattened himself against the RV, and Carlo ran to the truck for the shotgun. An old flatbed truck sped by, and someone tossed a rock with a piece of paper out of the passenger window.

"Good lord! Do you think he was trying to kill us or just scare us?" asked Carlo excitedly.

"God only knows what they were doing. I guess it was the man from last night, but what a crazy situation. I don't know what to do. Should we report this shooting or leave it alone?" asked Mario.

"Let's see what message he sent on the rock," said Carlo.

Carlo picked up the rock wrapped with torn paper tied with strands of string. It was brown wrapping paper, with a note written in bold letters with a black Scripto pen.

The message read, "Them bullets was just to get your attention. You boys have messed with the wrong clan. I wanted to teach you a lesson last night, but you beat me to the punch. This ain't over, and you won't know what I am going to do next until it's done."

"Oh shit! What has happened here? Can this man be totally nuts?" exclaimed Carlo.

"Well, it is clear that he knows who we are. Why would he get so mad at seeing NY license plates? Maybe he has us confused with someone else? It seems he knew he could catch up with us because he had the note ready," said Mario.

"Well, we did kick his ass last night. We need to stay alert, and we will continue to drive without stopping to spend the night at a rest area," said Carlo.

Mario changed the tire while Carlo stood guard with the shotgun handy. They decided not to repair the damaged tire until they were far down the road. When they finally stopped for gas, Mario discovered the blown tire could not be repaired. They bought another tire and once again had two spares in case of a double blowout.

They had just experienced two strange incidents that were hard to fathom. Mario and Carlo both wondered, what did it mean for their future?

Mario thought about incidents that had recently happened in Kingston, and a blurry thought crept into his head. Maybe something had triggered this craziness, but he would need to do some investigating to be sure.

# CHAPTER 4

# Three Months Before
# the Trip to Florida

O N THE FARM near Kingston, Mario had been preparing
a new field for the last two days. It was not hard or hot
because the tractor had an enclosed cabin with air-conditioning. A
large corporation owned the farm where he worked, and they wanted
the most productive crops possible. They used the latest equipment,
irrigation systems, fertilizers, and insecticides to produce exceptional
yields of everything they planted. He was proud to be an employee of
this company, and he received many benefits that only a large farming
company would provide.

Several hundred employees worked various jobs, and there was an
unusual amount of camaraderie among the men and women on the
farm. The workers frequented a few local bars after work, and lots of
fun and laughter were usually in play. There were rarely any fights or
arguments; and if one occurred, it was over quickly, and the merriment
resumed.

Carlo would often join Mario and his friends at the bar, and
frequently a group of them would go to one of the local restaurants and
continue their drinking and fun. Carlo spent so much time with the
farm crowd that any casual observer would think he worked with them.

Mario was a calm man, with short black hair, muscular arms, an
average-looking shaven face, and a height of six feet. He was not fat and
not thin, but any observer would notice his tanned skin from working in
the fields and sense his powerful strength. Mario had a habit of waiting
a couple of seconds to respond when asked a question. Some thought

he might not be too smart, but those who knew him were aware of a thoughtful man who often gave unusually intelligent answers.

Carlo was an active and hyper man who could hardly sit still, and he loved to talk fast and tell loud stories. He was almost six feet, and he was stocky with muscles that bulged beneath whatever shirt he wore. He wore his hair long and tied it back in a ponytail, but he had no tattoos; and despite first impressions, he did not belong to any gang or ride a motorcycle.

On those few occasions, when fights broke out, Carlo was usually one of the fighters who either started or ended the fight. Mario had warned Carlo about the fighting and how he was making himself unwelcomed to drink and eat with the farmworkers. Carlo did not think Mario saw things in the light of the real world. Carlo believed that tough, hardworking farmhands admired his fighting and aggression and that they liked men who could win a fistfight.

A few months prior, the tomatoes were ready for harvesting, and the crop was incredibly large. The farm had planted a new variety and used a unique combination of fertilizers and irrigation rotations. The result was the most abundant crop they had ever produced.

They needed some extra workers, and they could not find as many migrant workers from Mexico as in the past. The Mexicans were harder to find each year because of the immigration policies in Washington.

As a result, the agent they used to supply temporary farm labor recruited a group of workers from Cherokee County, North Carolina. The men had lost their jobs when an iron mine closed, and they needed work badly. The agent said they did not know how to pick tomatoes, but they had worked hard in the pit, and they would learn fast. The farm manager agreed to try them, and the agent brought twenty-five men to the farm, on a bus, at no cost to the workers.

The farm owners had used transient workers during the summer months for years. To house these large numbers of temporary workers, the owners had built over fifty small cabins. The little cabins were comfortable, and each accommodated three men. The pay was not great, but several communal meals were provided each day, and there were no living expenses. Most of the men were happy to have work, and they sent a large part of their money home to their families.

A few of the young men were not married; and when they had time-off, they spent their money at the bars and strip joints. A couple of these young men looked for trouble, and more often than not, they found it.

One day, Mario and a group of his friends went to a local hangout to have a few beers. There were four men with Mario when Carlo arrived, and he joined them. Several of the men had previously expressed concerns to Mario about his brother's behavior, but Mario promised he would cause no more trouble. Everyone was having fun when six of the North Carolina men arrived at the bar.

Mario and his friends recognized the men as the temporary tomato pickers and nodded hello as they passed their table. The North Carolina men found a pool table in the back, and two began a game while the other four took a nearby table. Suddenly one of the men playing pool started swinging his pool stick at his opponent. At first, Mario and his friends thought the man wielding the pool cue was playing, but then he hit the pool table and broke the stick into two pieces.

It no longer looked like a game but a serious fight. The other man broke his pool cue over his knee, and they moved around the table like two swordfighters. Carlo jumped from his chair and ran over to the first man wielding the broken pool stick and snatched it from his hands. Carlo had approached the man from behind, and so he took the stick away easily.

"What are you doing? This is none of your business. Give me back that damn pool cue!" yelled the man.

"Stop fighting! This is a peaceful bar, and we don't want any violence or trouble. You and your friend just pay for your beers and the broken sticks and then get the hell out of here," advised Carlo.

"You can't tell me what to do. We have as much right to be here as you Northern boys. You think just because we are Southerners, you can push us around," said the man.

"This is about jerks and punks, not North or South. Get out of here before I teach you a real lesson in proper conduct." Carlo laughed.

"I won't forget you. You had no right to interfere in our little dispute. Give me your name so I can put you down on my shit list," challenged the man.

"I want you to write it down. It is Carlo Moretti, and be sure to write it down in bold letters. I would love to meet you anytime, anywhere, you simpleton," said Carlo.

# CHAPTER 5

# Discovering the Reason for the Trouble

MARIO RECALLED THE little incident with the pool cue as he drove toward Jacksonville, Florida. As he remembered, there was no fight, just a quick move by Carlo to disarm one of the fighters, and then he asked them to leave. The situation was over in less than ten minutes, and nobody was hurt. They paid for the broken sticks and left the bar.

"Carlo, I have been trying to think of what could be the cause of our trouble on this trip. I may have an answer," said Mario.

"What are you thinking?" asked Carlo.

"Do you remember when you took away a pool stick from a guy in the bar? Those guys were from North Carolina. The guy in the wifebeater shirt was from North Carolina. I think it might be the same guy," said Mario.

"That seems like a reach. Why would he care, and how would he know who we are?" asked Carlo.

"I remember, when you took the pool cue, he wanted to know your name for his shit list. You gave him your name and told him to write in down in bold letters. Well, the note is written in bold letters," said Mario.

"How would he know we are on the road? Why would he be so intent on revenge for something so simple?" mused Carlo.

"I think I will call the farm and ask Milly in the payroll department if any of the workers who came up from North Carolina was named Buford Stratton," said Mario.

Mario made the call; and sure enough, one of the summer workers from North Carolina was named Buford Stratton. Buford had left the farm a few weeks ago with a friend named Dan Noland in an old flatbed truck they bought from the farm for a few hundred dollars. Milly mentioned that a few of the best workers from North Carolina had remained to work for the farm during the winter months. Just before Mario hung up, Milly mentioned that the farm manager had fired Stratton and Noland for shoddy work and constant complaining. The manager did not want them to return next summer. The two men had left angry.

"Well, that is the definitive answer on who is causing our trouble," said Mario after the phone call.

"Do you think it was just a coincidence he saw us at the rest stop?" asked Carlo.

"No, I think he was waiting for us. My friends at the farm threw a small going-away party for me the day before I resigned. So the word went around the farm that I was leaving for a new life in Florida and that you were coming with me," offered Mario.

"I told them about our plans and when we were leaving. I even told them how we were planning to travel and the routes we would be taking. I was excited about our trip and shared it with my buddies over lunch and drinks at the bar," said Mario.

"I guess we can conclude that Buford is mad about me taking away the pool stick and that he knows our travel plans. I think we should take a different route," suggested Carlo.

"I agree. Let's pull over and check our travel options," said Mario.

After checking numerous alternatives, they decided to leave I-95 and pick up Route 84 just south of Savannah, and stay on 84 until they hit Route 27. They could take Route 27 to Miami. The backroads would slow them down, but it would be impossible for Buford to know their new route. Also, it would be more interesting to see the small towns along the way.

"That Buford guy must be insane. I just don't see why he is so upset," said Mario.

After leaving I-95, they decided to put Buford out of their minds and start making plans for their arrival in the Redlands.

"Mario, what kind of work are you going to look for?" Carlo asked.

"I think I am going to try something new. I have worked on the farm for years, and I learned a lot about farm equipment. I know how to use tractors, plows, disc harrows, mowers, hay balers, harvesters of all kinds, and most fertilizer distributors. I think I will try to get a job with a farm equipment dealership. Maybe even try my hand at sales," answered Mario.

"I think I might try to get work on a farm. Not driving a tractor but working with the field manager or owner responsible for the planting and harvesting of vegetables. At the Kingston Farmers Market, I saw every kind of vegetable imaginable, and I talked with so many farmers about their techniques and the things they did right or wrong. I also saw how to present the products most appealingly. I think I could help a farm with their production and presentation techniques," said Carlo.

The brothers talked about their hopes for work, and when they had Internet connections tried to research some of the farms and equipment dealerships that might be prospective employers. They were excited about the life that lay ahead and quickly forgot about the nut from North Carolina.

# CHAPTER 6

# Arriving at the New Property

THEY TRAVELED THROUGH the Florida backroads until they made it to Miami. Once in Miami, they took I-95 south to US1 then to the small community of Princeton before turning west through the heart of the Redlands. They were amazed at the endless number of nurseries, fruit, and vegetable farms. This was an agricultural marvel, not twenty miles from one of the largest metropolitan areas in the nation.

"Wow, look at these farms. I don't think we could have chosen a better area for our skills and our future," said Mario.

Their five acres was on the extreme western edge of the Redlands. One thousand yards farther to the west was the Everglades boundary, but it was almost in the middle of the Redlands when measuring from north to south. It might not be a prime piece of property, but it was a convenient location for most of the job opportunities they planned to explore. The property was a rectangle with the long sides running east to west; and the street frontage was around one hundred yards wide, running north and south.

It was laid out perfectly for a house to be set back from the street and still have lots of room for a garden and outbuildings. They put the RV where a home might be built in the future. They would need to dig a well and get a power connection to the Florida Power & Light (FPL) lines that ran along the front of the property.

Before they could move the RV into a permanent position, they needed to clear the land of trees, brush, and coral rock. The soil in the Redlands sits on a layer of coral rock (oolitic limestone). This rock needs to be "scarified" or basically pulverized to create flat land that could be farmed. They did not need to prepare their plot for farming at this time, but it did need a lot of clearing.

They had many of the tools for clearing, which they had used as kids to help clear the land in Kingston. They worked for three full weeks with chainsaws and machetes to clear underbrush and cut down small trees. They used the pickup with a heavy chain to pull up the stumps from the small trees they cut down. It was hard labor, but they enjoyed the work.

They cleared the one hundred yards of frontage left to right then back to a depth of one hundred yards. When they finished, there was plenty of room to create a small homestead. The coral rock was still a pain, but they made a two-track road from the paved frontage street to the place for the RV.

They cleared and flattened the RV spot of most rocks so that when it was put in place, there was no wobble, and the RV floor looked level. To be sure it was level, Mario put marbles on the floor in several locations to see if they would roll in any direction, but they stayed put. They were now ready to set up permanently for a while.

Living together in the RV was tight, but they each had a bedroom. There was only one toilet and shower, but they were used to sharing, and they had a routine that worked. The kitchen had everything they needed, and there was a living room with a TV and a small dining table. This setup would do just fine until they could get jobs and make enough money to build a house.

Mario took responsibility for getting the power hooked up, and Carlo found a well-digger to dig their well. The well-digger had a friend who also put in a septic tank for them. They were good to go!!

They had accomplished a great deal in a short time because they had worked day and night. Other than eating at a local restaurant, they had hardly left their property and had done no exploring. Now was the time to look around the area and begin their search for work.

"We need to buy one of us another vehicle. I am happy to drive the F250, but I will do whatever you want," said Mario.

"Fine, let's find me a used Ford Explorer or something similar," said Carlo.

The next day they went shopping for used SUVs; and in Homestead, they found the perfect one. It was a 2001 Explorer with only twenty thousand miles and was on sale for $14,000. They split the cost because everything they owned was in both names.

"I think we have everything we need to find a job," said Mario.

"Me too. I feel terrific that we got ourselves set up in less than a month, and because we did most of the work, it did not cost much," agreed Carlo.

"We still have over $30,000 between us, and I guess we should move our money from the bank in Kingston to one down here. I will take care of that tomorrow," said Mario.

Neither brother had any credit card or other debt. They were getting started in the Redlands with their land free and clear, two vehicles paid for, the RV, well, and septic tank installed, and $30,000 in the bank.

They looked at each other, did a high-five, and shouted, "We can do it!" It was 2010, and they were two confident young men with a bright future ahead.

# CHAPTER 7

# Finding Work and Anna

MARIO WENT TO the local Wells Fargo bank branch to open a checking and savings account in both their names. He was asked to wait and told that a bank officer would be with him shortly. He took a seat; and as he looked around, he noticed one sharp-looking young woman.

She had short blonde hair and was wearing a black skirt and jacket with a white blouse and high-heeled shoes. She had a trim figure; and with the heels, she was probably five feet ten inches. She must have been around thirty years old, and she looked like she was an experienced member of the bank team. He was pleased when she was the one to greet him.

"Good morning. I am Anna Rosado, and I will be glad to help you open an account. Please come with me to my office," she said.

She led him to her office and closed the door.

"I want to open a joint checking and savings account for my brother and me. We have only been in town a few weeks, and we want to move our money from Kingston, NY," said Mario.

"We would love for you to open those accounts with us. You and your brother need to fill out these forms. When you have them completed, you will both need to visit me here at the bank, and we will open the accounts," she explained.

She handed him the forms and began to rise from her seat to escort him out of the bank.

"Before you leave, may I ask you a couple of questions?" Mario asked.

"Of course, go ahead." She smiled.

"My brother and I bought a five-acre property in the Redlands, and we parked our RV there temporarily until we have time to build a house," said Mario.

"Congratulations, this will be a big change from New York for you, guys." She laughed.

"I am sure it will, but we are very flexible men, and we wanted a warmer climate where the crops grow year-round," he said with a grin.

"Well, the farmers do grow something all year long down here," she agreed.

"I am looking for employment, and I wonder if you could give me some tips on where to start. I am skilled at everything to do with farm equipment from the most sophisticated tractors and implements to the simplest hand tools. I want to interview a few farm equipment dealerships," Mario said.

"I know of three dealers in the area. Two of them have accounts with us, and I know the owners fairly well. I could write their names on the back of my business cards, and maybe it would serve as an introduction." She smiled.

"That would be terrific, and I am sure it will make it easier for me to speak with the top guys. I will let you know how it works out when I meet with them," he said.

"While I have such a helpful person in front of me, I would like to ask you about a position for my brother. He wants to work on a midsized vegetable farm. He gained a lot of experience in all aspects of vegetable farming while working at the Kingston Farmers Market," continued Mario.

"Mario, in this area, there are countless midsized farms and a few big corporate ones as well. Also, there are hundreds of family farms. I can give you the names of two farms that I know are successful and are often looking for workers. They are both tomato farmers with lots of equipment, and each has over five hundred acres of cultivated land," Anna replied.

"Anna, you have been so helpful. I am glad I had the luck to meet you today. My brother and I will complete the forms and return in a couple of days to open the accounts," Mario said.

As he left the bank, he could not get Anna out of his mind. She was competent, helpful, friendly, and attractive. She did not have on a wedding ring, and she was the right age for him to date. He would need to find a way to meet her away from the bank.

He was already in Homestead, so Mario decided to visit the two equipment dealers she had written on the back of her cards. His first stop looked like a first-class operation handling John Deere, Kubota, Bush Hog, and several other top brands. The showroom and equipment yard were both large and well displayed. Mario walked into the showroom and saw what looked to be a salesman.

"Hi, my name is Mario Moretti, and I would like to speak with Mr. Bailey. Ms. Anna Rosado from the Wells Fargo bank gave me his name," said Mario, with his best smile.

"Sure, just a minute. I will give Mr. Bailey her card and your name. I am sure he will be with you shortly," said the man.

In a few minutes, a short bald man in his fifties walked into the showroom and greeted Mario. He looked like a man who was always happy, and he had several laugh lines around his bright blue eyes.

"Hello, I am Gene Bailey. How can I help you? If Anna says I should speak to you, then I should speak to you. She is a sharp young lady," Gene said, smiling.

Mario explained they had just arrived, gave Gene his background and experience, and asked for a job either as a service rep or a salesman. Gene asked him to come into his office and fill out an application. As Mario was filling out the form, Gene started talking.

"So you decided to pick the Redlands as a place to live out your life. That is interesting to me because I have lived here all my life, and I often thought of moving to someplace cooler like the Catskills." Gene laughed.

"Well, I guess the grass is always greener, but we did want a year-round warm place to work and raise our kids. We came here debt-free with a nice piece of property paid for free and clear. We are hardworking people who stay out of trouble and stay out of debt," said Mario.

"Are you married?" asked Gene.

"No, but if Anna would marry me, I just might jump at it," joked Mario.

"She sure is a looker and a fine banker. She makes every customer feel special, and she tries to help in any way possible to connect local business people," said Gene admiringly.

"If I had an open position, how much would you expect in salary?" asked Gene.

"I don't know this job market, and you are the first person I have interviewed. It would be wrong for me to ask for an amount. You seem like a successful dealer who has been in business for a long time. I am sure you are in a better position to make me an offer than I am to ask for one," said Mario.

"That is an honest answer. I think I may have a job for you. One of our service reps is leaving for Texas to be with his wife's family. I can offer you $800 per week starting in ten days," said Gene.

"Thanks, Gene! I like the way you conduct yourself, and I am not going to look any further. I accept your offer on one condition. If I can show you that I am not only a good service rep but that I can sell, I would like a chance at selling for you," said Mario.

"That is a deal. It is hard to find sales reps that can talk details with the farmers. If I see that you can do that, we will give the sales job a try," promised Gene.

"I will do a background check during the next ten days, and unless something turns up, we are good to go," said Gene as he offered his hand to Mario.

Mario left the showroom on top of the world. He had a job, and he met a girl in just two hours. What a way to start the day!

# CHAPTER 8

# Carlo Finds work

CARLO TOOK A shower after Mario left for the bank, and he put on a clean pair of khaki pants and a long-sleeve casual shirt. He appeared younger than his twenty-eight years, and he seemed like the strong working-class man that he was. He was handsome in a rugged-looking way, and the initial impression he created was positive.

Before Carlo left the RV, Mario had called with the farmers' names that Anna had provided. Carlo wrote down Anna's name to use as a reference and the names of the two farmers. Carlo used Google to get the addresses and Waze to find the closest farm.

When he pulled up to the farm address, there was no farmhouse, but he saw a bustling fenced-in area with tractors and equipment of all kinds. Four wooden sheds with tin roofs looked like they held supplies, and a small building had a sign that read Office. Beyond the fenced-in area, there were large fields with planted crops.

Carlo knocked on the door, and a voice yelled, "Come on in!" Carlo walked into a small but neat air-conditioned office with three desks and chairs. Behind the largest desk was a weather-beaten man in his sixties who looked like he had spent his lifetime in the Florida sun. Two middle-aged women were occupying the other desks and chairs.

"How can I help you?" asked the man.

"Are you Mr. Newsom? Anna Rosado from the Wells Fargo bank suggested I speak to you about employment," asked Carlo.

"Yes, I am Jake Newsom. What kind of work are you looking for?" Jake asked.

"I am skilled in vegetable farming. I trained in agriculture at a vocational school, and I spent eight years at the Kingston, NY, Farmers Market," said Carlo.

"What did you learn while you worked there?" Jake asked.

"I worked with hundreds of farmers to improve planning, planting, watering, weeding, fertilizing, and harvesting almost every vegetable that can grow in the USA." Carlo smiled.

"When would you plant tomatoes in the Redlands?" Jake asked.

"I would guess September to November, but remember I just got here three weeks ago, and you are the first farmer I have met. I am sure I have a lot to learn about this environment." Carlo laughed.

"Do you think you can sell tomatoes?" asked Jake right out of the blue.

"I have never thought of myself as a salesman. Someone would need to explain who we want to sell, what price we want, our packaging and product presentation, and our frequency and method of delivery. Would I contact the prospective customers on the phone or in person? I guess I would need a lot more information to answer your question," said Carlo.

"I have been selling my tomato crops almost entirely to the supermarket chains, and I want to expand that market by selling to restaurants. I have watched some other tomato farmers get better prices from the restaurants, and I want to give it a try. I believe you would need to meet the restaurant owners face-to-face," said Jake.

"How far would I need to travel?" asked Carlo.

"I would start with just two counties: Miami-Dade and Monroe. Those two counties encompass all of Miami and the Keys. You might need to stay overnight if you go all the way to Key West, but most of the time, you would be home each night," said Jake.

"Well, Jake, that is not the job I had in mind. I thought I could be helpful in the production side of the business, not the sales side. But it is intriguing to think about learning a new skill. How would I be paid?" asked Carlo.

"This would be an experiment for both of us. I am willing to pay the same as I would pay for an experienced farm helper, plus some extras. I can pay $550 per week, plus a 1.5 percent commission on what you sell. Also, I will cover your gas and oil expenses, and when you are on the road, I will pay a $15 per day food allowance," said Jake.

"What if I need to stay in a hotel overnight?" asked Carlo.

"Sure, I will cover that cost up to $120 per night," said Jake.

"It sounds like you have given this a lot of thought. Why haven't you done it already?" asked Carlo.

"I have not been able to find anyone that I thought would represent the image I want to project. I want the restaurant owners to see that my salesman is, first and foremost, a farmer who knows his stuff. I want them to immediately feel that they can trust our farm to deliver the quality we promise. You impress me as that man," said Jake.

"Well, thanks for the compliment and the job offer. Let me think about it for a couple of days. Anna gave me one more name that I should visit, and I want to speak with them before I make a final decision. Jake, I must say that I am intrigued by your offer, and I thank you. Good day to you, ladies," Carlo said as he left the office.

Carlo left the Newsom farm, surprised at the discussion and the offer. His mind was spinning: Could he possibly make a go of it as a salesman? What if he failed? If he failed, would he get a bad reputation before he even got started in the Redlands? But if he could sell, then maybe it would open new doors for him that paid a better wage. He would need to talk with Mario.

# CHAPTER 9

# Learning the Business

CARLO MET WITH the second farmer, but he had just hired several new farmhands and did not have a place for him. The owner liked Carlo and asked him to fill out an application so that if something opened up, he could call Carlo. He also encouraged Carlo to remember to call him in a month and see if he had an opening.

"Where do you sell your tomatoes?" Carlo asked before leaving.

"About half of my production goes to the supermarkets and cruise lines, and the other half to restaurants all over South Florida," he replied.

"As you know, I am just learning about how things are done down here. I worked for eight years at a farmers' market in Kingston, NY. Up there, the farmers brought their produce to the market, and auctioneers sold their vegetables to buyers from supermarkets, restaurants, schools, and other companies. Do you have such a facility nearby?" said Carlo.

"We have a farmers' market here, but it is my experience that I can get a better price by selling directly to the supermarkets, cruise ships, school cafeterias, and restaurants," said the farmer.

"Wow! That is cool. How do you find customers?" Carlo asked.

"We use a company that specializes in selling products to these institutions," said the farmer.

"There are also many large repacking operations that have excellent contacts with these markets. Like every item in the world, there are many supply-chain options to get your product to the end-user," said the farmer.

"Good grief, I guess I have a ton to learn. Thank you for answering my questions, and I hope to see you again soon." Carlo smiled as he shook the farmer's hand and went back to his Explorer.

He thought to himself that Jake might be misguided to believe that one man driving around South Florida asking for business could be successful. The buying companies probably wanted a resource that could provide all their vegetable needs, not just tomatoes. That must be why the repacking facilities are so necessary. He would need to study the landscape before deciding to sell for a living.

"We had a productive morning. I will start working as a service representative for Gene Bailey in ten days. We need to complete these bank forms and stop by the bank to give our signatures and open the accounts," Mario said as he summarized his morning.

"I am not optimistic about selling after I met with the second farmer. I was intrigued when I met with Jake, and he wanted me to sell directly to restaurants. But that must be a very competitive market, and I bet the big companies control most of the sales," said Carlo.

"Well, you have only met with two midsized farmers. I would keep looking and maybe go to the big corporate farms in the area. Those big farms have production and repacking facilities and vast contacts for sales to all markets. I think they also buy from the local farmers to supplement their capacity. You could learn so much from them. I saw the power of a big farming operation when I worked in NY," said Mario.

"I think you are correct. I can see why farmers like Jake are frustrated that they are not getting the best price, but really, they don't have the facilities to meet the needs of the big buyers," said Carlo.

They were eating their lunch when a stranger approached their table. He looked as though he had just come from a field with his muddy boots and a sweat-stained shirt.

"Are either of you guys looking for work? I saw your NY license tags and wondered if you are new arrivals," he said.

"What kind of work?" asked Carlo.

"It is hard work, but I am under the gun, and I will pay extra good money. I contracted to clear an old forty-acre field that has been left untended for twenty years. It is overgrown with everything from briars to sturdy pine trees," said the man.

"I had a team of ten Mexicans helping me, but they got scared with all this talk of deportation and just up and left me. I get a bonus if I finish in the next two weeks, and I need the bonus to break even," he explained.

"What kind of equipment do you have?" asked Mario.

"I have two Ford tractors with front blades and one with a bush hog mower on the rear to help cut down the tall grass and small bushes. Plus, all types of assorted hand tools like chainsaws and machetes," he said.

"We are currently looking for work, and we know how to clear land. What are you willing to pay? We can start as soon as we finish lunch and change our clothes," said Carlo without consulting Mario.

"I can pay you $15 an hour, and I will feed you lunch," he said.

"We will work for $20 an hour and lunch," said Carlo.

"My name is John Wilden, and you have a deal," he said.

"I can only work for ten days because I have already accepted a job that starts then," said Mario.

"Okay, let's see if we can get the job finished by then," said John with a pleased expression.

They agreed to meet in the overgrown field in one hour, and John left. They finished their lunch and went to the RV to change clothes.

"Carlo, you did not even check with me," complained Mario.

"You know we should not pass up an opportunity to make $800 a week for the next two weeks performing work we can do in our sleep. We had nothing in hand, and this is a blessing." Carlo laughed.

Mario knew he was right, and they high-fived again.

# CHAPTER 10

# Anna

ANNA'S PARENTS IMMIGRATED from Cuba in 1959, and they settled in the Little Havana neighborhood of Miami to maintain their Cuban culture. Many Cuban immigrants settled in this area; and it remains the cultural, social, and political heart of the Cuban community in Miami. Their apartment at SW Eighth Street and SW Seventeenth Avenue was in the center of Cuban life in Miami.

Her parents were in their early forties when they arrived in Miami, and her mother was forty-five when she unexpectedly had Anna two years later. Anna's mother maintained an illicit relationship with her lover from Cuba, who also came to Miami in 1959. Her mother would continue her adulterous relationship for years, and Anna was aware of her promiscuity and infidelity. Her mother always worried that Anna might do a DNA test and discover the name of her real father: because she was not even sure who he was.

Anna's father got a job with a landscaping company, and her mother worked as a hairstylist. They put Anna in daycare as soon as they could find a school that would take her. As it turned out, Anna stayed in the same Catholic girls' schools from daycare to the eighth grade. Her parents moved to a Coral Gables apartment as she was about to enter the ninth grade; and she started at Coral Gables High, where she stayed until graduation.

Anna learned to be completely independent because her parents expected her to take care of herself and them. She had to make dinner for the family after she got home from school, and it was her job to wash the dishes and put them away. Anna was also responsible for her own laundry and any necessary ironing. Three days a week, Anna had to sweep the floors and vacuum the carpets.

She was by herself most of the time she was not in school, and it made her self-sufficient, and she learned to be happy when alone. Anna sometimes brought girlfriends to her house after school, and they were shocked at how much work Anna was required to do.

Because of so many household chores, she did not have the time to do her homework and study properly, and she was a C+ student. She was a popular student because she was always ready to help anyone with anything. Despite her household chores, it seemed no one in the school could do as much as Anna with team assignments. She was also cute, and boys were interested in her, but her mother did not trust Anna to date until she was a senior.

Her father came home each night, dirty from his day working in the yards of homes and offices. He took a shower, ate dinner, and left to spend time at a local bar or go bowling with his buddies. Anna never knew where her mother went after her father left the house, but Anna was alone for most evenings. Anna knew her mother had a lover, but her father did not seem to care, so Anna didn't care either. Still, to Anna, it was disgusting behavior; but it was what it was.

She thought she loved her parents, but she did not think they knew how to love each other or her. She accepted their indifference and became a supremely confident person who felt she could manage her life without help from anyone.

Anna graduated from Coral Gables High School and then got a two-year associate's degree (AA) from Miami-Dade Community College (MDC). MDC is the largest university in the nation, with over 160,000 students. It is proud of its reputation as the educational starting point for many hardworking, ambitious people who attend part-time. Anna worked while going to MDC as a waitress at Fridays three nights each week.

She met Juan her first semester at MDC; and for a change, someone wanted to spend every minute with her. As expected, her mother would not permit Juan to be in the house when no parent was home. She had Juan over for dinner a few times, but he soon tired of the restrictions, and he left her. She often wondered if she had loved Juan, but she wasn't sure.

However, she was positive that she would move out of her parents' home as soon as she had a job. Anna was frustrated with her self-absorbed parents, and she did not respect them or their behavior. She vowed never to be like them.

When she graduated from MDC with her AA degree in business administration, her parents did not attend. Her mother was on a "girls' weekend," and her father was on a drunken binge. The very next day, Anna started looking for a job and saw an electronic posting from Wells Fargo for an entry-level position. She called and got an appointment for an interview.

She was so impressive in the interview that the manager hired her on the spot for a starting salary of $29,000 per year. She took an apartment the next day; and for the first time in her life, she was out from under a strict rule. She would determine her own responsibilities and not be under the thumb and direction of dysfunctional parents. It was remarkable, but her childhood did not damage her. On the contrary, it taught her to rise above the shortcomings of others. She was sure she would grow into a beautiful, caring adult; and she did.

She met Larry a few weeks after starting at the bank. He was a junior loan officer, and he was Jewish. She had never dated much, and she certainly had never been with a Jewish boy.

Larry took her to the movies, restaurants, beaches, and once to the Everglades for an airboat ride. Early on, she rejected Larry's romantic efforts; but he was patient, and eventually, they had sex. She met his parents one Friday night and had Shabbat service and dinner with them. Their relationship lasted three years, and she matured in her romantic skills, and her self-confidence grew in one more area of her personality.

After three years and three promotions, she was an assistant loan officer in Miami. Then, an opening for a bank officer in the Homestead branch was posted; and she took the job. She knew the transfer would end the relationship with Larry, but she was ready to move on with her life and try something new.

Once in Homestead, she focused on being an outstanding worker; and she spent long hours at the bank, learning everything she could. She was a great team player willing to do anything that needed doing.

She would file papers, act as a teller, clean the break area, meet angry customers, open accounts, and simply make herself a helper for any task. After five years in the Homestead branch, everyone in the bank loved her; and her future looked bright.

# CHAPTER 11

# Mario and Anna

FOR THE NEXT ten days, Mario and Carlo worked from early in the morning until it was too dark to see. They were happy with twelve- to thirteen-hour days at $20 an hour. They would have worked until midnight if there had been any light.

"You are two of the best workers I have ever seen. You know what you are doing, and you never complain," said John.

"What is there to complain about when each of us is earning more than $250 every day?" Carlo laughed.

"Well, we finished the job on time, and I will get the bonus I need. Let me buy dinner tonight," offered John.

Mario and Carlo went to the RV, showered, changed clothes, and met John at the Outback Steakhouse in Homestead.

They got a booth and ordered a blooming onion and three beers. When the waiter brought the beers, they made a toast to the pleasure of honest hard work.

"You guys can work for me whenever you are between jobs. I stay busy most of the time because there is still a tremendous amount of uncleared land in South Florida," said John.

"That is a nice offer, and you can believe we will remember. You are a quality man to be around," said Carlo.

They were talking and laughing about a couple of tough stumps that were a beast to remove. They needed to use a front-bladed tractor to push and another tractor with a steady chain pulling to get the stumps out of the ground. They were startled when two attractive women stopped by their booth.

"Hi, Mario! Remember me?" asked a pretty girl.

"Do I ever!" Mario said as he jumped up from his seat.

"Guys, this in Anna Rosado. Anna, this is my brother Carlo and our friend John," said Mario as he made the introductions.

"Gentlemen, this my girlfriend Tammy Boone," Anna said.

"Please sit down and join us for dinner. We are just getting ready to order," said a smiling Mario.

"We just finished, but we can join you for a drink," Anna replied.

They asked the waiter for a new table with room for five people. The waiter moved the rest of their blooming onion and the beers to the new table, and they all took a seat.

"Gene Bailey came by the bank and told me that he hired you on the spot," Anna said.

"Yes, I start tomorrow. We have been so busy working on a rush job with John that we didn't have time to get to the bank and open our account. But we completed the forms you gave me, and Carlo can drop them by tomorrow morning with some new money we will need to deposit," said Mario as he toasted John.

"I know Anna works at the bank, but what do you do, Tammy?" Carlo asked.

"I work for an insurance agency as a claims clerk. When someone has a loss, I am the person who collects all the excruciating details to get them paid." Tammy laughed.

"Carlo, what do you do?" Tammy asked.

"I am looking for work. So far, I have only had time to speak to a couple of farmers. I had one offer that I am considering but nothing definite," answered Carlo.

The guys ordered their dinners, and the ladies ordered two glasses of white wine. The conversation was lively, and the girls did not seem in any rush to leave. They spent a couple of hours together, and then all said good night. It had been a fun few hours for everyone.

The next morning, Carlo gave the forms to Anna, who opened the accounts and transferred the money from their New York bank and accepted a new deposit of a $5,000 check from John. Anna and Carlo chatted a little about the previous night and exchanged a few comments about the weather before she was called away to meet with a waiting customer.

Mario started his first day with a tough assignment. One of Gene's best customers had an accident. He was moving one of his John Deere tractors from a field near Fort Lauderdale to the Redlands. The tractor was on a trailer pulled by a pickup truck. They were on a backroad when a child ran across the road, and the driver swerved to avoid hitting her. The tractor was flipped off the trailer and fell into a watery ditch.

The customer called Gene and asked for help. Gene sent Mario and another equipment service rep to the accident site. When they arrived, they saw two police cars and a AAA truck. The tractor was lying on its side with the hood pointing toward the trees.

"Wow, that tractor really took a dive. The first thing we need to do is get the tractor upright. Then we can try to start it and move it back to the trailer. If we can't start it, then the AAA guy can tow it to our dealership!" exclaimed Mario.

They attached three chains to the tractor at various locations. Then, they connected the other end of each chain to one of the three trucks that were on site. The drivers coordinated their efforts, and the three trucks slowly pulled the tractor into an upright position.

Once they had the tractor upright in its normal driving position, they needed to start the engine. The water must have damaged the engine while in the ditch, and it would not start. Mario and his partner worked on the engine for several hours and finally got it started. They drove the damaged tractor back onto the trailer, and the driver took it to the dealership to repair the bent hood and fenders.

Mario thanked the AAA rep for his help, and he and his associate returned to the office. The customer told Gene that his men had done an excellent job. It was a good beginning for Mario, and he was pleased that day one was a winner.

For the remainder of the week, Mario was so busy that he forgot that he needed to stop by the bank and give his signature in person. The next Monday, he called Anna and asked if he could come by the bank during lunch to sign his name and take her for a quick lunch. She said yes, and they walked to a nearby Subway for a sandwich and a Coke.

"Could I take you to dinner and a movie on Saturday night?" Mario asked as they were walking back to the bank after lunch.

"That would be nice. Would you like to double-date with Carlo and Tammy?" she asked.

"I would prefer to be alone with you if that is okay." He smiled.

"That would work for me." She laughed.

"I promise I will ask Carlo to give Tammy a call," he said.

That Saturday night was the beginning of a relationship between Mario and Anna that resulted in marriage twelve months later.

# CHAPTER 12

# Carlo Gets a Job

ARLO WAS ALMOST obsessed with the complexities of the vegetable supply chain. Jake's job offer for him to sell tomatoes directly to the restaurants had caused Carlo to think about the produce industry differently. He constantly wondered how vegetables got to all the people who were preparing meals. Before three weeks ago, he never considered how many consumers might be involved in buying produce: restaurants, hotels, prisons, educational institutions, hospitals, nursing homes, cruise lines, supermarkets, private homes, and even military bases.

Carlo did not go to a four-year college, but he was brilliant. In the eleventh grade, he had taken an IQ test, and the results were a score of 135, plus he also tested high in analytical problem-solving. Now, he kept thinking about how competitive it must be for the farmer to sell his products directly to an end-user. There were just too many elements and too much competition to sell direct as Jake had wanted him to do.

Since he had finished the land clearing with John, he had spent three weeks searching the web for ideas and job opportunities. He started by reading articles on the food industry supply chains and the processes from planting to consumption.

Among numerous interesting concepts, he learned there were companies called food distributors. These companies were organized to do the many of the things he was puzzling over. They bought the produce from the farmers; delivered the products to their distribution facilities; and, when necessary, repackaged them into saleable containers. They had enormous resources to buy, process, sell, and deliver.

In his research, Carlo found four public companies listed on the New York Stock Exchange with operations and distribution centers in

South Florida. Also, he found fifteen midlevel specialty distributors with a niche like fruit, meat, chicken, or cheeses. These companies had the organizational skills that Carlo had intuitively known were needed to succeed, and he concluded that one guy trying to sell tomatoes to restaurants did not stand a chance.

Carlo also thought that working for one of these companies would be much more interesting than working on a farm, and he felt his experience would be useful to such a company. He decided to take a chance and apply online for a produce buyer position at all nineteen companies. He thought he could do an excellent job of finding the best farmers and working with them to provide a steady source of products for his employer.

To his amazement, he was quickly given interviews with five of the companies; and two made him a job offer. He could not believe that his starting salary would be $52,000 plus benefits like health insurance and a 401K with matching contributions. He would start in the position of an assistant buyer.

He chose a listed company called Toco, which had annual sales of $45 billion. They had over 50,000 workers, 275 distributions centers, and a list of 500,000 blue-chip customers.

The local Toco headquarters was in Miami, but they needed someone in the Redlands to build a more robust output of products in that region. The recent emphasis on farm to table was making it even more critical for Toco to have an excellent relationship with the farmers near Miami.

To sell the idea of farm to table, they needed a local farmer to be within 250 miles of their distribution and repacking facilities. The Redlands was a perfect area to help promote this important new concept.

They also wanted Carlo to expand the list of products they could buy, including some of the exotic fruits grown only in the Redlands. Hundreds of nurseries in the Redlands also grew a wide range of plants, flowers, and trees. They expected Carlo to determine if there was a market for some of those products during special holidays like Christmas, Easter, and Halloween.

To begin his job, he would need to attend a three-week training class in Miami. After the class training, a senior buyer would accompany him for one month to introduce him to their existing farmer relationships and to help him learn how to approach new prospects.

This job was the best chance he had ever had to have an actual career. He thought back to just a few weeks ago when he was looking for simple farm work, and now he was part of a national organization with a good salary and benefits. It was almost too good to be true, and he would work hard to make his good fortune pay off. His supply-chain education had started when he met Jake, who wanted him to sell directly to restaurants. He would need to buy Jake a drink.

"Mario, you will not believe it. I have a job as an assistant buyer with Toco, who is a national food distributor. They buy, sell, process, repack, and distribute all types of foodstuff. My starting salary is $52,000 plus health insurance!" shouted Carlo as he saw Mario in the RV

"Great news. I think that is fantastic—way to go! You will do a good job, and I bet you can grow with them. You are the first in our family to work for a big corporation, and I am proud of you," said Mario.

They went to their favorite hangout, had a few too many drinks, but left the bar happy and on top of the world. Now, they both had jobs, and the future looked even brighter than before. Another high five and "We can do it!"

# CHAPTER 13

# Ten Years of Prosperity

THE TWO BROTHERS prospered over the next ten years. They both advanced in their careers, and their salaries were almost double from where they began.

Carlo was a senior buyer with Toco; and although he had been offered several promotions, he chose to stay in the Redlands to be near Mario and Anna. Carlo now had a salary of $120,000, with performance bonuses.

Mario stayed with Gene Bailey's dealership; and he was now their top salesman, usually earning around $60,000 each year. Anna was a senior loan officer at the bank, making $80,000 a year. Their joint income of almost $150,000 enabled them to comfortably pay the mortgage on their home, drive midpriced vehicles, send John to a private Catholic school, and save a few dollars each month.

As soon as they married, Mario and Anna rented a house in Homestead close to both of their jobs. Carlo stayed in the RV on their Redlands property. The brothers kept a close relationship and spent many hours together in their leisure time.

Five years after getting married and three years after the birth of their son, John, Mario and Anna decided it was time to build a house on the Redlands property. Carlo was still living in an upgraded RV, but he was also ready for a new home and more room.

The brothers decided to build two houses at the same time using the same builder. They already owned the land, so they were able to find a builder who would charge around $150 per square foot to build their homes. They made the interior layouts almost identical, but each exterior had a different architectural design. They placed their homes fifty yards apart and one hundred yards back from the frontage, and splurged on a shared screened-in swimming pool behind the two houses.

Mario and Anna agreed on a floorplan and designed a three-bedroom, two-bath home with around twenty-five hundred square feet. The builder finally agreed to build them what they wanted for $350,000. They had $75,000 in savings for a down payment; and Wells Fargo gave them a mortgage of $275,000 with a monthly payment of $1,250. When they added taxes, insurance, and utilities, their monthly nut was around $2,000. With their two incomes, money was not tight.

Carlo's expenses were about the same as Mario's; and with his salary, he was living as he liked with no financial pressure.

It was a great setup. The families did many things together. Carlo had a steady procession of women in his life but had not found one to marry, and one of the reasons was because Carlo and Mario went fishing almost every weekend. Anna and John spent lots of time together as she had promised herself she would do with her children. Anna kept John busy with playdates and did not seem to mind being at home alone to read and relax by the pool.

The brothers became experts in shallow-water backcountry fishing. Flamingo was only fifty miles away; and it provided easy access to some exceptional snook, redfish, tarpon, and sea trout fishing. Flamingo is the southernmost headquarters of the Everglades National Park, and it sits on the edge of Florida Bay and extensive backcountry.

This small facility has a unique feature with boat ramps for both "out front" into Florida Bay or "inside" to Whitewater Bay and the Wilderness Waterway. The Wilderness Waterway is a ninety-nine-mile route through some of the most remote areas in Florida. The beauty and tranquility of the region are so incredible that once a fisherman fishes it, they are often "hooked for life."

Among avid sportsmen, Flamingo is world-renowned for its shallow-water fishing on the "flats." The boats used for this type of fishing are mostly skiffs especially designed for floating in less than five inches of water. They are often made of lightweight materials so they can be pushed easily through the water with a pole. They are usually only sixteen to eighteen feet long. The person doing the poling stands on a platform over the engine while his fellow fisherman is in the front of the boat, waiting to cast his fly or lure to a fish. It is called sight fishing and is a method highly regarded by most sports fishermen.

The brothers bought a top-of-the-line Hell's Bay skiff, with a boat trailer. Hell's Bay builds a boat that is one of the lightest skiffs on the market, and it can float in four inches of water. They kept the boat parked behind Carlo's house, and it took them just under an hour to drive to Flamingo and launch the boat. As they became more and more skilled, they were consistent winners of many tournaments. They used the Winnebago to pull the boat trailer and often slept in the motorcoach at Flamingo to fish all weekend without returning home.

Anna and Mario had a small circle of friends who kept them busy on the weekend nights that Mario was not fishing. In addition to the friends that Anna had met before Mario, they later developed relationships with the parents of John's classmates. They went to all of John's school activities; and if there was some function on the weekend, Mario would not go fishing. He had promised Anna he would be an attentive and loving father, and he kept his promise.

Carlo had a large group of friends from work. He met many of the local farmers and their families when he was buying their produce. Carlo worked hard at building friendships with his suppliers, and he was good at it. He fished with his buddies when Mario was not available, and he also liked to hunt for deer in the Everglades. Sometimes they would take the Winnebago to Central Florida and hunt in the Gulf Hammock Preserve and the Ocala National Forest. During their childhood, Carlo and Mario had hunted deer with their father in the Catskills; and they loved venison on the grill.

It was a great life, and they counted themselves lucky to have moved from New York to Florida.

# CHAPTER 14

# Trouble Begins

"I THINK WE should take a cruise in January," said Anna, who loved to cruise the Caribbean.

"Where would you like to go?" asked Mario.

"I don't really care, but maybe we could go to Barbados for a couple of days and then cruise north for a week and return home from some other island. I just like to be on the boat with you, overeat the plentiful food, have some wine, and just read and relax. It doesn't matter where we are," she answered.

"Okay. Pick a ship, pick a date, and let's do it for one week," said Mario.

"You know, we could also take the Winnebago on a long weekend over Easter and go to Cedar Key or Homosassa Springs for some sightseeing. I would like to see those manatees at Homosassa Springs, and I hear that Cedar Key has some excellent seafood restaurants. Of course, we could also go down to the Keys if you wanted to fish with John," Anna continued.

Anna loved to go anywhere with Mario, John, and Carlo. They often traveled together, and the Winnebago enabled them to see lots of new places without spending a fortune. They even took the Winnebago to Disney a few times.

"Mario, I can't believe how hard it is raining. I hope it doesn't harm the crops," Anna said as she prepared to go to work and take John to the bus stop.

Carlo had come over for breakfast, and he and Mario were drinking coffee and looking at the rain. This was the third day of hard rain, and already some fields were flooded.

"We agree. If the rain keeps this up for long, the crops will be flooded for sure," said Mario.

It was late December 2019 when it started raining, and it did not stop for four days. When it finally did stop, it had flooded the fields and destroyed 80 percent of the vegetable crop in the Redlands.

The brothers toured the Redlands together in Mario's truck, and the devastation was incredible. Now the sun was out, and the tomatoes were rotting in the heat while lying in the water. The eggplant, cabbage, okra, and beans were also heavily damaged. It was the worst flooding the area had seen in a long time.

They stopped to visit farmers along the way, who expressed fear that their losses might be so significant they could not make their payments to the banks or equipment dealers. They would miss this season entirely because it was too late to replant.

"Mario, I need to go to the Toco office in Miami and give them a report on this region. I know it will impact our supply, and we will need to find other farm communities to pick up the slack," said Carlo.

"I will update Gene and compare notes on what he has seen. I know this will be tough on our business because he is so kind to his customers and extends credit when he should not. If they don't pay him, he could lose the dealership," said Mario.

There was a general malaise throughout the Redlands for days after the flood, and almost all small businesses were hurt. When the farmers had no money and no crops, the local economy took a hit. The migrant workers had left the area, the produce buyers were scarce, truck drivers who picked up the products were not around, equipment dealers were not needed to fix broken vehicles, and the restaurants did not need as many helpers. It was a tough time to be part of the agricultural community.

A few weeks later, starting in January and throughout February, the information coming out of China regarding the COVID-19 virus was disturbing. By mid-March, people were beginning to stay at home, and the schools were closing. By the end of April, almost everyone in America was staying home; and the economy crashed. The world had turned upside down, and nobody knew how long it would last.

The Redlands was especially hard hit with the flood in December and now the virus crisis. It was a community in bad shape.

"Mario, I am sorry, but I just don't need a salesman during this period. I don't need a service representative either. Nobody is buying anything, and most of the farmers are staying home until they see how deadly this virus is going to be. You know I respect you and love you and your family, but I just don't have the money to pay you. I can't even pay my bills," Gene said with sincere sadness.

"Carlo, we have lost almost all of our restaurant business. The cruise lines are not buying anything, the airlines have stopped flying, the educational institutions have closed, and the hotels are barely doing any business. Our sales are off over 70 percent. Unfortunately, we are going to furlough thirty thousand employees, including you. We will not be able to pay our furloughed employees during this crisis, but we hope it will be over soon, and we can bring back most of our workers. I am sorry this has happened. You know that we think highly of you and look forward to having you return soon," said Carlo's boss at Toco.

Later that day, Carlo joined Anna and Mario in the living room of their home. They had dinner and afterward decided to make some plans to cope with this confinement and loss of jobs. Anna had kept her position but was working from home.

"I don't see any reason for us to just sit here in the Redlands. We have a Winnebago, and we can travel around and enjoy ourselves while keeping our distance and, when necessary, wearing masks," said Carlo.

"I am just worried about our finances," said Mario.

"You don't need to worry yet. We have $150,000 in the bank, and I have my job at the bank. This crisis will not last forever, and they will rehire you as soon as the business picks up again. I am sure we will be okay. I can work from anywhere we have an Internet or phone connection," said Anna reassuringly.

Carlo was trying hard to convince the family to take a trip. "I have around $70,000 in the bank. That should be enough to last me over a year, and I do not think this thing will last that long. I just can't sit around here and do nothing. And look, John can't go to school or camp this summer. So I say let's plan a trip and reserve some campground spots before everyone in the country starts RV'ing it," suggested Carlo.

They all agreed to get out of the Redlands for at least one month. Anna was put in charge of the travel plans, along with John, who wanted to see some specific things. She made reservations at a few campgrounds in Central Florida, North Florida, and Southern Georgia. She reviewed the plans with each of the guys, and they thought her itinerary was just fine. If they changed their minds, there would always be someplace to park the RV for a few nights. If the trip was as much fun as they anticipated, they might stay longer. It would depend upon the virus's impact and their jobs returning.

# CHAPTER 15

# Campgrounds in Florida

AFTER MAKING THE campground reservations, the next step was to pack the RV with supplies. They were going to pull the Hell's Bay flats boat behind the camper, so they had lots of storage space between the boat and the RV.

"I want to avoid contact with as many people as possible. This virus is easy to catch if you encounter sick people," said Anna as she planned what they needed to be self-sufficient.

They put extra Igloos in the boat and iced them down to hold any perishables that could not fit in the RV. They took all their fishing and hunting supplies: rods, reels, lures, pistols, shotguns, and rifles. Crossing the state borders with firearms was a tricky business. However, they decided if they put most of the weapons under the floorboard of the boat, no law enforcement officer was likely to search that area. Mario was concerned they might encounter crazies along the way, and they could need their guns.

Because Carlo and Mario used the RV for fishing trips to Flamingo, the camper was well equipped with kitchen supplies and utensils. Anna added the kitchen appliances and tools she liked to use, and then she focused on food and drink. She wanted to limit the need for grocery shopping unless they were traveling between campgrounds and maybe not even then.

She decided to use lots of canned vegetables, soups, dried fruit, chips, bread, cheese, and a ton of beef jerky. She bought three dozen large eggs and enough bacon for five days. She loaded up on chopped meat and Idaho potatoes. Bags of salad went in one of the large Igloos.

The men liked coffee during the day and beer at night, so they put a few cases of beer in the boat and Folgers in the camper. John wanted fruit juices, and she packed plenty.

They brought two extra LP gas tanks for the camper and a four-person tent in case John wanted to go deeper into the woods at some of the parks.

The sleeping quarters were just right for four people: Mario and Anna would take the queen-sized bed at the rear of the camper, Carlo would sleep in a bed above the driver and passenger seats, and John would sleep on a pull-out sofa in the living room. It was not the roomiest of accommodations but not too bad, thought Anna.

The camper held more than enough gas for them to travel between campgrounds without refueling until they got to St. Augustine, which was their last campground in Florida. They left for the Fort De Soto campground near St. Petersburg early in the morning on a sunny day.

Anna had arranged for waterfront spots at all the campgrounds that had fishing and swimming facilities. They arrived at their campsite just after lunch, and immediately jumped into the water and started throwing a rubber football.

The park is on the edge of the nearby Gulf of Mexico, and it is an excellent place for fishing and swimming. There are more than a thousand acres with plenty of facilities such as a boat ramp, two fishing piers, concession stands, and lots of picnic areas.

It was a fabulous place to start their trip. The two brothers put the boat in the water using the boat ramp and then brought the camper back to the campsite and set it up for the four-day visit. They pulled the boat up on the beach near the camper and secured it to a nearby palm tree. It would be only a few steps away whenever they wanted to use it.

For the next four days, they went swimming, fishing, sunbathing, lazing in their beach chairs, drinking beer, and being happy.

"I am so glad we decided to take this camping trip. We have not had contact with anybody, and the weather has been perfect. I feel sure we are safe against a virus infection at this campsite. If we catch any more fish, I think I will have eaten a world record of sea trout and redfish." Carlo laughed.

"Our next stop is Juniper Springs in the Ocala National Forest," said Anna as they pulled away from Fort De Soto.

It was about a three-hour drive to Juniper Springs, and their GPS route took them through Ocala. Anna asked Carlo to stop at a Publix grocery store to resupply the camper. She maintained a detailed list of items she needed, which enabled her to spend the least amount of time in the store. She wore a mask as she did her shopping; and after forty-five minutes, she was finished for another four days.

They quickly set up the RV and left the boat attached to the camper. There was no fishing at Juniper Springs, but there was excellent bass fishing in nearby Lake George.

The highlight of the campground was the swimming hole, which was in the middle of the seventy-two-degree spring. It encompassed a large swimming area, and it was one of the most refreshing swims in the state. Because the springs were in the Ocala National Forest, there was no pollution; and the water was as clear as the sky.

The canoe run was also a favorite of many campers and one of the prettiest in the country. It takes about four hours to make the run from the springs to its exit near Lake George.

They decided to swim on the first day and take the canoe trip the next morning. Mario, Anna, and John would take two canoes and make the run while Carlo would pick them up in the camper. They would have a quick lunch in the RV and then fish for bass and crappie in the afternoon on Lake George.

On the canoe run, they saw six alligators, two deer, a raccoon mother with three pups, and many herons. Lake George is a large lake, and they had fun boating and fishing along the edge of the lake and once again saw lots of wildlife. They caught six largemouth bass which was enough to feed the group for dinner.

Four days of swimming in the cool, clear spring water and fishing in a productive lake were, once again, just what they wanted.

"How nice is this! I love this camping idea," said John, who spent hours in the swimming hole and turned almost blue from the water temperature. The cold water is a surprise and a shock for people who have never been swimming in the Florida springs.

"You would think you were swimming in the Arctic Circle the way you shake and shiver when you get out of the water." Anna laughed, pointing to John as he rushed for a towel.

Their last stop in Florida was Anastasia State Park near St. Augustine. They planned to do some limited sightseeing in the old city while staying away from other people when possible. When they got to the campground, they discovered it had been closed because of the virus.

"I guess we can go to our next destination a little early. We are only three hours from the campsite I reserved, which is near the Okefenokee Swamp Park. I just made a call, and they are open. I guess Georgia has more open facilities than Florida right now," Anna said.

# CHAPTER 16

# Campground near Fargo

FOR A CHANGE, Anna did not make a reservation in a government park but rather an independent campground near the Okefenokee Swamp. They all wanted to see this blackwater swamp and try their hand at exploring and fishing. Anna had decided not to go to the well-developed Okefenokee State Park because she felt it was too far on the upper limit of the swamp. The things she most wanted to see were more in the center of the swamp.

She found a private campground a few miles north of Fargo, Georgia, in a little community called Swamptown. The facilities looked good on their website, it was almost in the middle of the swamp, and you could easily take a boat ride to Billy's Island from a launch site at Fargo.

The Lee family settled Billy's Island in the 1850s. The Lees lived in the heart of the Swamp and lived off the land for years. In this remote, wild region, they grew corn, sugarcane, potatoes, and other vegetables. It is almost unbelievable but they survived by being fishermen, farmers, and hunters.

Eventually, the Lee family was removed by the government. But, their toughness to survive in such a wilderness is a legend among the Georgia people. Anna wanted to make sure they got to see Billy's Island and learn more about this incredible family.

It was almost dark when they got to the Swamptown campground. She was immediately disappointed because it was not as lovely as the photos had indicated. No other campers were in sight, and the office was unattended. They pulled the camper into a numbered campsite and decided they would pay the owner when he showed up. They left the boat attached to the RV because they did not expect to use their boat right away. They had planned to charter a trip or two into the swamp to learn the lay of the land and then use their boat to do more exploring.

Nobody showed up the next morning to collect the money or provide any information. Carlo left the campground and walked to the small community, which, according to the Internet, had a population of 214, and fewer than 100 households. At the little crossroad, there were no stoplights and only one general store, a small restaurant, and a gas station that were both closed. There was also an old brick building that advertised swamp tours, but nobody was in the office. Carlo walked into the general store, and the man behind the counter stopped him before he could enter. The storekeeper had on a mask and told Carlo that he must also put on a mask to come into the store.

Carlo did not have his mask with him, but he tied a handkerchief around his face and reentered the store.

"The town looks abandoned. Where is everyone?" asked Carlo.

"Three weeks ago, we had a group of motorcycle riders take twenty camping spots at the campground. Those guys had a great time drinking and touring and partying. They did not cause any trouble. In fact, they were some of the nicest people we have had here in a long time. Almost all the people in town attended a dance that the motorcycle group paid for and organized. They brought in a country band from Folkston that was really good," said the storekeeper.

"The next day, the motorcycle riders left Swamptown, and we returned to normal until people started dying. Without any warning, our entire community had been infected by the COVID-19 virus, and I think over eighty of our citizens are dead. The rest of the residents have either fled or will not leave their homes," said the man.

"We have no medical facilities for miles, and we did not know what was happening until it was too late to save many lives. If I were you, guys, I would get out of here as soon as possible," he finished.

Carlo returned to the camper and told his family the news. The virus had infected this place, and they should probably leave.

"If we leave, where would we go?" asked Mario.

"I am not sure. I was looking on my phone, and it seems the virus is increasing almost everywhere," said Anna.

"I have an idea. There is nobody here to infect us. We have plenty of supplies, and if we stay here, how could we get infected? This was a dangerous place before the residents knew to stay away from other people and to wear a mask if you get near someone. But now, it might be the safest place we could be," said Carlo.

"I think you are right. Let's stay right here and do our swamp exploring as planned. There are probably no people in the swamp, and it will be impossible to get infected. We can experience the swamp without the crowds that are normally around," said Carlo.

They went to sleep that night uneasy about their situation but mostly in agreement that staying at Swamptown was a good idea. Anna was the least enthusiastic about this idea. She and Mario were already in bed and about to go to sleep when she told him her concerns.

"Mario, I am concerned about something we did not discuss before. Remember when you said you were bringing the guns because there might be some crazies along the way? Well, I think there might be some crazies right here. Their little town has been hurt, and there seems to be very little at the crossroads for them to buy. There are no medical facilities and not even a pharmacy. Maybe they don't have any money, or the disease has made some of them nuts," she said.

"Go to sleep, Anna. We will be fine. If it makes you feel better, both Carlo and I will carry our pistols," Mario said.

The next morning, they decided to take the boat on an exploratory trip into the swamp. They had wanted to get some expert advice and help, but nobody was around. They backed the boat into the water at the old boat ramp and then returned the camper to the campsite.

Their first boat trip was exhilarating. The blackwater was so evil looking, and the alligators and water birds were everywhere. They only went into the swamp for a few miles and stayed on a well-marked waterway that must have been made for the canoers and kayakers. The mosquitoes were not too plentiful or annoying, plus each of the family had a full body suit of netting if they did get too bad.

"I knew this swamp would be of interest to you, guys. I hope we can either get some help or figure out how to reach Billy's Island. It is supposed to be amazing that an island that can support a family of people is in the middle of this vast swamp," said Anna, who knew the swamp covered more than four hundred thousand acres.

They returned to the camper midafternoon and had an early dinner and played some board games. They were getting ready to call it a night when someone knocked at the door.

"Hello there! Can you hear me? I would like to talk to you," said a man's voice.

"Yes, let me put on my mask. If you back away, I will come outside to speak with you," said Carlo.

Carlo went stepped outside and saw a man dressed in a freshly pressed pair of faded jeans and a clean Colombia fishing shirt. He looked to be in his late twenties, and he seemed clean-cut and friendly.

"Hi, my name is Dave Diamond. I am one of the swamp guides who work for the local adventure company. The owner died from the virus, and I am left without a job. I saw you guys have a boat, and I came over to see if you want me to show you some of the sights in the swamp. I would make you a special deal of only $100 for the day," he said.

"That might be a great idea! Come back in the morning, and let's talk about what you can show us. I will speak to my brother, and I feel sure we will want to use your services tomorrow. Thanks for coming by," said Carlo.

Carlo returned to the camper and explained what Dave Diamond had offered.

"How do we know he is not sick with the virus?" asked Anna.

"Don't you have a thermometer? I heard you have a fever if you are infected. We will wear our masks and take his temperature. If it is normal, then we should be okay," said Mario.

"It could be fun to have a guide. That is what I had planned for us to do in the first place," said Anna.

# CHAPTER 17

# Billy's Island

THE NEXT MORNING at 8:30 a.m., Dave Diamond arrived and tapped on the camper door. Carlo put on his mask and went outside to take Dave's temperature. He did not object when Carlo asked him to put the thermometer in his ear. When he gave the instrument back to Carlo, it was normal.

"Did you have any breakfast?" asked Carlo.

"Not really, I have been living by myself since my wife left with her mother for Atlanta. They took all the food and money," sighed Dave.

"Okay, have a seat in this lounge chair, and I will bring you some food and coffee. You will have $100 after today and can buy some food from the general store," said Carlo.

"That will be great." Dave smiled.

After all had breakfast, they began to plan their day. Dave felt it would be easier to get to Billy's Island if they took the Orange Trail, leaving Fargo. They pulled the boat to Fargo, launched it in the boat ramp, and prepared to get aboard. Anna took a group picture before they boarded the boat.

"You guys cannot go into the park today. The feds decided to close the national parks for a while. It seems too many people are not obeying the social distancing rules. We had to cancel all trips we had planned," said a worker from the canoe shop next to the boat ramp.

"I didn't hear you," said Dave as he pushed the Hell's Bay boat from the dock and started down the route to Billy's Island.

The Hell's Bay boat was designed for two people, three at the most. The five people on board today would need to sit close together, even with John sitting on the floor. They brought their mosquito netting, enough sandwiches for lunch, and a six-pack of beer. There was no room for a cooler with so many people in the boat.

Dave told them more stories about Billy's Island and the swamp as they made their way along the well-marked Orange Trail. In 1901 a family of loggers, named Hebards, actually bought the swamp from the State of Georgia and harvested the cypress trees for lumber. They created a large community on the island that had a store, a movie house, a school, and an unbelievable population of over six hundred. The logging operation lasted until Mr. Hebard closed it and left the island in 1926. The Hebards left all kinds of stuff that is still visible today. The US government purchased the swamp in 1937 and made it a national wildlife refuge.

As they wound their way along the trail, they saw countless alligators on the banks and in the water. There were beautiful water birds; and occasionally, they saw a deer flitting through the shallow water.

When they arrived at Billy's Island, it was more commercial than Anna had expected with picnic tables, restrooms, a small concession stand with a couple of canoes and kayaks and information displays. Dave took them around the island on a well-worn path and showed them some of the old structures and rusted-out equipment. They were glad they had seen the island but were hoping for something more natural.

"I was told it is a big island. Is there a way to visit a part of it that is not so heavily frequented by the tourists? I would like to see what it was like before they logged all the cypress trees," asked Anna.

"Sure, I can take you around to Devil's Island, which is just several miles off the main trail. It is the third-largest island in the swamp and was untouched by the Hebard company," agreed Dave.

Dave left the Orange Trail and took a small tributary that turned to the east. They had to duck under overhanging limbs and avoid the underbrush as he moved slowly along the little waterway. After thirty minutes, they arrived at an island with many large cypress trees.

The mosquitoes were continually biting, and the family put on their netting suits before leaving the boat. They decided it was a good time for lunch; and each had a sandwich, a drink, and some chocolate chip cookies. As usual, John put on his backpack, which had snacks and a drink because he was always hungry.

"Isn't this beautiful? Look at the size of those trees and their knees standing so beautiful in the water!" exclaimed Anna as they strolled along a narrow path.

"Let me show you a couple of the most towering trees in the entire swamp. They are just a few hundred yards up this little path. Wait right here while I run back to the boat for my netting. These mosquitoes are getting the best of me," complained Dave.

"I am glad we found this remote island because now I know what this area was like before man came along and destroyed it," said Anna as she continued to admire the natural surroundings.

Suddenly they heard the boat start and heard Dave laughing and yelling at them.

"You dumbass city slickers, you may not make it out of here alive, but I want you to know that if you do, your camper is already in a semi-truck container headed for Tennessee! Thanks to you, idiots. I think I will have more than $100 at the end of the day," he said as he drove the boat away and left them in the middle of the largest blackwater swamp in America.

# CHAPTER 18

# Devil's Island

"OH MY GOD! What have I done by insisting on seeing the cypress trees?" screamed Anna.

"It is not your fault, Anna. Remember, you warned me last night that there might be crazies in Swamptown. My answer was that we would carry our pistols, which we did, but they were no good to stop this disaster. This was a plan from the beginning. We were a target as soon as we pulled into the campground," said Mario.

"You are right. We were suckers to believe Dave Diamond. We did not accurately assess the situation after we met with the store clerk. He said we should leave, and he was right. We were just too confident we would be okay," agreed Carlo.

"We need to take a cold hard look at what we can possibly do to get out of here alive. Remember, the park is closed, and there will not be any visitors until it reopens, and even then, they may not venture this far off the main trail," said Mario.

"Let's find a place to sit down and think. This is a time to remember our family motto: We can do it! We need to stay calm and make sure we think clearly about our options," suggested Carlo.

They looked around and continued to walk down the narrow path until they found a fallen tree with a trunk large enough to use as a bench for all four of them.

"Let's make a list of what we have. Carlo, did you bring your pistol? How much ammunition do you have?" Mario asked.

"Yes, I brought it loaded with one magazine and ten bullets. I tossed another magazine in my tote bag, but it is in the boat," answered Carlo.

"I put my pistol in John's backpack before we left the camper, and I included an extra magazine, so I have a total of twenty bullets," said Mario.

"John, what do you have in your backpack?" asked Anna.

John emptied his backpack, which contained the pistol and an extra magazine, three bags of potato chips, some cookies, two apple juice boxes, one can of Coke, four sticks of beef jerky, a yo-yo, and a baseball cap.

"Anna, what is in that purse that you never let go?" Mario asked.

Anna emptied her purse which contained cosmetics, breath mints, her wallet, a mirror, a notepad, an ink pen, a small pack of Kleenex, nail clippers and a nail file, a couple of cough drops, nasal spray, eye drops, an old box of matches, and an extra pair of sunglasses.

"Well, we have two pistols, thirty rounds of ammo, very little food, and nothing in Anna's purse, except the matches that can be useful," said Carlo.

"Don't forget we have our mosquito nettings," said John.

"Good point, John. Without these nets, we would become sick from the massive number of bites we would get," said Carlo.

"Guys, before we left home, I read about the swamp for hours because I was so fascinated with the stories. One of the things that stuck in my mind was some interesting rumors. Some people believe that some of the families who worked for the logging company did not leave but are still secretly living in the swamp," said Anna.

"Well, that would be great unless they tried to kill us if we discovered them." Mario laughed nervously.

"Let's look around this island. If what Dave said is true, this is the third-largest island in the swamp. If there were any hangover people from the logging days, they would need a pretty big island to sustain themselves. They could have brought seed and even some livestock from Billy's Island," said Carlo.

"For sure, they would have needed some boats to get around. They probably would go back and forth in secret to Billy's Island to get the tools and lumber needed to build some houses," said Mario.

It was getting late in the day; and the swamp landscape was dense with trees and underbrush, which made the entire environment spooky looking. The mosquitoes were buzzing, and they had encountered two rattlesnakes that crawled away after giving their warnings with the rattles on their tail. John was a tough eight-year-old, but he was near to tears with concern.

"Mama, I don't think we can get out of here," John said.

"Yes, we can! We will find a way. Your father and uncle are experienced fishermen, hunters, and woodsmen. They will get us home safely. Don't worry," Anna said softly.

# CHAPTER 19

# Getting Settled

"WE NEED TO find anything to help us get some shelter. If it starts raining and soaks our clothes and netting, we will be miserable," said Mario as he looked at the darkening sky.

"We could build a lean-to with these fallen-down trees and limbs. The roof would not be completely leakproof, but we could put enough brush and leaves on top to stop a lot of the water," suggested Carlo.

There were many pine and oak trees on the island and lots of dead limbs were scattered on the ground. The heartwood of pine trees goes by many different names: lighter'd wood, fatwood, pine heart, and other names given by different locales. The heartwood is impregnated with resin and becomes hard and rot-resistant over many years. Because of the resin, the wood is excellent for starting fires. Also, if the lighter'd was used on the roof, it would not become soggy from the rain.

"We can use the root canopy of that fallen cypress tree as the backstop for our lean-to, and we can use the long limbs of the oak and pine trees to build the two sides and part of the top. Then we will crisscross the top with lighter'd wood filling the gaps with red bay leaves that are around six inches long and three to four inches wide to thicken the canopy. We can lap the leaves one over the other and build a tight roof. Then we can place lots of Spanish moss on top of that," said Carlo.

"Did you know that the fallen giant cypress tree we are going to use for the rear of our hut might be a thousand years old? They are one of the most amazing trees on earth. That is why I was so interested in seeing them," said Anna, continuing to explain her love of the old trees.

The four of them worked for the next three hours; and when they were finished, they had a hut about five feet wide and ten feet deep, ending up against the dirt wall of the fallen cypress roots. They made the top almost waterproof with the lighter'd wood, red bay leaves, and Spanish moss. They placed ferns, swamp tupelo limbs, and leaves on the sides plus more of the Spanish moss.

"John, go find some small pieces of lighter'd wood for us to use to start a fire. I will get some more cypress and oak limbs to feed the fire. A fire will give us light to talk and plan," said Mario.

They made a covered floor with fern, moss, and bay leaves. It would not be perfectly comfortable, but it would be better than bare earth. The moss might have bugs, but they would just need to ignore them for now.

They sat in the hut with a fire burning ten feet away from the front opening. They nibbled on the chips, jerky, and cookies and saved enough of the snacks to have a little breakfast.

Then it began to rain cats and dogs. The rain put out the fire, and their little world descended into darkness. Almost as soon as the rain began, the swamp sounds started all around them. The alligators and the pig frogs were grunting, and the many other unrecognizable frogs and toads were croaking. Occasionally, they thought they could hear the huffing of a black bear, but maybe it was just their imagination.

"Listen to the sounds, but do not be alarmed. There is nothing out there that can hurt us. Either Carlo or I will stay awake and look outward from our hut. We have our pistols, and if anything comes near, we will scare it away or shoot it," said Mario.

"Try to get some sleep. We need to do some exploring tomorrow to see if there are any remnants of people living here who could help us," agreed Carlo.

The roof and sides of the hut provided excellent protection, and only a few drops of rain interfered with the sleep of the family. They all tossed and turned with worry, but they did get some critical sleep.

Mario had taken the guard time from 3:00 a.m. to daylight. The rain had stopped, and the sun was not yet visible, but the early morning dawn was just starting when a young hog came to visit. Perhaps the pig was curious or hungry, but he came to smell the ashes of the fire.

Mario quickly aimed his pistol and shot the pig. He and Carlo knew how to skin wild animals; and in less than an hour, they had hog meat roasting on their fire.

"That pig was a gift from God! We would have been in trouble without any food, but now we have plenty to eat for a few days. Let's all look for any herbs or roots that might be safe to eat as we explore today," offered Mario.

"I wondered if that pig is a wild pig or an offspring of domesticated hogs used by people who lived on this island," asked Carlo.

"I guess that the pig is only a year old. I estimate he only weighed seventy pounds, and I can't tell if he is a domesticated breed or a wild one," said Mario.

It was not the perfect breakfast for people accustomed to eggs, bacon, toast, and coffee, but it was nutritious and filled their bellies. They left the hut and explored in a westerly direction for two hours and then returned to the shelter for lunch. Next, they would go to the north for two hours and return to the hut for their evening meal of hog meat. It was the time of year that it probably rained every evening.

They saw little sign of active human life, but they did find a discarded crosscut saw that must have once been used to cut down trees and big limbs. It was too rusted to be useful now, but it was an encouraging sign that people had been here before. They saw a small area where a few corn stalks were growing, and it must have once been a planted field, but there was no corn to pick.

The swamp looked the same as it must have looked for millennia. Anna had read that the swamp was under the sea around sixty million years ago; and then thousands of years ago, it became the swamp it is now. The Okefenokee Swamp was indeed an ancient forest.

They marked their trail by cutting pieces of low-hanging limbs with their pocketknives. Carlo and Mario always carried them for many common uses in their work, and they were handy in this crisis. Even John had a knife.

They returned to the hut for another meal of hog meat. They had no utensils other than their knives, so they could only cook the meat over the fire on a stick and then eat it with their hands. They needed to find something to supplement the meat, but so far had found nothing.

They were just finishing lunch when they heard a gunshot.

# CHAPTER 20

# The Encounter

"DID YOU HEAR that?" asked Carlo urgently. "Yes, and it was a rifle. I don't know how close, but it means there are people on this island, and they are armed," said Mario.

"Carlo, I do not trust anyone around here anymore. I want you to hide my pistol with the ten bullets and the extra magazine in the roof of our hut. If these people mean us any harm and should capture us, I do not want to be without at least one hidden weapon."

Carlo hid Mario's pistol in the roof, where it could be quickly reached if needed. Now Mario was without his accustomed feel in his lower back.

"Mario, why are you so suspicious?" asked Anna.

"I am suspicious for two reasons. One, from the moment we pulled that RV into Swamptown, we have been a target. I would not be surprised if some of these rednecks decided we might be worth a ransom. Two, another reason I am wary is if people are living here against the rules of the park, they may not want us to live to tell anyone," said Mario.

"What if they are just some hunters looking for deer or hog?" asked Anna.

"Nobody is supposed to be in the park. If they are hunting, they are poachers and probably dangerous. We just need to be incredibly careful and not trust anything they say if we meet up with them," said Mario.

"Should we try to find them?" asked Carlo.

"No. I think we should drag over a couple of logs that we can use for sitting by the fire. Let's make ourselves look comfortable and unconcerned. I have just thought of a plan," said Mario.

"Let's say to whoever finds us that we are on a survival experiment, and we will be picked up the day after tomorrow. Our assignment is to spend three days in the wilderness with only a few items: one pistol, five rounds of ammo, a few snacks, and five matches. Anna, hide the remaining matches in your bra. I do not want them to know we have an extra gun or any more matches. Carlo, hide our mosquito netting. I want them to think we need to keep our fire going because we are out of matches, and we need the smoke to stop the mosquito bites," said Mario.

They dragged over three logs and placed them near enough to the fire to roast the pig and eat it without getting up. The logs were also placed far enough away from the fire that the heat was not uncomfortable. They had prepared long pointed sticks for roasting.

When they left the camp to explore that morning, they made a deep hole with a bed of leaves and buried the hog in the ground. It had some dirt in a few places when they took it out for lunch; but they scraped it off, cooked it, and ate it anyway. They left a large piece of hog meat lying near the fire on a bed of red bay leaves for slicing as needed.

Their biggest problem had been something to drink. They used the Coke can to carefully boil water and then share a drink. It took around ten minutes to boil each can and five minutes to let it cool enough to drink. They were not sure how safe the swamp water was after boiling, but they had no choice. Water was essential to survival.

"John, go hide the Coke can. If they want to hurt us, they may not want us to have water," said Mario.

"Okay, I think I will fire my pistol to let them know where we are. The strangers might not have heard our shot this morning when we killed the pig, but they will hear it now. I will say I missed a deer that we wanted for dinner. Remember, do not believe anything they say," said Mario.

Mario fired his shot; and in twenty minutes, an older man and a young man walked into their camp from the swamp. They were dressed in ragged overalls and knee-high wading boots. The older man had a long white beard and appeared to be around sixty while the young man looked to be in his twenties. They each had a rifle pointing toward the ground, and the young man had two dead squirrels tied to his waist.

"Hello, folks. Can we join you for a spell?" said the old man.

"Sure, make yourself at home. Take a seat on our most exclusive log. Would you like a slice of hog meat?" Mario laughed.

"What are you folks doing here?" asked the young man without smiling.

"We are here as part of a survival training course we are taking from the USA Wilderness Survival Association," answered Carlo.

"What does that mean?" asked the old man.

"We have someone picking us up the day after tomorrow. We are supposed to survive three days in the wilderness with just one pistol, five matches, which we have already used, and a few snacks," said Mario.

"I was lucky to kill this pig this morning, so we started the three days with plenty of food." Carlo smiled.

"You killed my hog," said the old man without smiling.

"We did not know anyone was living on this island, and we thought it was a wild pig," said Mario.

"Well, it was not a wild pig. It belonged to me, and I want you to pay for it," said the old man.

"Okay, I am sorry we killed something of yours. How much do we owe you?" asked Mario.

"What do you think, Pa?" Junior asked.

"I think whatever they both have in their wallets will be enough," said Pa.

"Fellows, we are not rich people. We live modestly in a farming community, and we need our money to buy food and gas to go home. Let us pay you a fair price for the hog, but please don't take all of our money," said Mario.

"Well, I think both of your wallets, the pistol, and that big piece of my hog will be payment enough," said Pa.

"Junior, get his pistol," Pa said, pointing his rifle at Carlo, who had his pistol on his hip.

"Why are you treating us like this? We are just a simple farming family taking a course in survival. We will not be able to survive without that pistol or the hog meat," said Carlo.

"We do not like outsiders, especially ones with a Northern accent. If you can survive without your pistol and any meat, then you will surely pass your survival course exercise. If not, you will become alligator meat. Either way, I don't give a damn. By the way, we know there ain't nobody coming to git you," said Pa as he and Junior walked away with the pistol and the hog meat.

# CHAPTER 21

# A Plan to Escape

"WHAT THE HELL was that about? Was it just a simple robbery of our wallets, or was it something more sinister like murder? They left us with a little hog meat because he knew that was not all of the remaining pig. He did not search the hut to see if we had any other supplies. It's as if he is giving us a chance, but I think he plans to kill us if we are clever enough to survive," said Mario.

"Well, I have a thought! Pa and Junior must live in this ungodly place. Why would they choose to live here? They must either be crazy as hell or running from the law," said Carlo.

"Why is that important?" asked Anna.

"Because if they live here, then we can find their home and get our money back," said Carlo.

"Carlo, don't worry about the money. When we get out of here, I can arrange with Wells Fargo to send us money wherever we may be," said Anna.

"I have a lot of stuff in that wallet that I want. I say, let's find them, surprise them, and take back our property. They must have a boat they use to get supplies once in a while. Let's take it and get the hell out of here. I am pissed off and ready to kill the bastards if necessary!" yelled Carlo.

"I don't know how long we can last eating the rest of the hog meat and drinking boiled swamp water. We will probably need to kill something else and find some greens or roots to eat. Let's dig up every plant we see and hope we find one with an edible-looking root," said Mario.

The group pulled up every plant that had a green top. They were looking for plants with a rootstalk or a tuber. They found a group of plants that Anna thought were either wild potatoes or onions. She also found some tall plants growing in the water that looked like cattails and had long stalks with white roots.

"I am afraid to eat these things raw. But if we cooked them entirely over the fire, I am pretty sure we will be okay. We must eat something besides hog meat," Anna said.

"I don't think we should take a chance eating stuff that might hurt us. I think we should go hurt those hillbillies and get out of here with one of their boats," said Carlo.

"I think they have set us up. If we try to attack these people, they will kill us. The father-and-son act who came here might just be the tip of the spear. There could be many armed people in their camp with lookouts all over the swamp," said Mario.

"You are paranoid about these people," said Carlo.

"I see how they are playing us. First, they steal the camper, so there is no physical record of us having been at Swamptown. Remember, we never registered at the campground. Then they abandoned us here without any supplies, expecting us to starve to death. Next, when they see we have made a little progress to survive, they pretend we killed their hog. Now, they have our wallets but leave us with enough meat and fire to live for a while," analyzed Mario.

"One more thing, with no RV and no identification, who will even know we were here? They can kill us, and nobody will ever know," said Mario.

"I think they are tormenting us just for the plain fun of it. It is some perverted game to prove the swamp people are superior to the city people," said Mario.

"What if we changed our thinking a little? What if we tried to leave this place rather than survive here?" asked Carlo.

"How would you do that?" asked Anna.

"We could build two rafts and use some long, strong limbs from the oak trees as poles and pretend we are Tom Sawyer." Carlo laughed.

"How would we hold the log together to build a raft?" asked Mario.

"I don't know. I have another idea. What if just one of us tries to get out of here on a raft? Look at those three logs we have around the fire.

If we could somehow bind them together, I think they would support one person poling," said Carlo.

"I cannot think of any way to connect the logs into a raft," said Mario.

"We just need to get back to Billy's Island, and we can probably find enough things there to build a boat or just wait for the park to reopen. There may even be some canoes at the dock held in reserve for tourists who want another or different canoe for the return trip to Fargo," Carlo continued.

"All of a sudden, I have a better idea than a raft. How far do you think it is to Billy's Island?" Carlo asked excitedly.

"It took only thirty minutes to get here from Billy's Island, and we were not moving very fast. I bet it is three miles," said Mario.

"The water in the swamp is usually a max of three feet deep. I am going to walk back to Billy's Island," said Carlo.

"You are nuts. Did you see how many alligators there were in the water and on the banks?" asked Mario.

"I am not afraid of an alligator. I will not threaten them, and they will not bother me. I am more concerned about water moccasins, even though I think I will be able to see then if they swim toward me. They usually swim with their heads up, and I don't think they bite underwater," said Carlo.

"I don't know if they bite underwater or not, but they are poisonous, and you will be sick as hell if one bites you. What will you do if you make it to Billy's Island? You will starve to death without any food or water," said Mario.

"There are restrooms at Billy's Island where I can get water. There is even a small concession stand, and I will break in if I need to get food. I plan to find a canoe and come back for you, guys," Carlo said.

"I think I can make it to the island in three or four hours. I will take a five-foot pinewood limb with me to toss away snakes or to hit an aggressive alligator, if necessary. I want you to keep the pistol and ammo," Carlo said.

"I am concerned for you, but if you think this is our best chance, then I guess we should try it," said Mario.

"I would not be surprised if the hillbillies are watching us to see what we are going to do next, so I think we should split up like we are exploring. We don't want them to know you are wading to Billy's Island," said Mario.

"It is one o'clock now, and I should be at the concession stand by five o'clock. I will get a canoe, and I should be back here around dark. I think I can paddle the three miles in one hour or a little more," said Carlo as he picked up a pinewood limb and started walking into the swamp.

# CHAPTER 22

# Carlo's Walk

CARLO LEFT THE camp and walked west toward the swamp until out of sight. Then he turned back to reach the small tributary Dave had used to travel from Billy's Island to Devil's Island. Carlo had on his hiking boots and the upper body and face part of his mosquito netting. He was wearing long pants and a long-sleeve shirt.

He entered the water and found the bottom very soft and boggy. The swamp is basically on a bed of peat, and the bottom is not hard. The walking would be more complicated than he had envisioned. He would need to walk carefully not to sink deep into the peat bottom.

He had only gone a few hundred yards when he saw the first alligator lying on the bank not fifteen feet from him. Carlo watched the reptile, and the gator watched him. The gator did not move as Carlo walked slowly past the beast.

"I guess that is going to be the first of many gator encounters," said Carlo out loud to himself.

He disturbed countless water birds as he waded along cautiously. He saw many snakes on the banks and in the water and some in the trees. There were cottonmouth moccasins, rattlesnakes, and a host of non-venomous water snakes in the swamp; and it seemed to Carlo that every species was visiting the creek today.

Carlo was not afraid of many things, but he hated spiders. He was pushing aside an overhanging limb when a wolf spider fell on his head. Carlo immediately hit the spider with his hand, and she was carrying a large egg sack with hundreds of baby spiders.

He popped the egg sac when his slap killed the spider, and the babies started crawling all over his face and neck. He snatched off his face and body netting and frantically tried to brush away the small spiders. He tore off his shirt and ducked underwater.

He closed his eyes and held his breath while continuing to brush off the spiders. He came up for air and went down four or five more times before stopping to feel if they were all gone. After checking over himself carefully, he decided he was rid of the baby spiders. Then, he retrieved his shirt and net from the creek bank where he had hurled them. He washed off any remaining spiders and then put the shirt and netting back on his body.

"Good lord! I never thought I would need to deal with that situation!" yelled Carlo to the woods.

He saw a mother cottonmouth on the bank with her young around her, and he moved as far away as possible. He knew that disturbing any mother with her young created a dangerous situation. The snake did coil into a defensive position and hiss at Carlo, but she did not attack.

He felt he was halfway to his objective when he sank to his waist. He dropped so suddenly that he was barely able to keep his grip on the stick he had been carrying. He could scarcely move, and he was afraid to struggle because he might sink farther down.

"What should I do now?" he screamed in protest.

He stayed still, let his mind slow down, and let logic return to his brain. He must not panic. He must find a way out of this peat bog. He looked around to check his position in the creek. He was only five feet from one side of the narrow waterway, and tree limbs were reaching out toward the middle.

He could almost reach up and grasp a small limb, but it was about a foot too high. He took his long stick and put it on top of the limb and pressed down to bring it into his reach. But his leverage was wrong, and all his efforts only pushed the limb farther out of reach.

He was sweating profusely from the heat and from the fear of dying in that creek. He stopped to rest and realized how thirsty he was becoming. His mind was not thinking clearly, and he was getting desperate when one last idea popped into his swirling brain.

He would try pushing the limb upward and make it start bouncing. Maybe he could cause it to rebound enough to drop the one foot he needed. He pushed up over and over until he was able to grasp a few leaves at the end of a small branch. The leaves tore out of his hand as the limb bounced back upward, and he lost his grip. He kept trying, and finally, he succeeded in getting his hand around the limb that was only two inches in diameter.

Carlo figured with his usual weight, plus the pressure of the bog, there must be more than 250 pounds to pull up on that small limb. He stopped to think about what he could do to take away some of the weight.

He decided to push the stick into the peat around his body to see if he could create any space. He worked for over thirty minutes, pushing and leaning the stick outward around his entire waist and legs. He felt some space, and he could begin to move his legs from left to right. He kept working with the stick until he could move his knees. Throughout the pushing and leaning, he had held his left hand around the tree limb.

Once he could move his knees, he started pushing with them and pulling on the small limb. He made very little progress, but his feet were no longer stuck in the peat. He kept leaning slowly toward the near side of the bank, never putting too much pressure on the little limb. When he could finally lean even closer to the bank, he grasped a larger limb and was able to get out of the bog hole. He had been fortunate a little limb was there to help him.

After that near-death experience, Carlo strategized that he must stay near the edge of the bank so that if he bogged down again, he could reach a limb or a tree to pull himself out of a bog hole. He had lost a lot of time, and he might not even make it to Billy's Island before dark.

Being closer to the bank meant being closer to the alligators and the snakes. Carlo concluded he would move into the creek and away from the bank until he was past the reptiles.

He made it to Billy's Island without bogging down again, being bitten by a snake or spider, or being eaten by an alligator. All in all, he concluded he was very lucky to have walked that creek without being killed.

# CHAPTER 23

# Mario Finds Stuff

WHILE CARLO WAS walking in the creek toward Billy's Island, Mario and his family were exploring Devil's Island as they had planned to do the day before.

They went north from the camp, looking for anything they might use to survive if Carlo did not return. They did not see the hillbillies or any evidence of their living quarters. They did find some more rudimentary land-clearing tools too rusty to be of any functional usage.

"Look!" yelled Anna as she pointed to something in the distance.

They moved over to the object she had seen, and they could not believe their eyes. It was an old hand pump used to draw water. Anna cautiously moved the pump handle up and down, and it made a dry sucking sound, but no water came out of the spout. Mario and John took turns pumping repeatedly, but no water came from the well.

"Wait, let's think about this a moment. The old rubber washer or O-ring that sealed the sides to bring up the water has probably rotted away. If we take the top off the pump and place some smashed-up green grass down around the edge of the O-ring, we might be able to create enough suction to bring up a little water. Hopefully, the grass will clog the edges of the O-ring, which I know creates the suction," said Mario.

Mario unscrewed the top of the old pump and examined the O-ring, which was not as badly damaged as he had expected. They found some grass and mashed it into mush and packed it all around the fragile O-ring.

Mario replaced the top with the grass-packed O-ring and hoped it made the pump functional again. He waited a few minutes for the grass to settle and dry a little and then pumped the handle slowly.

It took many slow strokes; but finally, the water outlet began to drip small amounts of water. It was not the regular quantity one would get, but it would save their lives.

"I am not sure how pure the water is, but I am sure the swamp water does not contaminate it. This old well is down into an underground water table, and it will be okay to drink. We should probably still boil it, but it will be much safer," said Mario.

"We need a container to carry the water back to our camp," said Anna.

"There must be a reason for this pump to be here, and there must have been something around that needed water. There could have been an old homestead around here or an animal trough, or maybe this was just a water station for workers," said Mario.

It was John who found the old wooden foundation. It was too small to be a house, but it might have been a work shed. They looked everywhere, but someone must have taken away the lumber from the sides and roof.

"Look at this old water basin. It looks like it might have been used for washing the face and hands after work. If it doesn't leak, we could use it to carry water," said Anna as she picked up a dirty piece of tin.

Anna took the old tin water basin to the pump and added some water. It had two small leaks, but Mario plugged them with some twigs, and then there was just a small drip. It would hold the water for a while until they could devise another way to get water to the camp.

The family continued their exploration and their northern direction. They found wild tomatoes growing in an old clearing that had once been a cultivated field. Someone had lived here or farmed this island in days past. There must be some old stuff they could use somewhere.

"Wow, I am so happy to see some vegetables that we can eat," said Anna.

In another few minutes, they finally found an old, dilapidated farmhouse. The small front porch was broken into two pieces, and the steps were rotten. The roof was sagging, and the windows were all missing. It must have been abandoned for a hundred years or more.

"I am going to look inside to see if there is anything we can use and to determine if this place could be our shelter," said Mario.

As he approached the rotten front steps, a pair of bobcats jumped out of a window and ran snarling into the swamp. He drew his pistol and carefully eased up the steps and looked inside. Rats scrambled away, and there was the smell of animal and rodent dropping as looked into the three-room house. The floor was rotten and sagging in many places. The roof was full of holes, and this place would provide no shelter for the family.

He saw two fat rattlesnakes in a corner who must have been feasting on the rats. They slithered away as he walked into what would have been the kitchen and dining room. There was still an old pump where the kitchen sink would have been located, but no appliances of any kind remained. It was apparent that the house had been ransacked for anything of value. He saw bent and twisted forks and spoons near the pump. There were three broken water glasses and two broken mason jars next to the forks.

There had been no bathroom, and he looked into each bedroom and found only some old rotted wooden bedframes and one rusted metal coat hanger. He picked up the coat hanger, the spoons, forks, and the water glasses and then left the old house to join Anna and John under a mulberry tree.

Years ago, someone must have planted that tree for shade and for the yield of the berries. Mulberries are good to eat, and they were ready for picking. Anna and John had filled the water basin with the red berries, and they were smacking their lips and laughing. Mario ate several dozen before rubbing his stomach in delight.

Things were looking up. In one afternoon, they had found a water pump, a water basin, a coat hanger, some bent utensils, two water glasses, a tomato field, and a mulberry tree. If they could get some more meat, they could live for a long time.

"Let's take our stuff back to the hut, and I have an idea to try to catch some fish. I do not want to shoot my pistol to kill more meat because I don't want the hillbillies to know we have a gun."

It took forty-five minutes to return to the hut from the abandoned farmhouse. They had a basin full of mulberries and a dozen tomatoes. They would get water on another trip. They marked the way by breaking and cutting limbs so that it would be easy to find the pump and the other locations.

"I think I can catch some fish. I once read in a fishing magazine about a guy catching catfish on mulberries. I will make a crude hook from the hanger and use John's yo-yo string as my fishing line. If the mulberries don't work, I will try some of the hog meat for bait. I think we will have catfish for dinner," said Mario.

It was getting near sunset, so Mario quickly rigged his hook and line and was fishing soon after they arrived at their hut.

"Yahoo! I got a fish!" yelled Mario as he pulled in a fat two-pound catfish.

It seemed the hungry fish would eat meat or mulberries, and he caught six more fish before he brought them back to the hut for cleaning. He did not have water to wash them, but he gutted and filleted all seven fish. They cooked them well done and ate them along with the tomatoes. They pigged out on mulberries again and were satisfied with the day.

They saved two fillets for Carlo and three tomatoes. They figured he would be hungry if he made it back.

# CHAPTER 24

# Carlo Returns

CARLO IMMEDIATELY LOOKED into the concession stand to see if there was anything to eat. He saw lots of canned food, crackers, chips, beef jerky, pretzels, and ice cream. He tried the front door, but it was locked. He yelled to find anyone who might have stayed to watch the property while the park was closed, but nobody was around.

He broke a window in the rear, entered the concession stand, immediately found some bottled water, and downed two bottles before slowing down. He ate some ice cream to start and then filled up on assorted snacks and soda.

He moved one of the canoes to the stand and filled it with all the food, water, and soft drinks he could manage and still paddle the canoe. He tied a kayak to the back of the canoe.

He wanted to use the restroom to clean up; and to his surprise, it was open. It had one shower, and he shivered under the cold water, but he got the peat and other mud out of his hair and ears and off his entire body. He felt like a new man after the shower.

He found three paddles and put two of them in the kayak. To make the return trip to Billy's Island, they would put three people in the canoe, and Mario would use the kayak. One more canoe was next to the concession stand, and they would use it to go back to Fargo and plan a trip home.

Carlo was making excellent progress on his way back to Devil's Island when he encountered a mother black bear with her two cubs. Her cubs jumped into the water and started across the creek. The momma bear reared up on her back legs and growled. She did not immediately jump into the creek like her cubs but kept roaring and looking at the canoe. Carlo had heard many stories about not running from a bear, but he quickly decided to get out of the canoe.

A black bear has an incredible nose and can smell about seven times greater than a bloodhound. Many scientists have concluded that a black bear has the best ability to smell of all animals. The bear must have smelled some of the food that Carlo had put in the canoe, and she decided to take some of it. It was also possible she had smelled Carlo and would have been interested in eating him if there had not been food in the canoe.

Whatever caused her to want to investigate the contents of his canoe, he had to get out of it quickly. He snatched the rope that held the kayak, pulled it next to the canoe, and jumped in the kayak. He quickly paddled away back toward Billy's Island, and he kept paddling until he could barely see the bears.

He watched from a far distance as the mother bear, and her cubs tore open the food he had put in the canoe; and while he stood in the creek, they destroyed everything. They turned over the canoe and looked under it to see if there was more food. They did not linger around the canoe once the food was gone, and they ambled away into the swamp.

Carlo was still shaking from the near-fatal attack, and he waited for a full hour before returning to the canoe. He turned the canoe over, manually threw out most of the water, and continued to Devil's Island.

Carlo was getting close to his camp when he heard voices coming from behind him. He did not have time to make it to Devil's Island without being seen, so he jumped out of the canoe and pulled both the canoe and kayak into the swamp. He hoped the scars on the bank would look like gators fighting or breeding.

There were two men in the canoe, and they were talking loudly. Voices carry far on the water, and Carlo could hear them talking long before they passed and long after.

"Those city slickers that Dave left are either dead from mosquito bites or thirst, or they may have been killed already by the old man and his son," said one of the men paddling.

"I bet he has not killed them yet. He likes to torment them and let them think they can find a way to survive before he shoots them," said the other.

"I hope he got their money and anything else of value. If they are still alive, we need to kill them tonight to make sure they don't escape. Dave already sold the boat and got $2,000 for it in Waycross. The Winnebago was sold somewhere in Tennessee for $12,000," said the man in the front of the boat.

"It was smart of Dave to buy that campground in Swamptown. This is the third group of city slickers that we have fleeced and killed," said the man proudly.

"We have enough canned goods and liquor for the old man and boy to live for a month with what they can kill and find on the island. They are happy with this arrangement. If it weren't for us hiding them, they would already be in jail for killing that man in Folkston. We keep him and the boy hid, and he helps us get rid of our city slickers after we have picked 'em clean." He laughed.

Carlo could hardly believe his ears. This was a real organized setup to steal and kill innocent people. He decided to follow them to their camp. He stayed far behind; and when they turned off the little creek into an even smaller tributary, he could hear the old man and boy greet them as they parked their canoe.

The hillbilly camp was only a mile from where Carlo and his family were camping, but it was on the east side of the island. Mario, Carlo, Anna, and John had explored west and north but not east. Carlo returned to his camp and was greeted with hugs and high fives.

# CHAPTER 25

# Getting into Their Camp

MARIO, ANNA, AND John were so happy to see Carlo that they could hardly control their enthusiasm; but Carlo looked upset. Carlo was shaking his head and looking at the ground.

"We are so glad to see you. You made an incredible trip, and now we can get out of here. What is wrong with you? Are you hurt?" asked Anna with great concern.

"We have a serious problem. The people on this island are killers, and we are scheduled to be killed tonight. We need to make some quick plans and decide what we want to do," said Carlo.

"What do you mean? Decide what to do? Let's leave right now in those two canoes," said Anna.

"It is not that simple in my mind. I need to tell you what I accidentally heard as two hillbillies passed me on the creek. I was well hidden, and they were talking loudly," said Carlo.

"We are the third group of campers they have fleeced, and they killed the other two groups. This whole thing is well planned and has been working for several years. The old man and boy are on the run for killing someone. There are three other men involved. Dave Diamond and the two men I heard talking," said Carlo.

"Dave owns the campground in Swamptown. He doesn't harm every group, just the ones that look like they have some money. When Dave takes the campers on the sightseeing tour, his associates steal all their camping equipment, including the RV, if there is one. Dave takes the campers to Billy's Island and then here under a pretense to see the big cypress trees, and you know the rest. By the way, they sold our boat in Waycross for only $2,000 and our camper for $12,000, and they took all of our money," continued Carlo.

"I still say let's get out of here right now," said Anna as she grabbed John and headed for a canoe.

"I think we need to stop this operation in its tracks. I am totally disgusted that people like this are still functioning in our world," said Mario.

"Well, we can leave now and tell the police what we know about their operation so they can arrest them and put them away," said Anna.

"I think we should raid their camp and capture them. I have some ideas what we should do to them once they are under our control," said Carlo.

"How do you propose to capture them?" asked Mario.

"I know where they are camped. I followed them and heard the old man and boy greet them. The two men from Swamptown brought lots of food and liquor to last for one month. They apparently replenish the man and boy once each month," said Carlo.

"My plan is for Anna and John to stay here. Mario, you will walk into their camp from this side of the island as if you have accidentally discovered them. I will wait until you have distracted them, and I will come in with your pistol from the water side. They will not expect anyone to come from that direction," said Carlo.

"What will you do if they resist?" asked Mario.

"I will shoot them all or one or two or none depending upon how mad I get." Carlo laughed in an evil-sounding way.

"Guys, this is not a good idea. I say we leave and tell the police," said Anna.

"I think we can do both. Anna, you and John get in that canoe and go to Billy's Island. Hide in the concession stand and wait for us. If we are not there by tomorrow, go to the police and tell them the story," said Mario.

"I am not leaving you," Anna said.

"Yes, you are. I am never firm with you, but I am going to be today. You and John need to be away from any danger. If you feel like going all the way to Fargo, just leave a note in the ice cream cooler at the concession stand. If you go, tell the police and ask them to hurry to Devil's Island," said Mario.

They argued about this decision for a few more minutes, and Anna finally agreed, and she and John got in the canoe and left for Billy's Island.

"Carlo, are you sure this is a good idea?" asked Mario.

"It may not be a good idea, but it is the right thing to do. We must teach these killers a lesson," said Carlo.

Mario and Carlo both got on the kayak, which was only designed for one person. But they only needed to go a short distance to the old man's camp. Mario got out of the kayak several hundred yards before the camp landing area. Carlo guided the kayak right up to the three canoes tied to trees.

Mario walked into camp and said hello.

"What the hell are you doing here?" asked the old man.

"I have been looking for your camp because I wanted to discuss something with you," Mario said.

"I thought you would be dead by now. How the hell did you avoid those mosquitoes?" asked the old man.

"We rubbed ourselves with crushed red bay leaves. They are a great repellant," answered Mario.

"I guess you learned that in a survival class." One of the men from Swamptown laughed.

"Where is the rest of your family?" asked the son.

"They are also looking for your camp," said Mario.

"What did you want to discuss with us?" asked a man from Swamptown.

"Guys, can I have a drink of that whiskey? I am a confirmed alcoholic, and because of you, gentlemen, I have not had a drink in days," pleaded Mario.

"Sure, why not? Sit down, have a drink, and ask your question before we decide what to do with you," said the old man.

"My brother and I have a lot of money, and we will give you some of it if you let us go home safely," said Mario.

"Well, now, that is interesting! How much are we talking about?" asked the boy.

"Between the two of us, we can wire you $500,000 if we get home safely," said Mario.

"Holy shit. Hey, guys, maybe we should listen to this man. That is a lot of money," said the Swamptown leader.

# CHAPTER 26

# Retribution Begins

CARLO APPROACHED THE camp from behind the old shack they were using for a house. The group was sitting around a table near a fire pit, and they were looking at Mario in amazement that he might have $500,000 for them. Carlo made sure he could see all four of them, and he saw that none had their guns near them.

"Good afternoon, gentlemen, please put your hands on the table, or I will shoot you dead," said Carlo as he approached with his gun aimed at the Swamptown leader.

"What is this?" yelled the old man.

"This is retribution for your sins. You will soon understand pain and suffering. You will soon yell out for help, but none will come. You will want water, but there will be none to quench your thirst. You will ache and wish to have the pain stop, but it will not. In short, you are about to get what you sorry asses deserve," said Carlo angrily.

"I will not put up with that kind of talk from a damn city slicker," said the old man as he went for his gun.

Carlo calmly shot him in the leg.

"You bastard!" yelled the old man as he moaned and screamed in pain.

"Mario, get their guns and train a shotgun on this man right here," Carlo said as he pointed to the Swamptown leader.

"Now, listen because I am only going to tell you what to do one time. Each of you take off all your clothes. I mean, all of them. I want you pretty boys to be buck naked," said Carlo with the pistol pointed at the other man from Swamptown.

"Now, I want each of you to find a rope that I am going to tie you with. If you do not bring me a rope in under five minutes, I will shoot another one of you in the leg or knee," growled Carlo.

Mario had their guns, and the men were naked and could hide nothing in their clothing. However, Carlo and Mario followed them around as they looked for ropes. They soon found several coils of ropes that were used for tying the canoes to trees to keep them from floating away.

"Mario, I want you to tie Mr. Big Shot to that cypress tree over there. When you finish, I want you to tie this young idiot to that tree," said Carlo as he pointed out two trees with three-foot diameters.

When Mario had tied those two guys, Carlo instructed him how to tie the remaining two men. He let the old man with the bullet in his leg sit on the ground while tied to a tree. The old man was screaming in pain, but Carlo and Mario ignored him.

Carlo went into the shack and looked for jelly or honey. He found a jar of grape jelly.

"You guys killed innocent campers who were just out to have fun with their friends and family. You are bums—nothing but disgusting bums," Carlo said to the four of them.

"You two not only killed campers but you killed a man in Folkston," he said as he pointed to the old man and young man.

Carlo spread jelly over every inch of each man's body. It only took a moment for the mosquitoes and flies to feast on the naked flesh.

"You can't do this. It is inhuman!" yelled the leader.

"Mario, take their guns and put them in one of the canoes. I think it is time for us to leave," said Carlo.

The men were screaming from the torment of the bugs, but Carlo and Mario paid no attention. They each got into a canoe and left for Billy's Island.

They arrived at the island in just over an hour. They found Anna and John in the concession stand, and there was another session of hugging and high-fiving.

They spent the night in the concession stand and ate most of the things Carlo had not taken before. There was lots of ice cream, and that was about all John needed.

The next day they made it to Fargo around noon.

# CHAPTER 27

# Retribution Continues

"**B**EFORE WE TALK to the police, I want to take a trip back to the Swamptown campground. I hope to see Dave Diamond for a few minutes," said Carlo.

Anna and John waited by the boat ramp while the two guys looked for a ride to Swamptown.

Fargo had only one taxi, and they soon found it. They had the cab stop at a local greasy-spoon restaurant where Carlo made an unusual purchase. Carlo and Mario asked the driver to drop them a couple of blocks before the campground and to wait thirty minutes for them to return.

They walked into the woods and did not approach the campground through the front entrance. They surprised Dave, who was sitting in a lounge chair in front of the small office. He leaped up when he saw them, but Carlo already had his pistol pointed directly at Dave's chest.

"Sit back down, Dave. We are going to have a little talk and then a short trip," said Carlo.

"You made every effort to harm my family and me. You wanted us to suffer and then be killed after you stole our possessions. You put my brother, my wife, and son in fatal danger. We plan to tell the entire story of your evil scheme to the Fargo police," said Mario.

"Mario is right, but I want you to know that, in addition to that, you have thoroughly pissed me off," said Carlo.

"Now, I want you to get up slowly, and we are going to walk to the back of the campground where it meets the swamp," said Mario as he made Dave get out of his chair.

As before, no campers were in the campground. They walked about five hundred yards to the extreme back of the property. The solid ground in the campground gave way to the wet boggy swamp.

"Carlo, it is your job this time to tie him to a tree after he removes his clothes," grinned Mario.

"You guys are lunatics. I own the police, and they will lock you up as soon as you show up at the police station," said Dave.

"Don't worry about that. We have already typed up the story and sent a copy to the *Miami Herald*. I don't think you control them," said Carlo.

"What do you want from me? I have some money, and I can repay you for the loss of your equipment," pleaded Dave.

"We haven't lost anything. We got our wallets back from your stupid goons, and insurance covers our boat and camper," said Carlo.

"Well, you can come out ahead if you let me give you some cash I have hidden in the office," said Dave.

"Money can't buy what we want. We want you to suffer and maybe die unless you are lucky," said Mario.

They tied Dave to a tree on the edge of the swamp. Then Carlo took the gallon of old cooking grease he bought from the restaurant. All bear hunters know that one of the best baits for attracting bears to a shooting site is cooking oil. With their exceptional smell, the bears can detect the cooking grease for over two miles away. One sure thing about bears is that they love to eat.

Carlo poured the grease on the ground all around Dave's feet and smeared it on the limbs of the tree above his head.

Dave was screaming because of the mosquito bites and the fear of a bear eating him. Mario and Carlo ignored his screams. He tried to kill their family, and he deserved their retribution.

"We will tell the police where you are and your situation. They might get to you before the bears, but who knows?" said Carlo.

They left Dave in the woods and took the taxi back to Fargo. They told the police the entire story and suggested they hurry to Devil's Island because the naked men were suffering. The police said these men had been troublemakers their whole lives, and they were in no rush to help them.

They also told them that Dave was tied to a tree at the back of his campground and that they should get him soon. The police laughed when they heard about Dave's predicament. But the police chief sent his only deputy to cut Dave down and arrest him before the bears had him for lunch.

When the deputy found him, Dave was screaming in pain and fear. "Cut me down from this damn tree!" he yelled when he saw the deputy.

"Dave, you idiot. How did you guys let these damn Yankees get off Devil's Island alive? You have spoiled our entire operation," said the deputy as he was cutting Dave down from the tree.

"I have no idea what happened. I sent our two friends with the supplies, plus the old man and his son were there to kill them," said Dave as he scrambled to put on his clothes.

"Those Yankees outsmarted you, boys! Now, what am I supposed to tell the chief? He sent me here to arrest you!" said the deputy, who was part of the scam from the beginning.

"Tell him I was not here when you arrived. Tell him I must have escaped or been dragged away by the bears." Dave grinned as he raced for his SUV.

"Okay, but I don't know if he will believe me," said the deputy.

When the deputy arrived back at the police station, he told the chief exactly what Dave had told him to say. The chief listened carefully to the deputy and asked him to relax and have a seat until they could decide their next step.

Mario waited inside with the chief and the deputy, but Carlo disappeared. Anna and John sat outside in the chairs the chief had provided for them. It was hot on the little porch, but the sense of freedom was enough to calm their nerves and make the moment pleasant enough.

"Chief, I have a present for you and the deputy," said Carlo as he handed the chief a cell phone.

"Whose phone is this?" asked the chief.

"When I tied Dave to the tree, I also tied his cell phone to the back of the tree near his head. I put the fully charged phone on record and left it to document Dave's predicament and his rescue," said Carlo.

"I suspected there was some type of police involvement to help them with this evil scam. I figured that whoever came to rescue Dave would be a part of the scam," said Carlo, laughing at the stupid deputy.

The phone battery was running low, so the chief plugged in the phone and played the recording for Mario, Carlo, and the deputy to hear. After listening to the recording, it was clear to everyone that the deputy and Dave were part of a criminal enterprise designed to fleece unsuspecting campers.

"I want to thank you for helping us find this group of bums. Over the past couple of years, I have received several inquiries from families who wanted to know if we had seen their relatives, but we never had any indication they were even here," said the chief.

"Deputy, where is Dave?" asked the chief.

"He left in his SUV headed toward Folkston," said the deputy with his head hung low.

Several hours later, the Georgia Highway Patrol arrested Dave. The chief and some officers from the Georgia State Police also arrested the four men on Devil's Island. These six guys would spend many years in a Georgia prison.

After they had exposed the group of criminals, the exhausted family left the Okefenokee Swamp with a sense of relief and good fortune they had escaped such a crazy ordeal.

The closest place with an Uber was Valdosta, and they arranged for one to pick them up. Once they arrived in Valdosta, they rented a car and drove to Jacksonville. They knew they were lucky, but they did not plan to let that crazy experience stop their camping trip.

In Jacksonville, the family rented the largest Winnebago available. They planned to extend their trip another month and then return home to wait out the virus and get rehired or find new jobs. They were not worried because no matter what challenges they encountered, they believed in their motto: "We can do it!"

# ACKNOWLEDGMENTS

I WANT TO thank some special friends and family. It was so much fun to listen to the various inputs from my group of early readers. I particularly want to thank the following people: my fantastic wife, Nancy, most of all, for her encouragement, editing, and fabulous suggestions; our daughter Bonnie; my sister Sara McEvoy; my brother-in-law Richard McEvoy, Fred and Karen Buchsbaum; my cousin Baker Brooks, Dr. Stan Shapiro; Karen Weidenfeld; Dr. Lloyd Wruble; John Finguerra; Barry Frank; Dr. David and Linda Frankel; my cousin Vann Anderson and his wife Ann; Carl Pinkston; and Naomi Petteway.

This book was written during the 2020 COVID-19 pandemic, and I want to thank all of the health care professionals for their fantastic assistance in taking care of the sick.